IMMACULATE CORRUPTION

A MAFIA ROMANCE

NICOLE FOX

Copyright © 2021 by Nicole Fox

All rights reserved.

No part of this book may be reproduced in any form or by any electronic or mechanical means, including information storage and retrieval systems, without written permission from the author, except for the use of brief quotations in a book review.

❦ Created with Vellum

MAILING LIST

Sign up to my mailing list!
New subscribers receive a FREE steamy bad boy romance novel.

Click the link below to join.
https://sendfox.com/nicolefox

ALSO BY NICOLE FOX

Romanoff Bratva

Immaculate Deception

Immaculate Corruption

Kovalyov Bratva

Gilded Cage

Gilded Tears

Jaded Soul

Jaded Devil

Mazzeo Mafia Duet

Liar's Lullaby (Book 1)

Sinner's Lullaby (Book 2)

Bratva Crime Syndicate

Can be read in any order!

Lies He Told Me

Scars He Gave Me

Sins He Taught Me

Belluci Mafia Trilogy

Corrupted Angel (Book 1)

Corrupted Queen (Book 2)

Corrupted Empire (Book 3)

De Maggio Mafia Duet

Devil in a Suit (Book 1)

Devil at the Altar (Book 2)

Kornilov Bratva Duet

Married to the Don (Book 1)

Til Death Do Us Part (Book 2)

Heirs to the Bratva Empire

Can be read in any order!

Kostya

Maksim

Andrei

Princes of Ravenlake Academy (Bully Romance)

Can be read as standalones!

Cruel Prep

Cruel Academy

Cruel Elite

Tsezar Bratva

Nightfall (Book 1)

Daybreak (Book 2)

Russian Crime Brotherhood

Can be read in any order!

Owned by the Mob Boss

Unprotected with the Mob Boss

Knocked Up by the Mob Boss

Sold to the Mob Boss

Stolen by the Mob Boss

Trapped with the Mob Boss

Volkov Bratva

Broken Vows (Book 1)
Broken Hope (Book 2)
Broken Sins *(standalone)*

Other Standalones
Vin: A Mafia Romance

Box Sets
Bratva Mob Bosses (Russian Crime Brotherhood Books 1-6)
Tsezar Bratva (Tsezar Bratva Duet Books 1-2)
Heirs to the Bratva Empire
The Mafia Dons Collection
The Don's Corruption

IMMACULATE CORRUPTION
BOOK TWO OF THE ROMANOFF BRATVA DUET

THE TRUTH WILL SET ME FREE…
UNLESS HE KILLS ME FIRST.

Dima Romanoff knows everything now.

All my sins.

All my scars.

All the skeletons in my closet.

The only thing I have left is our baby in my arms…

And one last shot at freedom.

But Dima is coming for me.

I can't run fast enough or far enough.

And when he catches up to us…

He'll take everything I have to give.

IMMACULATE CORRUPTION is a secret baby romantic suspense novel. It is Book Two of the Romanoff Bratva Duet. Make sure you've started with Book One, IMMACULATE DECEPTION.

1

DIMA

It's been two weeks.

Two weeks since Arya's lies came to light.

Two weeks since a dying man tore my world apart with his last few words.

I've dreamed every night about the last moment I saw her. The way her eyes looked, wide and fearful, as she stared down the barrel of my gun.

Run, I told her. *This is my final mercy.*

And she ran. She took my son and fled like her life depended on it—because it did.

So now, that backstabbing Albanian bitch, that liar, that traitor… she's out there somewhere. When the time is right, I'm going to find her and make her pay for everything she's done.

But now is not that time. Now is the time to take care of the other traitors who think they can snatch away what's mine.

Zotov Stepanov's days are numbered.

I pull out my phone and call Ilyasov. The phone rings and rings. I'm about to hang up when he finally answers.

"Do you have good news for me, little brother?"

"Your man is dead." No need for pleasantries.

"Where's my proof?"

"How about your brother's word?"

Ilyasov chuckles like I've made a funny joke. "What good is that to me?"

"Do you think I'd lie to you?" I growl.

Ilyasov tuts as if he's pretending to think. "It wouldn't be the first time, would it, *sobrat?*"

I snort. "Says the man who claims he holds no grudges."

"Not a grudge. Just a long memory, that's all. You've always been quick to forget about the past. Me? Oh, I remember things. I remember *everything.*"

I grit my teeth. Ilyasov can deny it all he wants, but we both know that what happened ten years ago still burns in his blood like poison. He's defined by how much he hates the outcome of that night.

By what he did to me.

By what I did to him.

By what we both did to a man who deserved so much worse.

"I'm talking about the present. Not the past."

"One thing bleeds right into the other, Dima. You can't separate them."

"Enough with the fortune cookie bullshit, Ilyasov," I snap. "I killed the man you wanted dead. I held up my end of the bargain. Now, it's your turn to hold up yours."

Ilyasov ignores my prodding. "Tell me more. Did he put up a fight?"

"What does it matter? I put my boot through his skull. He's a fucking bloodstain now. The body is gone and his house is burned to a crisp."

"That's becoming a trademark of yours, isn't it?"

My blood runs cold. "What are you talking about?"

Ilyasov laughs again. "You think I wouldn't catch wind of what you did here? Chicago is my city, Dima. I know everything that happens here."

He's talking about Taras Kreshnik's house. After I saved Arya from that fucking beast, we turned the Albanian's house into a funeral pyre. In retrospect, it's obvious that Ilyasov would learn about that kind of thing quickly. But I don't like the idea that he's keeping such a close watch on my movements.

"Fine. Whatever. I don't give a fuck what you do or don't know. That shit's all irrelevant anyway. I only care how you're going to act. Where's my army, brother?"

"Oh, Dima, Dima, Dima..." Ilyasov sighs, like I'm some stupid little kid who isn't understanding the conversation. "This 'shit,' as you called it, is all extremely relevant. I can't give you your army."

I freeze. "What did you just say?"

"Listen to yourself, brother. Think about what you've done. Are these the actions of a careful man? You killed an Albanian underboss in his own home, kidnapped one of his whores, and burned down the house with his body still inside it. Then, as if that wasn't enough, you went and did the same thing to another one! What kind of killer starts a bonfire to let the whole world know what he's done?"

"I didn't—"

"You've made a mess of things. A big fucking mess." Ilyasov's tone grows frigid and sharp. "And just like always, Big Brother Ilyasov has to come clean it all up. So no, you don't get a fucking army right now. You have to wait until all this 'shit' is sorted out."

"I can't fucking believe what I'm hearing. Tell me this is a joke."

Ilyasov barks out a harsh laugh. "There's no joke here. Every single one of my men is busy putting out the fires you started. Tending to things to make sure the Albanians don't come slaughtering every Russian man, woman, and child they can find. You think I'm going to divert them all to come fix *your* petty little problems? The world doesn't revolve around you."

"This is your problem, too," I snarl.

"How so?"

"You're a Romanoff just like I am. We share a heritage, a name, the same blood in our veins. If I go down in New York, you don't think they'll come for you?"

"I'm safe. I'm protected. I take care of the snakes in my garden. You should've done the same."

"This is fucking bullshit, Ilya."

"No, this is how the world works. It's time you started to understand that. My answer is no. Not now."

Fuck.

I tighten my grip on the steering wheel. I'm parked outside of a lowkey motel where I've been staying the past few days, coordinating things and slowly trying to stockpile ammunition.

But has it all been for nothing? Is this a death blow? Everything Gennady and I have been planning revolved around Ilyasov's army. If he pulls the offer—even after everything I've done for him…

We're fucked.

"I can feel the brotherly love, Ilyasov."

He laughs. "We haven't been brothers in a long time. The first time I saw you in ten years was when you needed my help. If your Bratva hadn't been taken out from under your nose, you wouldn't have even thought twice about me."

"I don't remember getting a Christmas card from you, either."

"There's no room for love in our world, Dima. You know that better than anyone."

I sigh. Ilyasov isn't there anymore. The brother I knew? The brother I grew up alongside? The brother I learned the ropes of this world with?

He's dead.

Now, I'm dealing with a cold-blooded mob boss. I'm working on his terms with no special treatment. If I want his help, I have to follow his damned rules.

"Surely something can change your mind."

He sighs. "I don't even understand why you're doing this, Dima. Give it up. Skip town and let it go."

"Give me a name," I growl. "Tell me who you want dead. One more kill. Then you give me my army.

Ilyasov scoffs. "What's the point? My men are good and they can get you your Bratva back. But your reputation is ruined. You let one of your underlings wrench control from you. Now that the weakness has been revealed, more and more people will try to manipulate it. The wars will never stop. You'll be defending your heritage for the rest of your life. Which, I'm sorry to say, may not be very long."

Ilyasov isn't speaking out of his ass, which only makes what he's saying that much worse.

It's happened to other dons. As soon as it looks like their control is slipping, every snake within striking distance decides to take a bite.

The Bratva life is all about power and control. If it looks like you don't have enough of each, you're done. Your men won't respect you. Your enemies won't fear you.

Which is why there's only one way to handle this: scorched earth.

I have to slaughter every single person who betrayed me. The streets will run with blood when I'm done. If anyone doubts my strength, I'll show them what happens to *ublyudki* who cross me.

And then the world will go back to the way it's supposed to be.

No Zotov. No Arya. No Jorik.

Just me and my empire, unchecked and unchallenged.

"Dima..."

"Give me the goddamn name."

"A real man knows when to retreat," Ilyasov muses.

I shiver at the saying. Ilya sounds so much like Father. And to hear him echo Father's words in a time like this... it's unnerving. As if the man who gave us life is back from the dead.

"I won't ask again, Ilyasov."

Ilyasov is clearly tired of arguing with me. He's just as headstrong as I am.

So, with a sigh, he finally concedes. "Very well. One more task it is. The name is Giorgio D'Onofrio. He runs a casino in Atlantic City. Kill him and you'll have your army."

I nod and hang up without another word.

A real man may know when to retreat.

But a don knows when to launch a war.

I go inside the motel room and shower. Then I drop onto the shitty mattress and close my eyes.

I want to sleep. Fuck, I *need* to sleep. I haven't gotten more than a couple hours a night for two weeks running.

Partly because I've been busy amassing support from anywhere I can get it.

And partly because, every time I fall asleep, I see her face.

Aryana Georgeovich. A wolf in sheep's clothing.

I should hate her—and most of the time, I'm successful at doing exactly that. But sometimes, a different emotion rises. One I refuse to name.

A longing. A hunger. A desire.

One eye cracks open. I feel the tingle, the urge in my fingertips. I try to resist it. But in the end, the instinct wins out. I reach over to the nightstand and grab my cell phone. Swiping through the apps, I pull up the tracking software. A map pops open, centered on a little red dot somewhere in eastern New Jersey.

The night of Jorik's death, I told Arya to run. I told her it was only a head start, and that when the time came, I'd pursue her relentlessly.

I meant that. The war comes first. But once I have my Bratva back, I'll chase her down to the ends of the earth if that's what it takes.

In the meantime, however, I just can't bring myself to let her disappear completely. Even if she's nothing more than a little red dot on a map, emanating from a tracker in her things I had planted by a hired operative.

I sit and look at it for a while. Wondering what she's doing. Who she's with. What she's thinking.

It lulls to me to sleep. My eyes drift closer and closer to closed.

Until, just before I succumb to the darkness, I notice something.

The red dot has begun to move. It's been in the same place for almost two weeks. But now, tonight of all nights, it's picking up speed along a highway. Headed south.

I frown. And, all alone in the empty motel room, I murmur under my breath, "Where are you going, *krasavitsa?*"

2

ARYA

A MOTEL IN CRESTWOOD VILLAGE, NEW JERSEY

Ernestine stirs her tea, her spoon clanking against the side of her cup. "June asked where Dima was last night after dinner. You didn't seem to hear her. You were a little distracted."

Tears well up in the backs of my eyes. I blink them away.

I'm not going to cry. There is no need to cry. Everything is fine, right?

Wrong. Wrong, wrong, wrong.

For one beautiful morning, I let myself be fooled into thinking I could have a normal life with Dima. That we could be safe and happy. That we could splash in the lake and cook in the kitchen and take naps with Lukas.

I let myself fall in love with a fantasy. So when Dima popped my bubble, I wasn't prepared.

The two weeks since I ran have been a nightmare. I can't sleep at night. I can't function during the day. I'm a mess around the clock—and the only thing holding me together is this strange little family I've become a part of.

When I fled Dima, I got into Brigitte's car with Lukas and just started driving. We drove and drove and drove until we were as far away as I could get. I pulled over to the side of the road, slept for a few hours, and then kept driving some more.

Most of the days that have followed are a blur in my memory. I found Ernestine and June and told them we had to move. We've been on the run since then. Never more than one night in a single place. Just moving, constantly, and looking over my shoulder all the while.

It's no way to live. And it's wearing me down to the bone.

A hand lands on my shoulder. I jump and shriek.

"Did you hear me, dear?"

"I'm sorry, Ernestine. What did you say?"

"I asked if you were okay. You seem distracted."

I nod, unable to speak until I clear my throat and pull myself together. "Yeah. I'm fine."

Ernestine's eyes say she doesn't believe me, but that's okay. She knows what it's like to suffer under tough circumstances. She's been doing it her whole life.

She guesses what I'm thinking about without having to ask. "You and Lukas are safer without him, you know. He's trouble."

"I know," I mumble.

But do I?

I've seen sides of Dima that say that exact opposite. That he's not trouble. That he loves us. That he wants to keep us safe and protected, to be there for me and for his son, to take care of us. Somewhere deep inside him is a good man.

But the Dima who put a gun in my face and told me to run for my life is anything but that.

"It's late, darling," Ernestine says. "Get some sleep."

She shuffles off to the bathroom to get ready for bed. June is already asleep. I'm glad. I don't want either of them to see me cry.

It's not just Dima that is tearing me apart from the inside out. It's Brigitte; it's Jorik; it's a whole world of lies and violence I thought I escaped. So many skeletons in my closet now—Rose and Taras, too, of course. My mother as well. It's getting awfully crowded in there.

But Dima is still the star of the show.

Lukas fusses in the bassinet shoved into the corner. I swipe tears off of my cheeks and hurry in to give him his bottle.

It's a good reminder: no matter what, I have to do what's best for Lukas. Always. He is my only priority, the only thing that matters.

My plan since the moment the pregnancy test showed positive was to raise Lukas on my own. I knew I could do it back then. I know I still can.

It's harder now that I know Dima, of course. Now that I'm aware of what could have been.

But it doesn't change the reality.

Dima's heart will always belong to the Bratva, and mine will always belong to Lukas.

It can't be any other way.

Once Lukas has finished his bottle, he goes back to sleep in the cradle. I let June and Ernestine have the bed and curl up on the filthy armchair with a spare blanket and pillow.

But sleep eludes me. The motel room is silent and still and yet my mind is racing a million miles an hour.

Where are we going? I ask silently. I'm doing the same thing I've been doing for weeks now: talking to Rose as if she can hear me. As if she can answer me. As if I didn't watch her die.

I like to pretend she's talking back, though. The swish of the fan, the hum of the A/C—when I'm half-asleep and as desperate as I am right now, those things can almost start to sound like a comforting voice answering me.

Somewhere safe, Rose says.

Where is that, though?

You'll know it when you find it.

I laugh bitterly. I thought I was safe in my boring life in New York, long before Dima ever kicked in the clinic door and claimed my body at gunpoint. Long before I begged him to take me.

Harder. Touch me. Make me come. Those were the words that sealed my fate.

Even now, after all the shit that's happened, I can't bring myself to regret them.

I hear a noise in the bassinet. Lukas is starting to shift around again. I sit up hurriedly. I don't want him to wake up June or Ernestine, so I scoop him up, blankets and all, and slip outside of the room.

It's a chilly night. There's a plastic chair just outside the door, facing the mostly-empty parking lot. I sink into it and hold Lukas close. He's a little furnace, so his body heat keeps me warm.

We're in a little town called Crestwood Village, somewhere in eastern New Jersey. We've mostly bounced around here the last couple of weeks. I pulled all the cash I had from my bank accounts and we've been trying to keep our heads low to avoid any unnecessary attention until I can figure out what to do next.

Not exactly a fun vacation.

My head is constantly whirring with paranoia. *Is that person following me? Has that car matched our turns?*

Even now, there's a pair of headlights at the gas station across the street that have my attention. I eye them for a while as Lukas snoozes on my chest.

"It's nothing, Arya," I tell myself. "You're just tired, that's all. No one is following you. Dima has better things to do. He doesn't care about you anymore."

But the headlights stay right where they are. Almost like they're watching me.

That creepy, tingly feeling on the back of my neck picks up more and more with every passing second. What if I'm wrong? What if that *is* Dima? Or worse, what if it's someone else?

Zotov? The Albanians?

Too many possibilities. Each one worse than the last.

I shudder and cast my eyes down. Looking at Lukas's little toes, I start to count out loud under my breath. "One little piggy… Two little piggies… Three little piggies…"

It's stupid and silly, but weirdly, it calms me down. I do it ten times through, slowly. Then I pick my gaze up again.

The headlights are still there.

When the motel room door creaks open behind me, I almost scream. I twist around in my seat to see June shuffling out. Her eyes are bleary and there's a blanket clutched tight around her shoulders.

"June, honey, what're you doing awake?" I ask. My heartbeat is pounding a million miles an hour in my eardrums.

"Couldn't sleep," she mumbles. She comes over and rests her head against my shoulder. Her free hand reaches out to stroke Lucas's fine, dark hair.

"Bad dreams?"

She nods. "I miss Mommy."

My heart clenches. I pull her in close with one arm. "Me too, darling. I miss your mommy every single day."

June turns her eyes up to meet mine. "Are we going to be okay?" she asks.

"Of course," I answer fiercely at once—even though I have no way of knowing if that's true. "Why would you even ask such a thing?"

"I hear you crying sometimes. Mommy used to cry a lot, too."

I shudder. June has taken to me as a sort of surrogate mother since we reunited. She needs it, too. Someone to tell her that the world isn't such a harsh and ugly place. That there's room for love. There's hope for a happy ending.

But how can I tell her those things if I don't even believe them myself?

I had a happy ending there for the taking—and then it slipped right between my fingers.

"Sometimes, we have to cry. And it's okay. Because it means that happiness is right around the corner."

It's cheesy enough to belong on a fortune cookie or in a Hallmark movie. But it's all I've got right now. I sure as hell can't burden this poor little girl with all the real questions churning around in my head.

Questions like, *Where can we run? How can we hide? What will I do if he finds us?*

"Okay," June says simply. As if that lame answer was good enough.

She's so trusting. So pure. It's my job now to keep her safe. Which is why, after I say, "Let's go to bed now, okay?" and follow her back to the motel room door, I check over my shoulder one more time to make sure the world is safe for her.

But the headlights are still there.

Watching.

Waiting.

3

ARYA

I make a decision when I wake up the next morning—we have to run.

And not just run the way we've been running. Circling from motel room to motel room in the same general area, buying Poptarts in bulk from Wal-Mart and making them last as long as possible so we don't have to show our faces in any of the local restaurants.

No, we need to run far, far away from here.

I need to put a whole goddamn ocean between Dima and us.

So I dial a number I hoped to never, ever dial again.

When I left Jorik and the Albanians, I cut ties with almost everyone, but that doesn't mean I lost all of my connections. If there is anything I learned during my time with Jorik, it's that knowing the right people can quite literally save your life. I made sure I kept the numbers of the right people.

Arnie Fleishman is one of them.

I met him through Jorik, but he always liked me best. Jorik was an asshole until his very last breath and Arnie doesn't suffer fools.

Arnie doesn't answer the phone himself, of course. He'd never do that because he's not stupid, and you never know who's listening to a call. But when I say the right things to the right people, I get slowly passed from hand to hand until I'm talking with Arnie himself.

His raspy smoker's voice is unforgettable. "Hello, dear."

"Hi, Arnie. I—"

"Come see me. We don't talk on the phone, okay? Not safe."

Then—*click*. He hangs up.

Looks like we're taking a trip to Atlantic City.

~

Atlantic City, New Jersey

The boardwalk isn't as busy as in the summer, but there are a fair amount of people and families enjoying the day, eating funnel cakes and lining up for rides. I walk past all of it and make my way to the striped carnival tent.

Ernestine is watching June and Lukas while I take care of business. I gave her one of my last twenties to buy a hotdog or a funnel cake for the little ones.

The rest of the money I take with me. Arnie's help will come at a steep price.

Arnie has operated the carnival on the boardwalk for years. Kids love to see the elephants and the trapeze artists. They've got clowns, face painters, the whole nine yards. It's a magical world unto itself.

It's also a cover for Arnie's actual business.

During the day, the tent is filled with kids and families. At night, it's the biggest black market on the Eastern Seaboard.

Anything anyone wants, Arnie can either get it or he knows someone who can. That's why I memorized his number. For something exactly like this. To help me find a way out of the nightmare we're trapped in.

When I walk into the tent, I know immediately I came to the right place.

"Arya, sweetheart ," Arnie greets, his Brooklyn accent thick. "It has been too long. Look at you, you're gorgeous. Even more beautiful than the last time. I hear you're a mother now."

I gawk at him. "How on earth did you hear that?"

He waves me away with a mysterious smile. "I hear everything, love. It is my job." He surveys me with a careful eye. Then his smile curdles into a frown. "But if you're here to see me, then things are not good, eh?"

I give him a sad smile. "I've been better. I'm sorry it took trouble for me to come see you, though."

He shakes his head. "Nonsense. I'm glad I haven't seen you. I hoped you got yourself out of this messy little corner of the world. A good girl like you, you deserve someone better than that slug you were with. He's dead, did you hear?"

I saw, I want to say. *I was there. I watched Dima snuff his life out.*

Instead I just nod. "I heard. I'm not surprised."

"Me neither." Arnie wrinkles his nose. "He rubbed me the wrong way from the beginning and I'm sure he did other people, too. That's the thing about this life—you have to be tough, but you have to be likeable, too. Otherwise…" Arnie runs his thumb in a straight line across his neck.

I shudder and plaster a fake smile on. I like Arnie. But he's been immersed in this world for so long that he doesn't even realize anymore that death shouldn't be treated as such a casual thing.

"Anyway, come back to my office," Arnie says. He holds an arm out for me to take and leads me around the side of the carnival floor.

We walk through a curtain into a hallway. The walls are a pale blue-gray color with flat wooden doors. The office at the end of the hall is Arnie's.

His desk is piled high with papers and the shelves behind him are stacked with manila folders and binders. I'm sure it would be a treasure trove should the police ever show up to raid him.

Lucky for Arnie, the police are some of his best clients.

"Sit, please." He gestures towards a chair on one side of the desk, then walks around and slumps into his wheezy rolling chair on the other side. Once he's settled, his expression turns serious. "Now, Aryana, tell me why you're here. I'm a curious man and your voice on my phone was a surprise to me. It's not drugs, is it? God, don't let it be drugs. You're a mother now. That baby needs you."

I cut him off. "It's not drugs, Arnie. You know what my mother did. I don't touch the stuff."

He presses his hands together in a silent prayer. Strange for a religious man to be in his line of work, but I suppose it takes all kinds. "That's a blessing. What brings you here, then? You know old Arnie has anything you could need. I just had one of those Aryan Brotherhood, white supremacist bastards in here with his whore of a mistress, buying blood diamonds. That's nasty business. Let's see, what else, what else… I have weapons, but my supply isn't up to my usual standards right now. A group just came through and cleared me out of the best stuff. Some kind of turf war, I think."

"Who?"

"Darling, you know I don't ask questions. And even if I did, I wouldn't repeat the answers. Bad for business. Bad for my longevity, too."

I laugh politely, but part of me is dying to know. I wonder if it could be Zotov or the Albanians. I wonder if it has anything to do with Dima.

"No, not weapons, either." Though it could be smart to get a gun eventually. For protection. I push the thought away and focus. I'm trying to get out of this underworld, not deeper into it. "I need passports. Documentation. For me and my son. And two friends."

His brows raise. "You want to disappear. A new identity. Leave the old Arya behind."

I nod. "Something like that."

If I'd been smart, I would have done this the moment I left Jorik. I would have gotten a new identity, fled the country, and started over.

But then I wouldn't have Lukas.

And I wouldn't know Dima.

My heart aches at the thought of Dima. At the thought of taking Lukas so far away from him. Of the two of them never knowing each other.

But I can't have it all. I can't keep my son safe and let Dima be in his life. Not like this. Not the way things are now. Most likely, not ever.

Arnie sighs, his lips flapping with the exhale. "That's a shame. You're a good girl. I don't like that you'll live your life on the run."

"Better than being dead."

"You're right there," he concedes. "Okay, fine. Yes, I'll do it. It will take me a week, though. If you want good docs no one will question, I need a week."

I could wait a week.

Honestly, it might take me a week to talk myself into actually going through with this anyway. Right now, I'm only half-convinced it's a good idea. By the end of the week, hopefully I'll be three-quarters convinced, at least.

"Okay, a week it is. How much will it run me?" I start to shuffle in my purse for the money I have left.

But Arnie shakes his head and reaches a huge, hairy hand out to rest lightly on my wrist. "No, sweetheart. Nothing."

"Arnie, no. I don't want to owe anyone anything. I won't be here to make it square, remember?"

"We're square," he says, lowering his chin and looking in my eyes. "I remember when you came to me after you left that son of a bitch. You brought the engagement ring and asked me for anything I could give. I gave you some money, but it wasn't enough. I conned you, darling, and in my old age, I'm trying to make amends."

I'd almost forgotten about the ring. I was such a mess when I left Jorik's that I hardly remember what I did for the next few weeks. Everything was a blur.

"That was a long time ago. Are you sure?"

He nods and waves a hand, dismissing the matter in full. "Positive. Call me in a week and I'll have what you and your little boy need."

"Thank you, Arnie. You're a lifesaver."

He winks at me and scoots me towards the door. "No, I'm an old crook, and that's all I'll ever be. Some people never change, Arya. No matter how hard they try."

4

DIMA

When I wake up, I call Gennady.

"*Dobroye utro*," he greets. "Up and at 'em early this morning, I see."

I glance at the window. Through the slats and the blinds, I can see it's still dark outside. The alarm clock on the side of the bed reads 4:45 AM. I've slept barely two hours and I feel like I got hit by a truck.

But there's a fire burning in my chest, too. I'm still fucking livid at Ilyasov for reneging on the terms of our deal—and yet, at the same time, I can't help denying that it feels good to have a target again. A singular purpose. One life to snuff out.

It makes shit so simple. The whole world of possible actions narrowing down to two steps.

Find Giorgio D'Onofrio…

And kill him.

Nothing more. Nothing less.

"I have a work trip to take," I rumble. I explain quickly to Gennady everything that happened with Ilyasov.

When I'm finished with the story, he whistles softly. "Can't trust a fuckin' Romanoff, am I right?"

I can't help but laugh. "Watch it, *mudak*."

He's right, though. My family history is steeped in blood and lies. There's always another twist, another secret hiding around the corner.

Arya trusted a Romanoff. Look what it cost her.

"So," Gennady continues, "where do you wanna meet up for the ride down to Atlantic City? I'm in Flatbush right now—staying above an awesome pita shop, by the way, which you gotta check out once we get this whole rebellion situation sorted out—but I could find my way to Newark if you want to just scoop me up from there, so whatever you—"

"Gennady..." I interrupt.

His tone sours at once. "No. No, no, no. Hell no. Don't fucking say it. Don't say what I know you're about to say."

I sigh and say it anyway. "You're not coming with me."

On the other end of the phone, Gennady explodes. "What the fuck are you talking about, Dima? Of course I am! You're not about to go fucking Rambo on enemy turf without any backup. Are you out of your mind? Have you completely lost your..." He lapses into Russian, "*Vy dumayete, chto sobirayetes' popast' vo vnutrenneye svyatilishche v odinochku, ubit' dona i vernut'sya obratno, ne buduchi ubitym po puti?*"

I let his anger burn itself out until he's huffing and puffing on the other end of the phone.

Then I say quietly, "It wasn't a question, *sobrat*."

"You've done a lot of dumb shit in your life, Dima Romanoff," my best friend grimaces. "But this might top the list."

"I'll take that as a compliment."

"It wasn't. At all."

He can hear it in my voice, though—I've already made up my mind. There's no going back. No changing route.

"I wasn't calling to argue with you, brother," I tell him. "I was just calling to let you know."

"Thanks for the fucking heads-up," Gennady grumbles. "We really have to work on your team-building. As of now, your biannual performance review would say, 'Needs to develop listening skills.'"

"Take it up with Human Resources," I fire back. "They're located at the bottom of the Hudson River."

"*Shob tebe deti v sup srali*," Gennady retorts. It means something along the lines of, *I hope an orphan shits in your soup.* Sounds better in Russian than it does in English.

"Time's wasting. I have to go."

"Dima…"

"Yes, brother?"

"Just be safe, okay?"

I laugh bitterly. "There's no such thing as safe in our world, Gennady. There never has been. There never will be."

Almost three hours later, I'm nearing the outer boundaries of Atlantic City. Gennady always jokes that New Jersey is the armpit of America. If that's the case, then Atlantic City is the asshole of New Jersey.

I can't stand this fucking place. It's all dirty casinos and cheap hookers. Everyone desperate to separate fools from their cash. They do it remarkably well, too. It's good business for the men in the shadows who control things.

But for Giorgio D'Onofrio, that lucky streak is about to dry up.

His casino is called The Lady Fortune. It's nestled on Brigantine Boulevard between the Borgata and Harrah's. Not the biggest or the fanciest place in the city. But it's by far the most corrupt.

Anyone who knows anything knows that all the criminal shit takes place at The Lady Fortune. Money gets laundered. Lives are bought and sold. Guns, drugs, and girls move through here like sewage through pipes.

It's sickening.

And the man who makes it all happen is Giorgio D'Onofrio.

Decades ago, he was an ally of my father's. After my brother and I came to power, that ended. He retreated into his cozy little empire. Left New York and Chicago to the two of us.

Smart man. Neither Ilyasov nor I would've taken kindly to him meddling with our shit.

I wonder what he did now for Ilyasov to decide his life had to end. Then I shove the thought aside. Ilyasov has said again and again that it doesn't fucking matter what a target has done. All that matters is his death. For a change, I'm willing to agree with him.

It's easier to ignore that stubborn little voice in my head.

I pull into a parking spot outside the casino and watch for a while. And as the minutes tick past, I like what I see less and less.

Security roves past at irregular intervals. Sometimes, they're thirty seconds apart. Others, two to three minutes pass before the next pair of rifle-toting guards rounds the corner. It's a deliberate tactic—so no one can guess when shit is about to hit the fan.

The armed patrols are supplemented with roving cameras fixed to every surface. The cameras pivot from side to side and up and down, preventing blind spots. I note motion sensor lights and biometric security pads at every point of entry and exit.

The place is a goddamn fortress.

Getting in will not be easy. But that's not even the hard part.

It's getting out where my life hangs in the balance.

What I need is a distraction. A way to draw all eyes in one direction while I slip past in another. Something flashy, something big…

But what?

I'm coming up blank. A bomb would attract every mobster in the tri-state area. An assault would end in needless bloodshed. No, it's gotta be subtler. Something more like…

My phone pings. I glance down at it to see a notification from the tracking app. Swiping it up, my breath freezes in my chest.

Target within pre-defined radius, it says. The map shows Arya's little red dot.

And it's only a few miles away from mine.

Suddenly, it all clicks together. Arya is how I'll crack open the casino. And the casino is how I'll crack open Arya.

I set her GPS marker as my destination. Then I fire up the car and head out.

"Can't wait to see you again, Arya," I growl. "But I doubt you'll feel the same."

5

ARYA

THREE DAYS LATER—A CHINESE TAKEOUT PLACE IN
ATLANTIC CITY

There's a feeling I can't shake. Ever since we arrived in Atlantic City, it's been following me around like a shadow.

Like I'm being chased. I know I'm not, but the feeling persists anyway. I check over my shoulder constantly. I take weird routes around whenever I have to go out for food or supplies. And if I can help it, I don't go out at all.

It's no way to live.

None of this is, really. We've been holed up in yet another dingy motel. I'm dreaming of the day we get to say goodbye to these shitholes and go somewhere else forever. Somewhere bright and sunny and European, where no one has ever heard of me and no one gives a damn what I'm running from. Somewhere my son, Ernestine, and June will all be safe.

We'll get there. It just takes time.

Arnie Fleishman said one week for the passports. Three days down, four to go.

"Anything else for your order?" asks the little old woman behind the cash register.

"Umm, yes, please," I stammer as I survey the Chinese takeout menu overhead. "Can I get a pork fried rice, and, uh…"

My eyes pass over the dumplings and I shudder.

Ever since the night at Brigitte's brother's house, the mere thought of dumplings makes me nauseous. It's the last meal I had before my son was ripped from my arms and my best friend sold me into sex slavery. Not exactly a heart-warming memory.

So yeah—if I never have dumplings again, that'll be fine by me.

"Four eggrolls, please. And a sesame chicken. That's all."

"Forty-nine sixty-two," the woman says.

I hand over my cash and step out of line to wait for my food.

The other people waiting in line mostly ignore me. Except for one man. He's ridiculously tall, at least six and a half feet, with a scraggly beard and sunglasses on even though it's nighttime.

And every time I glance away, he shoots a quick little look over at me.

I shiver. *Relax, girl,* I tell myself. *It's nothing. He's no one. And you're no one to him.*

But my body doesn't want to listen. The hairs on the back of my neck stand on end and a chill surges through me.

I wonder if I'll ever be able to trust anyone again. My makeshift little family—Ernie, June, and Lukas—are the only pure people left in this world, as far as I'm concerned. Everyone else is a threat until proven otherwise.

I sink to a seat in one of the hard plastic booths and keep my eyes in my lap. *Hurry up,* I beg silently. *Just let me get out of here before I have a very public meltdown.*

The clock on the wall ticks out the seconds. I count them to try and soothe my fragile nerves.

One... Two...

Two hundred thirty four...

Two hundred thirty five...

"Order number fifteen!" crows someone in the kitchen.

I check my receipt. *That's me.* I stand up and slip through the queue to the food counter. The man in sunglasses doesn't move out of my way, so I have to turn and awkwardly inch by him. He watches me the whole time.

Without looking up, I mumble, "Thanks" to the old lady handing my food over. I put a dollar in her tip jar, then turn and leave.

It's just a few steps to the door, I urge myself. *Put one foot in front of the other and get the hell out of here. Back to your son. Back to safety.*

I can still feel those eyes burning a hole in the back of my head. But I ignore them and focus on the floor. One foot in front of the other. Just a few more steps.

I'm reaching out for the door handle. My fingers touch the cool metal. I lean into it, start to step out into the night...

And then a hand clamps down around my other wrist. A big, strong hand.

I stifle a scream and look up to see the man in sunglasses glaring down at me.

"P-please, just leave me—" I start to stutter.

He holds out his other hand, palm up. "You dropped this," he rumbles.

I look down to see him offering me a paper-wrapped eggroll.

I don't know whether to laugh or cry. I almost just had a full-on, five-alarm nuclear meltdown of a panic attack because a big stranger picked up my dropped eggroll for me.

I suppose I should say thank you. Instead, I just pluck the eggroll from his hand with trembling fingers, stuff it in the plastic bag with the rest of the food, and sprint out without so much as a word of gratitude.

Only when I'm breathing in the night air again can I start to relax.

"You're okay," I mumble to myself. "Nothing is wrong. Everything is fine."

Lies, lies, and more lies, but I'll tell myself whatever I need to in order to make it through this week from hell.

The motel is about six blocks away from the Chinese place. With every step I put between me and the man in sunglasses, I start to feel better and better.

In just a minute, I'm going to get back into the motel room. I'm going to see June's smile, hear my son's giggle, feel Ernestine's reassuring touch on my shoulder. And everything really will be fine.

I have them and they have me and that's all we need. That's all that matters.

The first half of the walk goes quickly. The air is still a little brisk for mid-spring, so I put some pep in my step. The very last stretch of road is completely dark and empty. No cars. No pedestrians. And the whole block of streetlights is burned out.

I can see the gold pot at the end of the rainbow, though: *Sunset Motel* written in bright pink neon on the sign at the far intersection.

I'm almost home. I'm almost safe.

I'm halfway down the darkened block when that familiar feeling strikes me again. The one I haven't been able to soothe since we got here three days ago.

Eyes on me in the darkness.

Shadows close on my heels.

But when I whirl around, there's no one. I'm all alone out here.

"Get a grip, Arya," I scowl. I brush my hair out of my face with my free hand, then turn back to finish the walk.

That's when I hear it.

A voice I hoped I'd never hear again in my life, cracking out of the darkness like a whip.

"Hello, Arya," Dima Romanoff says as he separates himself from the shadows. "Did you miss me?"

6

DIMA

She looks like a fucking angel.

Standing there in the near-darkness, her hair catches what little light there is and her green eyes gleam bright like emeralds. Her skin is as smooth and pale as ever, except for the row of scars along her chin.

She told me she got them when her mother's meth cooking went wrong, caused an explosion, and brought the roof of the house down on top of them. I wonder how much of that bullshit was true.

But fuck me if I'm not drawn in by her anyway.

She told me lie after lie after lie and I swallowed them all whole. Now, they sit like poison in my gut. Harsh. Scalding.

And yet I can't resist the temptation to touch her. To claim her. To show her why she'll always belong to me, no matter how far she tries to run.

I'm addicted to this beautiful fucking liar.

"I asked you a question," I growl.

She blinks and—slowly, slowly, slowly—raises her eyes up to meet mine. Even though she's clearly terrified, she's as defiant as she was the night we met. The night I kicked in the door of her clinic and tore her world to pieces.

"I don't want to talk to you," she retorts.

I laugh bitterly. "That wasn't the question I asked."

"Yeah, well, it's the answer you're getting. Leave me alone, Dima. Let me live my life in peace."

"Is that what you did to me?"

"I didn't ask for anything that happened!" she snaps. Her voice wavers with choked-up emotion. "*You* were the one who put a gun in my face! *You* were the one who threw me and a newborn baby in a stolen car and headed out for god-knows-where! I was fine before we met! You… you…" She lowers her gaze, quivering with rage now. "…You ruined everything for me."

I reach out and grab her chin. She flinches at the contact, but she doesn't run away like I thought she might. She doesn't want to show weakness, I bet.

Or maybe she's just feeling the same shit I've been feeling since Jorik revealed everything. A mix of fury and temptation that's drawing me closer and closer to doing some shit I know I will live to regret.

"I haven't even started ruining you the way I intend to, Aryana," I snarl.

"Don't call me that."

"It's your name, isn't it?"

"It *was* my name. Not anymore. I left all that behind. Just like I left you behind."

I bark out another laugh. "You didn't leave shit behind on purpose. You fled because I told you to run for your life. I warned you that I'd be coming for you, didn't I? That this was just a head start?"

She juts her chin out towards me. "Yeah, so?"

"So," I say, spreading my hands out wide, "here I am. Where are you going to run now?"

Arya glances over her shoulder, first left, then right. There's no one in sight. This is the shittiest part of a shitty town, and even if there were people nearby, not a single living soul would be willing to intervene in whatever the hell is happening here between us.

She's completely and utterly alone.

Trapped with me.

She knows it, too. Her shoulders sag. Her fingers release the bag of Chinese food in her hand and it plops to the cracked pavement beneath our feet. Her head drops down to her chest.

Her voice wobbles as she starts to whimper, "Dima, I…"

And then she swings a vicious knee up towards my crotch.

If I were any other man, she would've had enough of a surprise advantage to do what she wanted to do: cripple me and run.

But I'm not any other man. I'm Dima fucking Romanoff. I've trained my whole life to be goddamn untouchable. And this petite little veterinarian, as fiery as she is, will not be the first one to catch me by surprise.

I leap out of the way of her flying strike. At the same time, I grab her by the throat and use her momentum to swing her into the brick wall behind her. She slams into it hard. All the breath rushes out of her lungs.

She tries to beat me with her free hands, but she's too weak to do anything close to real damage. They swat helplessly at my shoulders until I snare one wrist in my grasp and pin it to the wall next to her head.

"We've been here before, haven't we?" I hiss in her face. "Me choking the life out of you. You begging me for mercy. But you've used up all of the mercy I had for you, Arya. When you lied. When you hid. And now it's time to pay the piper."

"You're going to kill your son's mother?" she rasps with the last of her breath.

I squeeze tighter, tighter, tighter…

Then I step back, release her, and let her slide into a sobbing puddle on the ground.

I can't admit, even to myself, what that pitiful sight does to me. I want to pick her up and clean the dirt from her hands. I want to take her in the shower like I did after I saved her from Taras's house of horrors and rinse all the pain away.

But I can't. She *has* to pay. It's the only way. It's how I was taught, how I was raised, how this world works.

If I forgave her, what kind of man would that make me?

Weak. Cowardly. Not fit to be don.

So it has to be like this. She has to burn beneath the full heat of my rage.

"No," I breathe down towards her. "I'm not going to kill you. I'm going to use you instead."

∼

Fifteen minutes later, Arya slinks out of the motel room. I'm standing in the shadows beneath the awning. Just out of sight of the people in the room. But I can see them through a crack in the blinds.

The old woman. The little girl.

And my son.

The little girl—June, I think her name was—is playing with Lukas. Tickling his toes and blowing raspberries on his round belly. I can't hear any sound from inside, but I can imagine the sound of his laughter.

It tears my fucking chest apart.

That is my son. My boy. My *malyshka*.

He's only a few feet away. I could easily rip this door off the hinges and take him away with me.

But the same question that stopped me from doing that the first time around still persists: what kind of life would he have with me?

I've seen so much blood. Both my own and the blood of men I've killed. I've always tried to use my power to make the underworld a better place. To rid it of the true filth. But there's only so much one man can do. Even a man like me.

If I took Lukas into my empire… I'd have to mold him the same way I was molded. And I remember all too well how that went. I still have the scars to prove it. Ilyasov does, too.

"How long are you going to keep lurking in the shadows like the world's biggest creep?" Arya scoffs.

She's leaning up against a chipped stone pillar, arms crossed over her chest, watching me.

I scowl. "I wouldn't be cracking jokes if I were you."

"That's because you're not as funny as I am."

"What about this is funny to you?"

She sobers up quickly. "None of it. Not a single fucking bit."

I nod, satisfied. "That's what I thought."

"Is this the part where you explain what you want from me? Or are you going to keep pretending you're Batman for a little while longer?"

I resist the urge to roll my eyes. "Not here. Come with me."

I turn and leave, not bothering to see if she's following. After a moment, I hear her footsteps trailing mine.

I lead Arya to my car. Opening the passenger door, I gesture for her to sit. "Get in."

She eyes me warily. "So this is actually the part where you kill me and dump my body in the ocean?"

"If I was going to do that, I would've done it a long time ago. So I didn't have to put up with your sass."

She snorts. "It was my sass that got us here in the first place, Dima," she mutters sort of forlornly.

"What does that mean?"

"Nothing. Nothing at all." She gets in the car and crosses her arms over her chest again. Her eyes are distant. Searching.

Frowning, I swing her door shut and walk around to my side. I get in, but I leave the engine off for now.

It's crazy how quickly her presence seeps into the small space. It smells like her, that delicate, flowery fragrance I could pick out of a crowd. It sounds like her, that soft, subtle breathing. It feels like her, too—in the way my skin prickles when she's near. The way my cock hardens at the sight of her lips.

Kontsentrirovat', Dima, I scold myself. *Focus.*

"I'm waiting," she says.

I can't help wondering how much of this is just a brave front she's putting on. And what she's really feeling underneath.

Is she as wet as I am hard?

Is she as hungry to fuck as I am?

I shake my head in disgust. I'm getting off track again. This woman does that to me without even having to try. It's fucking infuriating.

"Well?"

"I'm thinking," I snap.

"Don't hurt yourself trying," she mutters sarcastically.

"Christ, you are a pain in the ass."

"You're just an ass, period."

I blink and snap out of it. It's way too easy to slip into this role again. This fiery back-and-forth. As if none of the shit that's happened between us matters anymore.

But it *does* matter.

It *did* happen.

It cannot be forgotten.

"Anyway," Arya says, "I'm still waiting for you to explain what you want from me."

I nod grimly. "You're going to help me kill a man."

She laughs out loud, right in my face. "Absolutely not."

"I wasn't asking."

"Yeah, well, I'm answering anyways. It's a hard no for me. Thanks but no thanks, great to see you again, I'll just be on my way now so if you could be so kind as to—"

CLICK. I lock the doors of the car just as Arya reaches for the handle.

She rattles it a few times, then glances back over her shoulder at me. "That's not funny, Dima. Let me out."

"No, *krasavitsa*, I don't think I will. And I don't think I want to hear you talk anymore, either. You're going to sit the fuck down. Shut the fuck up. And listen to what I have to tell you. Am I understood?"

Arya's fingers slowly slip from the car door handle and flutter down into her lap. She looks at me, and for an instant, the fire fades away and there's just a mournful kind of longing in her eyes.

"You're serious, aren't you?" she asks quietly. "You really want me to help you kill someone."

"Very fucking serious."

"And you won't take no for an answer."

"No, Arya, I will not."

She blinks like she's weighing all the implications of that. Then she sighs. "But why?"

"Because this is how you pay off your debts to me."

She does a full-body shudder that ends in a tiny, terrified little gasp. "Don't say it like that," she whispers, barely audible. "That's what Jorik told me."

I clench my fists at my side. "I'm not him."

"But when you say that, you sound like him."

"I'm not him. I'm not a fucking rat. Not a fucking backstabber. I'm a man of my word, Arya. Do this and you'll be free."

She looks at me again and sighs. Those perfect lips part like she wants to say something important.

Then, at the last moment, she changes her mind. "Do you promise?" she says instead.

I shake my head. "No. But you don't have any other choice, do you? Now, listen up. Here's what you're going to do."

7

ARYA

Dima drops me back off at the motel, then drives away without so much as a goodbye.

I feel dizzy, nauseous, overwhelmed. For weeks now, I've been hoping I'd never see him again—until my dreams, when I saw him again and again.

I never knew exactly what would happen if fate brought us back together. But I never could've imagined it would go like this.

You're going to help me kill a man. This is how you pay your debts.

The words ring around in my head again and again. It's sickening. But like Dima said, what other choice do I have?

If I want to be free, I have to do this.

So, with a sigh, I duck back inside the motel room and get to work.

∼

Twenty-four hours later, I'm a different person.

For starters, I've gone from brunette to blonde. The shirt I wore for the bleaching is a disaster, but my hair actually looks okay.

After the first bleach, my hair was as yellow as straw. So, I went in with a thick layer of bleach, got it down to a warm white color, and then hit it with a toner.

The whole time, all I can think about is when Brigitte and I bleached her hair a few years ago. We spent hours watching video tutorials online, but her hair still turned green. We ended up dying it turquoise just to cover the mistake.

It would be a fond, silly memory with my best friend... if said best friend hadn't turned out to be a backstabbing traitor I was forced to kill to save my son.

I've had nightmares of tightening the rope around Brigitte's neck. Of the way she gasped and gulped for air.

I know I did the right thing, but that doesn't make it any easier to live with.

Thankfully, even if the memories hurt, I learned a lot from Brigitte's botched dye job, so my hair turns out pretty damn good, if I do say so myself.

After a deep conditioning treatment, I blow dry and style my hair, running a circular brush through it to give me loose, breezy waves. Then I do my makeup for the first time in weeks.

I took a trip to the drug store this morning to replenish my supplies, so I can do an entire glam look. Foundation, concealer, setting powder, contour, blush, fake lashes, and glittery eyeshadow.

I feel like a Barbie doll, but when I slip into the slinky silver dress I also picked up at a nearby boutique, I end up looking more like a high-class escort.

It's the first time I've seen myself done up in a long time. Certainly since Lukas was born.

And it's… nice, actually.

I feel sexy and powerful, ready to take on anything the casino has to throw at me.

The first step of the plan Dima described sounded simple enough. *Go into the casino and get a look around.* How hard could that be?

It's what's at stake that's got me shuddering every time I think about it.

A man will die eventually because of what I do tonight. I'll be responsible for that. For as long as I live, his blood will be on my hands.

Just like Tommy's.

Just like Brigitte's.

The Hippocratic Oath flashes across my mind. Vets don't usually take it, but we learned about it in my classes at Cornell. The main tenet: *First, do no harm.*

Is that what I'm doing here?

Is that what I've done these last few months?

Not by a long shot. I'm becoming a person I never wanted to be. I'm tumbling head over heels into a fate I fought like hell to escape.

But I don't have a choice. I have to do this so my son can have a better life than I've had. So Ernestine and June can find the safety and freedom we deserve.

I lift up my chin and look at myself in the mirror. "You can do this, Arya," I whisper fiercely.

I wish I believed what my reflection is saying. And, for a moment, I do. The girl looking back at me in the mirror is strong. Powerful. Confident.

But when I walk out of the motel room and see Dima standing outside of his car, waiting for me, my confidence grows shaky.

It's the first time he's seen me like this. Around him, I've always been in sweatpants or covered in blood or days without a shower. He's only ever seen me at my worst.

Dima's eyebrows raise when he sees my hair. I can see he's taken aback by the sudden change. But as his eyes drift lower, a familiar hungry look slides into place. I recognize it well.

"Well, do you like it?' I ask. Even though I know the answer.

He grumbles. "Maybe too much. You'll be a distraction the moment you walk in."

"I think that's a compliment. Isn't that the point?" I spin in a circle and pop my hip. "Do I look rich?"

"You look fucking priceless." Something about the way he says that raises goosebumps on my arms. He walks towards me, eyes gliding up and down my body. Then he reaches for my hair and picks up a strand. "Except the hair. I hate the hair."

I pull my hair out of his hand and swat him away. "Not nice."

"It's not you," he says, his thumb brushing along my jawline. "Dark hair suits your skin tone much better."

My body flushes at his touch. It feels like he's trailing fire across my face. I tuck my chin down and clear my throat. "I'm not trying to look like myself, though. I want to look different. So do I?"

Dima stands back and studies me, tipping his head one way and then the other.

His hair has only gotten longer over the last few weeks. I like it. It softens him, although his eyes are still like hot coals, black and fiery. I want to run my fingers through his tangled locks and rough beard.

Instead, I curl my hands into fists at my side while he looks at me from all angles.

"It'll work. Especially if people aren't looking at your face," he says. "In a dress like that, they'll be focused… elsewhere."

I suddenly feel the urge to cover my breasts, but I resist. I have to be confident.

"That's a little objectifying."

He shrugs. "That's men for you."

He's not wrong. And the dress does really highlight my assets. The neckline is cut dangerously low, giving off a considerable view of my cleavage. If I lean too far forward, my tits will fall out completely.

"Anyway, here's what's happening. Tonight's goal is reconnaissance. I need to know how many visible security guards there are inside and what kind of security you go through before getting into the casino proper."

I nod. "Can do."

"Try to look for cameras, especially in the lobby and around the edges of the room, but don't be obvious. If they see you looking for cameras, they may think you're trying to cheat, and they'll boot you before you even get through the door."

I feel like I should be taking notes, but I don't think that would give Dima much confidence in me.

"Don't drink," he continues. "You want to make sure you're sharp in case anything starts to go wrong. If you think they're looking at you twice or being shady at all, get out of there. Do you hear me?"

I nod, but that isn't enough for Dima. He grabs my chin and turns my face to his, gray-blue eyes piercing. "Do you hear me?"

"Yes," I say, knocking his hand away from me. "I'll be careful."

"Good. You'll have your phone so you can call me if anything goes wrong. I won't be coming inside tonight, but I'll wait for you in the parking lot."

"I can handle it on my own. You don't have to come with me."

Dima gives me an unamused look. "I'm not letting you out of my sight for long, Arya."

He says it's like it's meant to be a threat. But the way my body reacts is anything but scared.

When he first showed up in the alley, I was terrified. Part of me still is. That's what he wants, of course. He's said as much. He wants me to fear him. To hate him.

Is it possible that it's because he can't bring himself to hate me?

Even after all my lies... All my deceptions...

Part of Dima still cares.

I can't deny that I feel the same about him. My body is drawn to his. It's the same way bubbles are drawn to the water's surface. It's science, nature, physics.

It's irresistible.

"Time to go," I croak quietly to break the tense silence. I take one look back over my shoulder. I can see Ernestine giving Lukas a bottle through the crack in the blinds.

She asked a lot of questions when I came back to the room and told her that Dima had found us. I didn't have great answers. I still don't. So I just told her we had some things to take care of. That everything would be fine. That I'd be home tonight and we'd be on a plane somewhere beautiful by the end of the week, just like I promised.

I hope to God that all comes true.

For now, this is the only path forward, though. So with a gulp, I turn and follow Dima Romanoff—on our way into the lion's den.

8

DIMA
THE LADY FORTUNE

"You know what you have to do?"

Arya nods. "I think so."

"And you know what's at stake."

She bites her lower lip and nods again. "Yeah. I know."

"If you fuck this up—"

"I won't." She raises her gaze from her lap to meet mine. I can see fear in her eyes. But I can see bravery, too. The same intoxicating mixture that drew me to her in the first place.

"Alright then," I rumble. "I'll be here."

Arya scowls as she unbuckles her seatbelt, opens the door, and starts to slink out of the car.

I can't help staring as she goes. She's mesmerizing in that dress. I like her better with her natural dark hair, but something about the blond dye job keeps my eyes riveted to her.

I'm supposed to hate her.

I'm supposed to destroy her.

But, fuck me… all I want to do is bend her over and taste her instead.

She's almost all the way out of the car when I move. I don't even realize I'm doing it until I'm already lunging halfway across the seat. Until my hand seizes her wrist and freezes her in place. It's just an automatic instinct. An impulse I've never been able to control.

She looks down at my hand clamping on her wrist and then up to my face.

I know what I want to say. What I ought to say.

Don't get yourself killed.

Our son needs you.

Hell… I need you.

The words are right on my lips. It'd be so easy to say them. To forgive her for all her lies and take the first step towards a different kind of future with Arya at my side and Lukas in my arms.

But I can't. At the last moment, I falter.

"Hurry the fuck up, okay?" I snarl.

Then I drop her hand and break the eye contact.

Arya stands in place, lingering for one long moment. Then she sighs and walks away.

I tell myself I'm not going to look at her as she goes. Not even one fucking peek. But at the last second, just before she pushes through the doors of the casino, I can't help glancing.

And it's a fucking vision.

Her in that metallic dress. Gleaming under the lights. Curves like sin. A stride like a goddess. Full of fear and fire and fury.

That's the mother of my child.

What the fuck am I going to do with her?

Time passes slowly while I wait. A million different scenarios flash through my head. Each one crazier than the last.

Arya's been caught. She's in a basement room right now, getting tortured for information.

Arya's betrayed me. She's in Giorgio's office, telling him everything, and he's calling an army of guards to come slaughter me right here.

Arya's abandoned me. She's shacked up with some high roller, sucking his cock and moaning for him the way she once moaned for me.

What does it mean that it's that very last image that hurts the most?

I growl wordlessly and flip on the radio. Anything for some distraction from these intrusive fucking thoughts.

It's a true crime podcast. The story of some suburban *mudak* hunting down the men who killed his wife and son.

By the end of it, I'm sick to my stomach.

Motherfuckers came into this man's home and slaughtered his family in cold blood. Like any good man should, he went after the bastards. Stalked their trail. Hunted them down.

And when he finally had them in his sights, did he avenge the deaths they caused? Did he unleash holy fucking hell on the people who dared touch what's his?

No.

He calls the cops. Reports them for drug smuggling or some bullshit like that.

And then he *leaves.*

As if his job is done.

In the final interview, he talks about showing the killers mercy. "They needed to be taught what mercy is," he says.

"*Ootebya nyetu peeski*," I snarl at the radio. *You have no fucking dick.*

His wife and son didn't get any mercy. Why should the motherfuckers who killed them?

It's supposed to be some grand morality tale. A story of taking the high road. I can't relate in the slightest.

When Taras Kreshnik touched what's mine, I put a bullet in his goddamn skull. As soon as I catch up to Erik Arnaud, I'm going to do the same.

Same for Zotov. Same for Fyodor.

Everyone's who's ever betrayed me can expect nothing but pain in return. Not mercy. Never any fucking mercy.

Except for Arya. She's the only one who's ever seen what Dima Romanoff's mercy can look like.

I turn my eyes to the casino doors. "Where are you, Arya?" I whisper.

The same carousel of images from earlier plays in my head. *Arya's blood dripping from her lips. Arya's mouth telling Giorgio that I'm coming for him. Arya's tongue, lapping up and down the length of someone else's—*

"No." I squeeze my eyes shut, doing my best to quiet the annoying voice in my head.

This will be fine.

She'll be fine.

A knock on the door interrupts my thoughts. I look up.

It's her.

I sigh in relief and reach over to open the passenger door for her. "How did it go?" I ask as she sinks into the seat.

Her eye makeup is slightly smudged and her curls are flatter than they were when she went in, but she still looks radiant.

She's breathing heavily, her chest heaving. I feel my dick stir and have to readjust in my seat just as Arya turns to me, a smile on her face.

"I won."

"Won what?"

She looks at me like I'm crazy and holds up an envelope of cash. "Money, obviously. Turns out I'm good at poker."

"You won," I repeat flatly. "You won?"

"Two grand," she says, grinning with pride. "And I was still able to do everything you asked."

Arya starts gushing about everything she went in to observe. She explains the floor plan, promising to draw pictures later, and tells me where guards are stationed, where security checkpoints are located, where the visible cameras look.

It's some of the best reconnaissance work I've ever seen, right up there with my most reliable men in the Bratva.

Arya knows what she is doing.

I frown when she's done. "Did anyone notice you?"

It's dark in the car, but I can still see her cheeks flush. "I mean, a few guys noticed me, but I don't think they worked at the casino."

The jealous beast inside of me flares up. "Not what I meant."

"Sorry," she murmurs. Then she waves the money at me. "Are you hungry? I'm buying."

"I'm not sure if you remember, but I'm the one who gave you the money you started with."

Arya considers that for a moment and then hands me half the stack. "We'll split it. Finder's fee."

I can't help laughing. After a moment, she joins in.

It reminds me of the moment we first laughed together like this. After we'd fled the hospital with Lukas and ended up at a diner in the middle of fucking nowhere. We'd been at each other's throats—until it all became too much and the only thing to do was laugh until your sides hurt.

This isn't quite that intense. But the effect is similar. As I pull out, I feel a tiny fraction of weight lift off my shoulders.

I focus on driving, grateful to be moving, and steer us towards the highway.

"Is this the part where you rave about my work tonight?" Arya teases.

"Mm."

"Oh, no, stop it, you're making me blush," she deadpans.

I glance over at her. That smile is fucking infectious. I'm trying hard to hold onto my motivations here. To remember my hatred, my fury.

But it's getting harder and harder with every passing minute. She looks so goddamn good in that dress. That smile, that laugh—it's a drug I can't quit, can't resist. And the smell of her floating through the car is making my head swim.

"You did good," I concede.

"How good?"

"Good enough."

She laughs again. "Never say with ten words what you can say with a grunt and a middle finger, am I right?"

"Something like that."

She shakes her head as if this is all too crazy to comprehend. We keep driving. The highway whisks beneath the wheels of the car.

When she doesn't say anything for a while, I glance over again. This time, I notice Arya's hands fidgeting in her lap nervously.

"What is it?" I ask, pumping the brake as we slide down the off-ramp and into the quiet part of town near her motel.

Arya takes a deep breath, then looks at me. "I met with someone this week. Before you came."

Again, I feel that flash of jealousy hot in my chest. "Who?"

"A man. A guy who can acquire things."

I turn into a row of empty spaces behind the motel and put the car in park. "And?"

"I've known him forever. He agreed to make me some passports. Fake passports. New identities. For me and Lukas and Ernestine and June"

My heart stops.

When it finally resumes, it feels like I'm being hammered in the chest with a bass drum mallet.

"You're leaving."

"Yeah," she says, her voice breaking. "We are. They will be ready in a week."

"Why are you telling me this?"

She shrugs like she doesn't even know the answer herself. "I just... I thought you should know."

"Because I'm going to have to stop you, you know."

"That's what you keep saying, yeah."

"But you're telling me anyway."

"Yeah," she mumbles. "I don't… I don't know why. I just did."

I turn to face her. "Do you not believe that I mean what I'm saying?"

She nods. "I believed you. But I had to try running, didn't I? I still have to try. If you mean what you say…" She gnaws at her bottom lip again, and fuck me, all I want to do is suck it into my own mouth, to taste it, to palm her hips and grind my cock against her sweetness. "Do you mean what you say, Dima? Are you going to keep us here forever? Are you going to kill us?"

There it is. The question I've been avoiding—even in my own thoughts.

Can I do what I vowed to do?

I think about that man in the podcast. About mercy. About forgiveness.

And then my hands fall limp in my lap. "No," I rasp. "I'm not."

Love is a weapon.

Love is a fucking weapon.

And Arya has it pointed right at the center of my chest right now. I'm helpless against it.

"But it's not just me you have to fear," I add. "There are men out there who will do anything to hurt me. Even if it means hurting you. Not just Jorik—there are others."

"How will killing this Giorgio whatever help with that?" she demands. "How does killing someone stop violence? How does murder keep Lukas and me safe?"

"Once I have my Bratva back, I can protect you both. I just have to annihilate this threat, and then I can—"

"What about the next threat, though?" Arya presses. "Or the one after that? What about the next traitor, the next jealous rival? You can't protect us from everything, Dima."

"If you run across the fucking planet, I can't protect you at all!" My voice lashes out in the car, booming like thunder.

Arya flinches. But she doesn't back away.

Instead, to my utter surprise…

She reaches out and touches me.

It's the first true touch we've had since I found her again—assuming me pinning her against a brick wall doesn't count. Her fingers are soft and delicate on the underside of my forearm. My cock is straining against my zipper at this alone.

"Dima, please listen to me."

"I'm listening."

"What I'm asking you is, can this world—*your* world—be any other way than what it is? Think before you answer."

I open my mouth to offer the obvious retort: this world is whatever the fuck I make it. Once I have my Bratva back, once Zotov is dead, things will be made right.

But I know even before I say it that it's a lie.

The Bratva underworld has been soaked in blood for as long as I've known it. Either my blood or my enemies'. That's the only way it can be. That's the only way it's ever been.

"That's what I thought," she whispers. "And if you're killed, then what? Who takes over for you? Who keeps us safe?"

"My son," I say without hesitation.

It's the way every don ever has answered that question. And as soon as I do, I know what Arya is going to say next.

"But I don't want this life for him, Dima. And I don't think you do, either." She grips my elbow and then slides her hand down to my hand, her fingers intertwining with mine. "It's not safe. Even if you can protect us now, you and I won't always be there for him. Who will protect him when he's grown, when he's the one in charge? What will happen if he gets killed before that day even comes? Maybe he'd be out on a mission for you and he'd get ambushed. He could be attacked for no reason other than that he is the heir. Is that what you want for him?"

No. The answer is there at the forefront of my mind, but I don't say it.

"I can protect you both," I insist. "I can. I will."

Arya leans forward and presses her lips to my cheek. It's an apology. A sympathy kiss. An attempt to make me understand what I'm refusing to grasp. That the future I'm working for right now isn't possible.

She kisses a line down my jaw and down my neck. She tilts my head so she can suck my earlobe into her mouth.

She's trying to distract me from the hurt. Maybe she's trying to distract herself, too. I don't know which it is, but right now, I don't fucking care.

I've craved this for too goddamn long to say no.

I grab Arya by the waist and swing her around into my lap. As she kisses me, I slide my seat back as far as it will go.

This kiss is fire. It's quick-moving and destructive. We both know what we want, so there's no need to draw it out.

Arya slides her arms out of the dress, letting her breasts bounce free, and I palm them both as I roll my hips against her.

I'm ready. Beyond ready.

My erection is stiff against my zipper. When Arya slides it down and frees me, I growl into her kiss.

It's a tight fit with both of us in the front seat, but she shoves her panties aside and slides onto me like her life depends on it.

I bury myself in her to the hilt.

"Fucking hell, Arya. You're impossible. Goddamn unreal."

Her dress is little more than a band around her stomach now, and I grab hold of the soft flesh of her hips and spear myself into her.

We shouldn't be doing this here, much less at all, but there's no way I can stop it now. No way I can cut this short.

I need the release. God, do I need it.

Arya leans back, hands on the ceiling and rolls her body against me slowly, working herself on my length.

"Fuck," I growl. "Motherfucking fuck."

"Does that feel good?" she purrs, doing it again, her flat stomach tensing and curling with the motion.

Later, this memory will hurt like hell. But right now, it's fucking heaven. I might as well make the most of it.

I grip Arya around the waist and thrust into her hard. Our bodies slap together, the sound echoing in the car, though it's quickly drowned out by Arya's cry.

"Right there, Dima," she gasps. "God, give me more, I'm begging you."

I do it again and again, driving into her until her mouth is hanging open, her eyes are squeezed shut, and her body is convulsing on top of me and around me.

I can feel the pulsing of her body. I've never enjoyed someone else's pleasure so much in my life.

When she's done, she collapses forward onto my chest and nuzzles her face against my neck. She bites the skin beneath my ear and kisses me.

As her orgasm fades, she regains movement and picks up speed again. She slides herself up and down and up and down along my aching length.

I want to let go. I want to release.

But I know that, once I do, this moment will be over.

And I'm not sure what comes next.

So long as we're together like this, I know where we stand. I know what I want. I know what *she* wants.

But once she's back in the passenger seat, I don't know what she wants from me.

All I'll know is what she needs.

I'm doing what Arya needs right now. Not the sex—although, based on her moans, she needs that, too.

No, this mission—killing D'Onofrio, getting Ilyasov's army, taking back my Bratva—is what Arya needs.

Because I will be able to protect her and Lukas. The sooner I can show that to her, the sooner she sets aside this idea of hopping on a plane and running away. The sooner she realizes she belongs to me…

Forever.

Warmth is spreading in my body. I can't hold back much longer. She's too tight and too wet and too hot. I'm losing my grip.

But I want Arya to come with me.

I push on her chest until she's sitting up and I have better access to her center. I slide my hand between our bodies, circling my thumb over her clit.

She gasps, and I can already feel her shuddering. She's close again.

"Come with me, *krasavitsa*," I snarl. "Come for me."

Just as I lose control, jerking inside of her, Arya tips her head back and releases a long, loud moan. "Fuck," she gasps, her thighs shaking around my hips.

"Let me hear you come," I order. I rake my fingers through her blond hair and wrench her head back to expose her throat so I can taste her sweat.

She trembles. A shiver storms through her body. "I'm coming so hard. Again."

Once we're done, she collapses on me. We lay in the driver's seat together for a few minutes, catching our breath and shaking.

Then she slinks back into the other seat, rearranging her dress as best as she can.

Nothing is solved when it's over. Nothing has really changed.

But at the same time…

It feels like a whole new world.

9

ARYA

We go back to the casino the next two nights.

Each night is the same. I stumble in, pretending to be half-drunk as soon as I arrive, and pick a table. On the way to my seat, I count every man in a suit with an earpiece. I count every camera. I count every exit.

When I come out of the casino, Dima is always there, waiting. I brief him on what I saw, what I did, and then he drives me home.

There are no repeats of our car sex escapade.

I know it's for the best, but the short ride home is so filled with sexual tension that I have to disappear into the bathroom for fifteen minutes as soon as we get home to try and dispel some of the hunger in my body.

It feels like an exorcism. Except, instead of purging Dima from my mind and body, it only makes me want him more.

Every time I come with his face in my mind, he seems to take over a little more space in my brain. My body needs him to truly release. Nothing else will suffice.

I've tried thinking of something else, someone else, but it doesn't help. Until I imagine Dima inside of me, underneath me, pinning me down and fucking me senseless, I can't get there.

But as soon as his face swims into my vision, I come like a fucking geyser.

"Clock's ticking." Dima's voice yanks me out of my thoughts.

I look around and we're already at the casino. He's parked in his usual spot. Except tonight, he's wearing dress pants and a button-down shirt.

When he pulled up in front of the motel to pick me up in the business casual attire, I nearly jumped him. The nice clothes look dangerously good on him. The slacks are tight, showing off his muscular thighs, and the shirt hugs his broad chest and shoulders while emphasizing his tapered waist.

He looks like what he is—a don with more money and power than I could ever dream of.

"New orders tonight," he says.

"Aye-aye, captain."

He smirks but kills it a second later. "Pay attention. This is important."

"I'm listening."

"We're going to maintain an open call line. Keep your phone on speaker," he says. "When you say 'I always lose,' I'll start heading inside. From there, I'll need you to maintain the distraction for three minutes so I can get through the doors, past security, and into the building proper."

I nod, my heart suddenly racing. "So tonight's the night."

"Tonight's the night," he echoes.

I shudder. A man will die tonight. A man I've never met, who's never done anything to me, is going to die at Dima's hands.

He lays one of those hands on my shoulder. It takes everything I have not to flinch away.

"You'll be fine, Arya. You can do this."

"I know I can, but can you?" It's supposed to sound playful, taunting, accusatory.

But the truth is that I'm terrified.

Terrified *of* him.

Terrified *for* him.

Terrified of what happens next.

For the last few days, I've had Dima in my life in a way that feels almost… normal? Well, as normal as it can be to spend nights casing a casino and preparing to infiltrate for a murder. But I've had him here. I've seen him. Touched him. Smelled him. Fucked him.

So what if I have to leave this casino tonight without him? What if he doesn't come out and meet me at the car? What if *I* don't make it out?

A thousand thoughts and possibilities, most of them tragic, are circling around my head. I feel like I can't breathe.

"Yes," he growls, "I can. Do your job and I'll do mine." His voice is cold and certain.

I want to have his level of confidence, but when I get out of the car, my legs are shaky.

This is really happening. Actually happening.

I glance over my shoulder once just before I go in. Dima is watching me. I still haven't decided if that's my dream come true or a nightmare turned reality.

Out of habit, I scan the lobby on my way into the casino, trying to take note of every single important detail.

Then I remember it doesn't matter. It's too late. There will be no reconnaissance meeting tonight, no exchanging of information.

I've told Dima everything I'm going to tell him. There's nothing more to add.

I hope to God I've told him enough.

The casino is smoky and dim. Same as I've done for three nights running, I exchange my cash for chips and head to the poker tables.

The dealer at the first table is the same one I had the night before. He tips his head in recognition, but otherwise, doesn't pay any special attention to me.

I play a few rounds, losing each one. "Bad luck," I slur, gathering my chips. "New table."

The other losers at the table nod in agreement as they scatter, but the winner, a tall man in a cowboy hat, bids us goodbye as he stacks up his chips.

I order a drink. "Vodka soda, please." Contrary to Dima's instructions, I need some liquid courage to get through the evening this time around.

"Somebody pre-gamed," the waitress comments a minute later as she hands it over. I'm slumped forward on the table, my makeup purposefully smeared under my eyes.

I hiss at her and take my drink. The husband and wife next to me scoot closer together and further from me.

Eyes are definitely beginning to turn in my direction. Time to start dialing that up a little more with every passing second.

I play another two rounds, losing significant money in each, and slam my fist on the table.

"Tonight is not my night," I say, nudging the woman next to me with my elbow. "Mind kissing me for luck?"

The white woman has a middle-aged mom haircut and her shirt collar couldn't be any tighter around her neck if she tried. I doubt she's the type to be sexually fluid.

She grimaces at me and grabs her husband's arm. He pats her leg, but otherwise keeps his eyes on the table, eager for the next hand.

"Will anyone kiss me for luck?" I yell, throwing my arms up. "I could really use the luck."

"Ma'am." The dealer catches my attention and shakes his head. "Keep it down."

I waggle my brows at him. "Are you interested?"

He sighs and shuffles the cards with skilled hands. I'm sure he has dealt with his fair share of drunk gamblers, but I'm about to cement a permanent place in his memory. *Just give me fifteen minutes.*

The drink is warming my belly. Taking the edge off my prickling nerves and relaxing me.

The burner phone shoved in the side of my dress, on the other hand, feels like a third arm. I'm positive everyone is looking at it. At me. Like there's a spotlight aimed in my direction and the big neon sign out front says, **"Aryana Georgeovich Is Here To Help Dima Romanoff Kill A Man."**

Shut up, brain, I scold myself. *Focus.*

In the third round at the table, the man and wife win again. She claps politely in celebration. I take the opportunity to topple my chair over with a frustrated scream.

The woman freezes, the man pauses, arms wrapped around his winnings, and the people at the tables next to us gasp and turn.

Usually, the casino is a din of noise and bells and chatter and music. But right now, it feels deathly silent.

"I always lose!" I yell, angling my head towards the phone just in case the speaker on it isn't very good.

I always lose. Those are the code words.

Which means, in three minutes, Dima will take the first steps towards a murder.

Suddenly, I panic. I wonder if the phone died. Maybe Dima can't hear me. Maybe this whole plan will be for nothing.

If the phone is dead and I cause a huge scene, I won't be able to come back here. After what I plan to do in just a second, I'll probably be banned for life. The last few nights will have been for nothing.

"Calm down, honey," the winner says, tucking his wife safely behind him. "If you don't have any more to lose, then don't play. Just walk away."

I lean forward and bark out a laugh in his face. "That's what everybody does. Walks away. I'm not like everybody. I don't just give up when the going gets hard."

"No, you just throw a fit and ruin everyone else's night." The man's wife is confident now that her husband is a human shield between the two of us.

I pout out my lower lip at her. "Oh no, am I ruining your date night with my petty little problems? How fucking dare I! Attention, everyone: the world revolves around this woman and we all need to keep our problems to ourselves."

Her husband stands up, his chest puffed out. "Hey now, don't talk to my wife that way. We didn't cause your problems. Don't put it on the rest of us."

"No, you just stole my money and refused to kiss me good luck. Screw you, bitch."

I make a big show of struggling to pick up my chair, spilling my drink on the floor in the process. Then I stumble over the leg of the chair, catch myself on the edge of the table, and send everyone's stacks of chips flying.

The man next to me hurries to gather his fallen chips. I drop to my knees to help.

"I'm so sorry," I say, shoving one chip down the front of my dress. "Mind if I take one as a 'thank you' for helping?"

He eyes my chest suspiciously, obviously wanting his chip back, but not desperate enough to reach down my dress and assault me for it. I feel bad for him, for the situation I'm putting him in.

But there's no time for that emotion right now.

"Ma'am, I think it's time you cashed out and made your way home," the dealer says. "Or I'm going to call security."

He threatens me with security as if I'm not already being watched already. I know there's a camera behind his head. Over the top of the table and hanging from the rafters every ten feet apart. My breakdown is being observed from multiple angles in 4K resolution in some back room somewhere.

Security knows all about me.

"What is there to cash out?" I laugh, the sound turning into a choked sob halfway out. "I'm broke. There's nothing left. My ex was right; I never should have gotten down from the pole. That's where the real money is."

I stand up and plant one foot on top of my chair like Captain Morgan. My dress is short and riding high up on my thigh. I know the man and his wife are getting a nice close-up of my panties. The shock on the woman's face confirms it.

"I thought I'd come here and try to make myself some money with my mind, but Gary was fucking right. I'm not worth anything more than the cash that gets shoved down the front of my g-string during an act."

The wife is now trying to shield her husband's eyes, which are darting from my crotch to his winnings and back again.

I can hear the dealer saying something into a headset. I know they're coming for me now.

It's time to kick it up a notch.

I step up onto the chair and throw my arms in the air. "Ladies and Gentleman, back for a special one-night engagement, may I present Jazzy Jack-Off!"

Someone nearby cackles in obvious amusement. I smile in that direction while, at the same time, I slide down the strapless top of my dress and let my boobs fall out.

I catch the phone before it falls, holding it in my hand like it's nothing more than my cell phone. Not important. Not a secret. Just a plain old phone, hiding in plain sight.

The wife gasps and turns away, the dealer is shaking his head in disappointment, and somewhere, a camera flash goes off.

Voice slurred, movement unsteady, I start beatboxing my own dance music and shake my chest back and forth. A few drunk men whistle and catcall from the bar.

Just like Dima requested, every single eye is on me.

Which is why I'm the only one who sees the broad-shouldered, well-dressed man slip into the lobby, past security, and down a "Staff Only" hallway.

Just as Dima disappears down the hallway, a large security guard wraps his arms around my knees, picks me up off the table, and throws me over his shoulder.

I give a loud rebel yell and throw up a peace sign. "Jazzy Jack-Off, signing off!"

Mission accomplished.

10

DIMA

Arya is quite the actress.

All I can hear on the phone are the muffled sounds of her conversation and her slurred voice, but it's obvious she's putting on a show and people are buying it.

At least, I hope people are buying it.

I assured Arya before she left that everything would go to plan, but I'm not convinced myself. There are still so many unknowns in this scheme. So many places where I could make a mistake or be caught or be recognized.

Or maybe Arya won't simply be kicked out of the casino. Maybe she'll be taken to a back room where she'll be identified and interrogated.

Regrets surface the longer I sit and wait. I shouldn't have brought Arya into this. I shouldn't have involved her. I could have done the reconnaissance myself. I could have formulated another distraction.

I risked her life in an effort to save it.

How does that make any fucking sense?

When Arya yells out the code, I shove aside my doubts and regrets and start heading inside. There's no time to change the plan. It's happening, whether I think it's still a good idea or not.

It's well after midnight, so the lobby is mostly empty. The people working the teller stations are turned around watching a screen in the corner of the booth, which I realize is a security feed. They're watching Arya's show.

The people milling around in the lobby are craning their heads to catch a glimpse, too.

Arya quite literally has all eyes on her.

I use the phone to hide my face from the cameras lined up along the right wall inside the lobby. The cameras to the left, just as Arya told me, are angled lower to the ground. "If you stay in the center of the lobby," she said, "and hide your face on the right, you might as well be a ghost."

She paid attention to every detail.

Arya may not want anything to do with the mafia lifestyle, but goddamn, she'd make one hell of a mob queen.

As I approach the "Staff Only" hallway Arya told me about, I look up just in time to see Arya herself, standing on a table.

Topless.

She's far away, just a smudge, but it can't be anyone else. I feel two emotions at once. The first is the insane, chemical attraction I've felt for her since the moment we met. I want to take her down on that card table and fucking devour her—in front of everyone, if necessary.

The other is the insane, chemical jealousy I feel for her anytime anyone else so much as glances in her direction. I want to go around to every man in the room one by one and rip their fucking eyes out from the sockets.

But I have a job to do. Both the jealousy and the attraction will have to wait.

So I turn down the hallway, keeping my head low.

The security checkpoints in the lobby are cleared, the guards no doubt responding to the chaos inside. I slip through without a single hitch. And if there are cameras in the staff hallway, I have to hope everyone is too busy watching the impromptu strip show in the other room to pay any attention to me.

The hallway is long and curved, wrapping around the outside of the main casino. At the end of the hall, there are only two doors.

An emergency exit and an office door.

Everything past here is a mystery I don't know what I'm walking into or who will be waiting for me.

Grabbing my gun from my hip and taking a deep breath, I push open the office door. I find myself in an entryway of sorts that branches off into other staff spaces. All of them are labeled. There's an employee lounge, a restroom, a kitchen. And, at the back, a large metal door with a coded handle that says "SECURITY."

As I approach, I notice the door is propped open with a wooden doorstop. I say a silent prayer of thanks and push the door open.

This time, the room is dark except for the glow of a wall of screens.

Three bodies are hunched over the screens, pointing at the scene below.

I don't spend much time look at the screens, but I do see a lot of movement in one of them. It looks like someone is being carted away, kicking and screaming.

Good girl.

The hunched over man in the middle is wearing an expensive suit. I can see cigar smoke drifting up from his mouth. The shadows on his left and right look almost identical. Same black suit, same haircut, same corded earpiece leading up to their ear.

The two on the flanks are guards.

And the man in the middle…

That's D'Onofrio.

I lift my gun and take the first guard out with one silenced shot.

The bullet rips through his head and careens into the screen in front of him. Electronic shit breaks, fries, hisses.

There is a yell, but I don't notice where it comes from. I'm too busy taking aim at the other guard.

My second bullet enters his temple. He drops, lifeless.

D'Onofrio doesn't even turn around. He just lifts his hands into the air in surrender. His fingers are trembling.

"Who are you?" he rasps, still facing the screens. "What do you want?"

I press the gun to the back of his head. "Nothing you can give me."

He exhales a shaky breath. "Please don't kill me. My father is powerful. He can give you whatever you want. Anything. Money, cars, jewels, women. Just name it and it's yours. Don't shoot."

I roll my eyes at the shameless begging. I almost feel bad for D'Onofrio's pitiful final moments. A don should never go out so pitifully.

Then his words register.

My father is powerful.

D'Onofrio is in his sixties. His father is a nobody. This isn't a family business. It was built from the ground up by Giorgio himself.

Which means…

"Turn around," I bark, removing the muzzle from the back of his head and taking a few steps back. "Slowly. Keep your hands in the air."

The man spins around slowly, the tremors in his hands moving down to his arms until he's shaking like a leaf.

When he finally does face me, I curse under my breath. "Who the fuck are you?"

The man—no older than twenty-something, with jet-black hair and enough gaudy gold on his wrists to supply a jewelry shop—whimpers. "Ennio D'Onofrio. My father owns the casino. I can get you whatever you want."

I wave the gun at him. "Shut up. Shut the fuck up."

He smashes his lips together and then glances down at the dead guard on his right. He winces and turns to stare at my gun in mute horror.

This man is barely a man. He's a kid.

Twenty years old. Maybe less.

Jesus fucking Christ.

"Where's Giorgio?"

"He isn't here," Ennio says, lifting his hands higher. "I swear. He's gone."

Fuck. Not only is this a huge wrench in my plan…

But it proves that Arya was right.

She told me Lukas wouldn't be safe in my world. Even if I could keep him safe, eventually he'd take over for me, he'd start to lead what was once mine.

Lukas could easily be Ennio one day. The son of the don, caught in the wrong place at the wrong time.

I'm here to kill his father, but that doesn't matter now. I just killed two guards. So unless I want to be set upon by the entire security department of the casino, I have to kill Ennio, too.

He's innocent. Or, at least, not guilty of being his father. He isn't my target, but it doesn't fucking matter.

The boy has to die.

My grip on the gun is crushing and my palm is starting to ache. I adjust it. Just a tiny motion, but Ennio looks like he's about to piss himself.

He's a coward.

But that still doesn't mean he deserves to die.

I take a deep breath. "Where is your father?"

Ennio clenches his lips together harder until they begin to go white. His attempt at being brave, I guess.

I step forward, gun pointed at his forehead. "Ennio, listen very closely to me. You need to answer my questions and do it quickly. I don't want to have to kill you."

"But you will anyway," he says in a surprising show of courage. "If I tell you, you'll kill me and then go after him. If I don't, you'll kill me and then go after him. At least if I stay quiet, I won't betray my father."

Am I going to kill him? The fact that the question even crosses my mind is maddening. This should be easy. So fucking easy. I've killed people for far less. If they get in my way, I end them. It's not pretty or right, but it's business. It's my world. It's what I know.

Now, suddenly, I'm hesitant.

Because of Arya.

Love is a weapon. It slices through the most tender parts of you. It brings you to your knees.

A scenario plays in my mind of some unknown assassin standing in front of my son one day, threatening his life because he wants to get to me. It's entirely fictional, but I feel sick anyway.

Arya was right. I can't keep them safe. I can't protect Lukas from my world. From my life.

I can't fucking do it.

One half of my brain is descending into a thought spiral of self-loathing and pity. The other half is trying to figure out what in the hell to do with Ennio D'Onofrio.

I take a breath and ask him again, "Where is your father, Ennio?"

The man shakes his head. "I won't say."

Without hesitation, I lower my gun and pull the trigger. Shooting him in the knee.

Ennio cries out and drops to the ground, clutching his leg.

"Hands up!" I hiss. "Or I'll shoot you again."

Whimpering, he slowly lifts himself up on one leg, the other bent awkwardly beneath him. He's leaning back on the security equipment for balance and his forehead is drenched in sweat. Blood trickles down his ruined leg.

"Just kill me," Ennio begs. "I won't tell you anything. I'm useless to you."

I consider it for a moment. I need to get out of here. I'm running out of time.

Then I realize... he isn't completely useless.

If Giorgio feels about his son even half of what I feel for mine, Ennio could be quite useful indeed.

"Take me to the elevator," I order.

Ennio frowns. "W-what?"

"Elevator. Now. Don't even think of calling for help."

Ennio hesitates for a moment and then begins hopping towards the door. I follow close behind, the gun pressed against his back.

He leads me through the lobby area to a metal door on the other side. He enters in a code and then opens the door with one of many keys on his keychain. The door opens onto an elevator shaft.

"If there are guards down there, send them away," I order, blocking the buttons so he can't press anything. "If these doors open and we see anyone down there, I'll kill them immediately."

"And me too?" he asks.

I scowl. "By the time all this is over, you'll wish I killed you."

Ennio blinks and then grabs a walkie on his hip. "Antonio, go to front of house and check on the situation."

A voice crackles through the walkie. "Roger."

Ennio nods. "It's done."

We go down to the basement level and walk into a dark, concrete hallway. There is a door directly next to the elevator shaft with a glowing "Exit" sign above it. Ennio pushes it open and we emerge out onto the side of the building.

I yank Ennio back and slam him against the building. "Don't move."

I pull out my phone and call Arya.

"Thank God," she breathes as soon as she picks up. "I was getting worried. Where are you?"

"East side of the building. The keys are on the rear wheel-well. Go get the car and come pick me up."

I wait for a long minute. I can hear her feet pounding the pavement and her dress swishing. Then the sound of the car engine starting through the phone. "Are you hurt?" she asks.

"I'm fine."

"Okay. I'll be there in a second." She hangs up.

When she turns the corner, her eyes nearly pop out of her head as she sees the bleeding man with me. She reaches over and throws open the passenger side door. "What in the fuck is this?"

"Ennio, meet Arya. Arya, Ennio." I shove the bleeding man into the backseat of the car and follow after, gun still aimed at him.

Arya is turned around in her seat, staring at us with wide eyes.

"This is the part where you start driving," I deadpan.

Arya releases a heavy breath through her nose, whips herself around in the seat, and takes off.

She doesn't say anything the whole way back.

11

ARYA

I coast to a stop outside of the Sunset Motel.

Dima and Ennio are still squeezed into the backseat of the car. Ennio is curled up against the side of the car, as far from Dima's gun as he can get. Dima is a statue. His gun has not wavered since we left the casino. I wonder if he has even blinked.

"Go to the front desk," he orders. "Buy the adjoining room."

I'm furious as I leap out of the car and stalk to the front desk. I hardly say a word to the night manager as I hand over the cash and take the key to the second motel room.

When I return, I don't go straight back to the car. Instead, I slip into the room I've been staying in all week.

Lukas is in his bassinet with Ernestine and June. I didn't know how late we'd get back, so she offered to take care of him all night. Now, I'm beyond grateful for the offer. I don't want Lukas anywhere near this stranger Dima has kidnapped.

I creak open the adjoining door, slide through, and then come out the front. Marching out to the car, I rap on Dima's window.

"You can come in."

It's the first thing I've said to him since we left the casino. And even now, my words come out between gritted teeth.

What in the fuck was he thinking?

He wasn't thinking. That's what happened.

Taking hostages was not part of the plan. Holding a mobster hostage in the motel where Lukas and Ernestine and June are living was most definitely not part of the plan, either.

Driving home, I wanted to suggest we take Ennio somewhere else. Anywhere else.

Anywhere except where my infant child is, my mind screams.

Dima slides out of the car first, moving backwards so he can keep his eyes and gun trained on Ennio.

Ennio follows, hands raised. I can see he's shaking. I don't know if it's from exhaustion, pain, fear, adrenaline, or a mix of all of it.

"Walk ahead of me. Go into the room." Dima's voice is deeper than I've ever heard it. Almost like he's a different person entirely.

Ennio walks inside. Seeing him here, mere feet away from where my son is sleeping, makes me livid.

This should not be fucking happening.

I stand in the background as Dima rips out cords from the two lamps in the room, along with the extra bedsheets, and uses them to secure Ennio to the corner of the radiator that is bolted to the concrete floor and wall. So long as the ties hold, Ennio won't be going anywhere.

"Are you hungry?" I ask Ennio just before Dima and I turn to leave. "I can bring you something."

"He's our prisoner," Dima snaps. "Not a fucking houseguest."

"Hostages are no good when they're starved," I hiss back.

Ennio nods. "Actually, yes. I'd love something to eat. Anything you have."

Ennio D'Onofrio is a man, but chained up on the floor, he looks like a small child. I can almost imagine him as a little kid. A head full of dark hair, big brown eyes, a lopsided grin.

Does his father know he is missing yet?

I push the thought away and sneak back into my room.

We've got a cooler with some food items in there, so I get to work making a sandwich. When I'm done, I grab a bottle of water and take it all over to Ennio.

I set the plate on the floor and then scoot it into range with my toe so he can reach it with his bound hands. He thanks me sincerely.

I leave without saying a word.

I go outside instead of back to the room. I sure as hell can't sleep, not with all this nervous, angry energy racing through me.

So I pace. Dima is leaning up against the trunk of the car, deep in thought. I pass back and forth, back and forth, back and forth in front of him.

"Arya, stop." Dima is looking up at me now.

"I'm pacing."

"I can see that. Stop." He sighs and looks up at me. "We have to talk."

I fold my hands in front of me. "About what?'

Dima snorts and gestures to the sky overhead. "The weather. I'd love to know what you think of this unseasonably warm day we had."

I grimace at him. "Don't talk to me like that. I'm not an idiot."

"Then don't act like one. We have to decide what we're going to do."

"Oh, it's 'we' now?" I snap. "Do I suddenly get a say in what happens around here? How nice. How exciting for me. It's like a promotion."

Dima lifts his head. It looks like he has aged ten years in the last two hours. There are dark circles under his eyes, his lips are chapped, and the lines around his mouth seem deeper. "Always with the jokes," he murmurs.

"Not a single thing about this shit is funny, Dima!" I yell. "I told you I didn't want my son being part of this world. I wanted all of this shit as far away from my family as possible. And yet *you brought it here*."

"I didn't plan this. I thought Giorgio would be back there. I had no idea it would be his son instead. I did what I thought was best."

I clench my fists. "You thought ten feet away from our son would be the best place to hold a mafioso ransom? Are you deranged or just stupid?"

Dima takes a sharp lunge forward. The car creaks without his weight leaning against it. He's still a yard away from me, but I startle back anyway.

"What was I supposed to do, Arya? I'm on the run, if you remember. I can't exactly take him back to my mansion or the Bratva cells. I also can't take him to the safehouse because it would no longer be a safe house if he knew about it, would it? I'd have to kill him if he saw that." Dima runs a hand through his hair, the curls standing on end in every direction. "I brought him here because it's a shithole motel in a corrupt fucking city. We're paying with cash, so it's not tied back to us at all. I regret that Lukas is here, but it was my only option, and I don't regret the choices I've made. I never fucking will, so don't ask that of me."

Some of what he is saying makes sense, but it doesn't do anything to ease my anger.

"This is exactly the kind of shit I was talking about before," I say somberly. "There will always be a surprise. Something unplanned.

There will always be something that crops up and puts my son at danger. So long as we are near you, we aren't safe."

Dima looks like I just slapped him across the face. In a way, I did.

When we had sex in the car the other day, it was because I could see the hurt in his eyes when he saw I doubted him. I could see how much it pained him to want to take care of us, but for me not to trust him enough to let him do it.

I wanted to comfort him. To give him some part of me even though I couldn't give him all of me.

Now, that instinct is gone.

Dima needs to hear me. He needs to understand me. He has to know that I'm serious when I tell him I don't want my son subjected to these kinds of dangers. So long as this shit is his life, it can't intersect with ours.

"I did this to keep you safe!" he hisses.

I stare at him, baffled. "How? How is this keeping us safe? How is this not purely motivated by your own selfishness and desire for power?"

His blue eyes flare, the pupils dilating wide. "Selfish? If I was being selfish, I would have shot Ennio back at the casino the second he didn't give me what I wanted. And then I would've disappeared before his dear old dad could do anything about it."

"Sounds great to me," I lie, throwing my hands up. "Why didn't you?"

Dima points his fingers at the side of his head like a gun. "Because your voice was in my head. *'What happens when Lukas takes over for you?'* he mimics in a high-pitched voice. *"'What happens when someone goes after him to get to you?'* That's all I could hear while I stood there with my gun pointed at my target's son. It's all I could think about. You fucking broke me, Arya."

My heart tears slightly. I feel it happen. The fabric of it ripping apart, tearing in two.

I want to wrap my arms around Dima and try to protect what's left of the gentle soul inside of him. The last bit of innocence that his dark and twisted life hasn't yet stained forever.

But I also want to slam my fists against his chest and demand to know why he won't just leave with me. Why he won't run away with us and leave this all behind.

"And now, I have a way forward," Dima continues. "If I'd killed Ennio, I would have had nothing to lure Giorgio out with. He would have been on high alert, knowing someone was coming for his family, and I never would have reached him. This way, I have a chance to still make the hit."

"Are you serious? That's what you're thinking about right now? The goddamn *hit*?"

"Of course it is!" he roars. "Because I can't keep you safe until Giorgio is dead. I can't protect you and Lukas until I'm wielding the full power of my Bratva again. And I can't do that until I have my brother's army. It's the only way."

I sag forward and drop my head against my fists. "It's not the only way, Dima. It's not. You could leave with me. You could start over with me and Lukas and leave this all behind. This is just the only way that gives you what you want."

The air between us descends into a deathly silence. We sit there in it for a long time.

Finally, Dima leans back against the car and folds his hands in front of him. "I don't have to pick between the two. I'm Dima fucking Romanoff. I can have everything I want."

There's a barely restrained frustration in his voice. I wonder if I shouldn't leave it alone. I'm not afraid of Dima, but I don't want to purposefully poke the bear. However, I also don't want to lie to him. Not anymore.

"*You* can have everything," I correct. "Lukas and I don't have that option."

I turn around and walk into our room before he can figure out how to respond.

Inside, Ernestine and June are snoring in the bed and Lukas is asleep in the bassinet. I lay down on the floor at the end of the bed. I close my eyes, begging for sleep to come and wash away the horrible thoughts rushing through my head.

But sleep never comes.

12

DIMA

I stand outside for a long time, thinking. How did things get this fucking far?

The rational part of my mind understands where Arya is coming from, but I'm too angry to be rational. I'm too angry to understand.

No one makes a don choose between his empire and his family.

I'd die for Lukas and Arya, of course. But I'd die for Gennady, too. I'd die to protect my men and my family name. Can she really expect me to give all of that up?

When sitting still becomes impossible, I march into the adjoining room.

Ennio is the problem. Ennio is the reason this argument came to a head. The sooner I get rid of the D'Onofrio runt—not to mention the weakness that led me to kidnap him in the first place—the better.

When the door opens, Ennio hurries to sit up. He looks behind me, like he's hoping for someone else. I notice his face fall.

He was wishing Arya would be here. Because she was kind to him. Because she calmed me.

Unfortunately for Ennio, though, he has to face me now. Just me.

And I'm not nearly as kind as Arya is.

"Where is your father?" I ask. I've tucked my gun away in my waistband in favor of a tire iron that I fished out of the car. I toss it back and forth from one hand to the other. Ennio's eyes follow it every time.

He swallows and shakes his head. "I'm not talking."

I sigh. "Don't be stupid, Ennio. Your father is an old man. He has lived a long life. And you're set to inherit, I presume? You're young. Imagine what you could do with the business in your lifetime."

"Like you'd let me survive longer than it took to tell you his location? I know how this game goes. I'm a loose end."

He isn't wrong, but he doesn't have all the facts. Ennio doesn't realize that I have a woman just inside who, whether she admits it or not, is rooting for Ennio to survive.

Time will tell who gets to decide his fate.

"You don't know anything about my game."

"I know more than I'd like," Ennio mumbles.

I step towards him, wrench clenched in my fist. "What does that mean?"

"Just that these are thin walls," he says. "I heard everything."

I frown. I don't like that. Uncharacteristically careless of me. "It's rude to eavesdrop."

"Well, you shot me in the knee and kidnapped me, so I'll say we're even."

"How about I say when we're even?" I snap, raising the wrench. "Or would you like me to take out your other knee, too?"

Ennio's eyes widen. He pulls his legs closer to his body. "My parents had a lot of similar discussions. It isn't anything I haven't heard before. It certainly didn't surprise me."

"I don't know if you're aware or not, but we aren't your parents. How much blood have you lost? Are you going to die on me?"

"It's not a happy story," Ennio continues as if he didn't hear me. "No happily-ever-after for them."

"With a pussy like you for a son, I'd imagine not."

Ennio actually laughs at that, but I assume it's for my benefit. If he thinks flattery will soften me, he's sorely mistaken.

"My parents were in love once. A long time ago. Mamma was an idealist, a dreamer. She imagined she could take my rough, violent father and soften him. She thought he would calm down once he was older and had a family."

"Let me guess: it didn't work that way."

He looks up at me, one eyebrow raised. "Do assassins like you usually target nice, quiet, suburban fathers? No, Papa never changed. Mamma put up with it for a long time, but then she started pushing back. She didn't want this life for me or my sisters. She didn't want us to be in danger."

"Too late for that."

Ennio lets out a breathy laugh and then sighs. "They fought about it all the time. Mamma wanted Papa to retire and hand the business over to his brother or his second, but Papa refused. So Mamma threatened to leave him."

"How did that work out for her?" I have a creeping feeling that I already know the answer.

Ennio looks down at his bloody knee and shakes his head. "She never got the chance. Just before she was going to take us back with her to see family in Italy—one-way tickets—she had a bad fall down the stairs. She broke her neck. Died instantly."

I whistle. "You weren't kidding. That's not a happy story at all."

"It's even worse when you grow up with the rumors of what really happened," he says. "Papa made it so there was no investigation into the accident. He cremated Mamma's body. Buried her quickly. He wept at the funeral. And then he never shed another tear again. It was as if Mamma never existed."

"People deal with grief differently."

"People deal with murder differently."

I suspected as much, but I'm surprised to hear Ennio say it so bluntly. "You think he did it?"

Ennio shrugs. "I think Papa helped the accident along. How would it have looked if his wife and his heirs ran away from him? A don must be able to control his family just like he controls his business. Papa couldn't control Mamma, so he did what he felt he needed to do."

The events of the day seem to catch up with me all at once. I feel the urge to sit down, but this is not the time. It's an interrogation, not a confession. I shake my head slightly and grip the tire iron tighter.

"If your father is as bad as he sounds, why don't you tell me where he is? Some would say it's karma."

"Some would say it's patricide," he snaps back. "I have hopes to be better than my father. Not just like him."

I groan. "Every son wants to be better than his father. None of us are. Apples, trees. It's nature."

"You think I'm a murderer?"

"I think you'd murder me," I suggest, "if you had the chance. If it came down to just one of us, you'd kill me just as easily as I'd kill you."

Ennio's dark brows pinch together. "That's self-defense. I'd never break into your place of business, kill your guards, and attack you. That makes me better than you."

"It makes you weaker," I say simply. "It means that between the two of us, I'm the one willing to do what needs to be done. No matter what."

He raises his brows and leans his head back against the wall. "Like my father."

Suddenly, the ease that had settled over me shatters. Anger, burning hot, floods my chest and sends pinpricks of energy to my hands and legs.

"I am not your fucking father, *mudak*."

Ennio doesn't seem to understand the danger he is in. Either that or he no longer cares. He shrugs. "I see it differently. My father was also willing to do whatever needed to be done to protect himself, his image, his position. He didn't let my mother take everything from him. Some say it makes him a monster. Others say it makes him strong. Who gets to decide which one of those is right?"

I'm tempted to hit him upside the head with the tire iron just to be done with this conversation. "There are other ways to deal with the people we love."

"Less efficient ways. Murder is the fastest." Ennio readjusts on the floor, tucking his legs in even closer and sliding his hands under his thighs to keep warm. "My father always said that sentiment is a dangerous game in the mafia world."

"Funny that you are so loyal to him. That is a form of sentiment, isn't it? And it's the reason you're bleeding out in this repulsive motel room instead of warm and safe in your bed."

His eyes widen for a second, like he's found what I've said amusing. Then he controls his expression and meets my gaze. "I suppose you were right before. No matter how we try, sons will never be better than their fathers. In my case, I hope that means I'm stronger than you think. I hope that means I'm going to survive."

Before I can even formulate a response, Ennio leaps off of the floor, landing on his good leg, and lunges for me.

One of his hands goes for my neck, the other for my wrist, trying to pry the tire iron out of my hand.

Somehow, he slipped out of the ties. While he eased me with idle chatter, he was escaping right before my eyes.

Bad move. Now I have to hurt him.

I lift my arm and bring my elbow down on the crook of his arm. Bone crunches somewhere. Ennio's arm retracts, letting go of my wrist, and I swing the tire iron at him.

He throws up his arm to protect his face, and I hear the metal make cracking contact with his wrist. Ennio cries out in pain.

He spins away from me and lunges for the door handle. He manages to grab it and rip it open. The door swings wide, letting in the first trickles of dawn light.

I scramble after him, but Ennio is ahead of me—and he's screaming like a fucking banshee.

As I burst out of the motel room, I see more doors opening up and down the rows.

Fuck. That means witnesses.

I know I'm up shit creek, but there's no bailing now. Regardless, I'm fucked. And I'd rather be fucked without an eyewitness account of my murdering two guards and kidnapping him.

This can only end one way now.

For a man with a bullet in his knee, Ennio is moving remarkably fast. He's twenty, thirty yards away from me now. The tire iron is useless.

I drop the tool on the concrete, grab the gun from my waistband, and take aim.

BANG. BANG.

Two shots ring out.

And Ennio D'Onofrio hits the ground. Once he falls, he doesn't move again.

I hear Arya's door open behind me, but I'm already racing across the parking lot towards Ennio, unsure if I hope to find him dead or alive.

Turns out he's well on his way from one to the other. There's a wound to his neck, blood gurgling out in a pulsing rhythm. His eyes are rolled back in his head. Mouth open. Arms limp.

He's got a few seconds left to live.

"Fuck," I growl.

How could everything have gone so wrong? I risked everything to bring Ennio back here, to find some way to right the botched hit. Now, he's useless to me. Giorgio won't show his face for his dead son.

And as I turn around and catch sight of Arya's horrified face standing in the doorway, I know something else: Arya will never forget what happened here.

13

ARYA

I feel like I'm almost asleep when I hear the gunshots.

BANG. BANG.

A pair of them shattering the pre-dawn silence.

I jump up from my nest on the floor and sprint to the door. Throwing it open, I take one step out into the cold air—and then I freeze.

The concrete is cold on my bare feet, but I barely feel it. There's too much adrenaline pumping through my veins for me to pay attention to anything other than the two shapes in the parking lot ahead of me.

One of them is Dima. Standing tall, with a gun in his hand.

The other one, crumpled at his feet, is Ennio.

I don't have to get close to know that I'm watching him die. I see him twitch once or twice like a fish on a boat. Blood bubbles up around his throat.

From that point forward, he doesn't move anymore.

"Dima?" I call out to him, but he either doesn't hear or ignores it.

He's dead. An innocent man is dead.

I can see the truth of it in the way Dima leans over the body and then, after a second, takes a staggered step back. He runs a hand through his hair and shakes his head.

My first thought is pure anger. *I told him this would happen. I told Dima this was a bad idea.*

My second thought is something new for me: an impulse for action. *We have to fix this.*

I look around the U-shaped motel building. I can see filtered lights shining out from the windows in the houses around us. Blinds lift and fall as people too afraid to come out and investigate the clamor for themselves peek out at us.

The gunshots woke people up. The police will be coming soon. We have to get out of here.

I grab Dima's car keys from just inside the door and run to him. He looks up at the sound of my footsteps. "Arya, I don't know—"

"Get out of here!" I scream, pitching my voice to sound as panicked as possible. "Who are you? What have you done?"

Dima's face is confused. Shocked, really. His mouth falls open and he blinks rapidly. "What are you talking about? He escaped and—"

"Dima, you have to go," I whisper, slamming him in the chest again, this time pressing the keys against his shirt. His hand falls over mine, clutching at my fingers for just a second before I pull my hand away, leaving the keys. "Get out of here. I'll make up a story, but you can't be seen here. Go."

All at once, he realizes it's a ruse. Color comes back to his face. He releases a long, ragged breath. "I can't leave you and Lukas now."

"Go!" I order, pushing him towards the car. Then, louder, I add, "Don't hurt me! I'm calling the police!"

Dima opens his mouth to argue, but before he can say anything else, I spin around and run back into the room.

Ernestine is awake now, June pressed tightly to her side, trembling. There's no time to explain. No time to ease them into this situation. We're in the thick of it and I need them to cooperate without question.

"We're leaving. Now. Get everything and be in the car in five minutes."

It's almost sad how quickly June and Ernestine follow my orders. There is no hesitation, not even from the little girl. Ernestine hurries June back into the bedroom and they begin gathering the few items they've accumulated since we went on the run.

I can't help but feel guilty for dragging Ernestine and June into this. No matter what, Tommy would have showed up at their door, whether I was staying with them or not. But my presence made things much more complicated.

I have to get them away from this life, too. It's my fault they're here. I have to fix it. I have to fix all of it.

As I pack up the room, getting rid of any trace of us, I pull out the burner phone Dima gave me earlier tonight and call the police.

"9-1-1, what is your emergency?"

"A man was just shot," I gasp, breathing heavily into the phone. "I heard yelling, so I went outside to see what was going on. There was an old Italian man yelling at a younger man, saying all kinds of horrible things. I think it was the guy's father. Then he shot him. It all happened so fast and—"

"What's your address?"

"The Sunset Motel."

"I'll have a unit dispatched right away. Is there anything else you can tell me? Are you safe?"

"The man saw me and came after me, but I fought him off. He took off in his car. The body is still in the driveway."

She asks for my name. I hang up and continue packing.

We paid cash for these rooms, so as long as we get out of here before the police arrive, there is no tying us back to this. It will look like Ennio was taken out by someone in his own mafia. If the cops follow the clues I gave the 911 operator, they'll finger Ennio's father for the crime.

As soon as the police ID the body, they probably won't even launch a large investigation. The assumption that he died in the midst of mafia business will be the logical conclusion. There will be no connection back to Dima.

"We're ready," Ernestine calls.

I meet her in the hallway. "Me too. Let's load up."

June is carrying Lukas, cradling him gently in her tiny arms, while Ernestine and I throw our scant belongings in the back of the van.

Police sirens are getting closer, the wails piercing the silence. We don't have any time to waste. I tell Ernestine to buckle in the kids while I take the keys and hop in the driver's seat.

I wonder where Dima is.

I want to kiss Lukas's face, cradle him against my chest, remind myself that he is healthy and okay and complete. And then I want Dima to do the same thing to me.

But there's no time for any of that. Right now, the best thing I can do for Lukas—and for myself—is stay focused on the mission ahead.

Ernestine is just finishing getting into her seat when I hit the gas and take off through the parking lot.

As we pass where Ennio's body is laying, I try not to look.

I've seen enough death to last a lifetime.

∼

As we get on the highway, I see police cars, sirens flashing, fly past us and take the exit towards the motel. I white-knuckle the steering wheel and mash the gas pedal faster until we're clear of the madness.

We drive in silence for a while, but as the excitement of the evening fades away, June begins asking questions.

"Who was that lying in the driveway? That wasn't Dima, was it?" she asks, her voice cracking.

It's been hard cobbling together stories that will make sense to June and to Ernestine. When I first found them again, I told them that Dima and I were taking some time apart, but that the kind of people who took Rose were after me again. They'd believed me, no questions asked, and we went on the run together.

But how long can they trust me blindly?

I have so many innocent people relying on me. Part of me wants to break down and tell them everything.

Everything I am. Everything I've done.

But I can't do that. So for now, we just have to get away. One day, I'll explain it all. Today just isn't that day.

Ernestine can sense my hesitation, my fear. She shushes her granddaughter gently and I reach a hand back to pat June's knee. "No, honey. That wasn't Dima. I promise."

Just then, a text flashes on my phone. I peek down at where it sits in the console and see it's simply an address texted from an unknown number.

1453 Wilton Avenue.

It's Dima. I feel like I can breathe.

I read the address twice more, committing it to memory. Then I power down the phone, roll down the window, and hurl it into the drainage ditch alongside the road.

Tonight did not go at all how I expected. Nothing about today did.

But I fucking took charge.

After feeling powerless for so long, I have to admit... It feels damn good to be in control.

14

DIMA

After I text Arya the address, I press my forehead against the steering wheel for a moment and take a deep breath.

Ennio was right: sentiment is a weakness.

It's also a pain in the ass.

If I was smart, I'd still be driving. I'd ditch my car, steal a new one, and be out of the state so fucking fast.

Instead, I'm parked in the back of a twenty-four-hour strip club parking lot, waiting for the mother of my son to come meet me.

I can hear my father's voice snarling in my mind.

Coward. Pathetic. Weak.

You've let this girl and her runt get you all twisted around her finger, eating out of the palm of your hand. No wonder your Bratva has been snatched from you.

You don't deserve to be called a don.

"Fuck you, Father," I say softly into the silence of the car. "You deserved everything that happened to you."

Lights flash across my face. I look up, momentarily blinded, and then see a van just ahead of me.

I'm about to get out of the car, but then the van reverses and pulls out of the lot. I shift my car into drive and follow.

We stop at a deserted park a few blocks away. The streetlight nearest is burnt out, so the park is pitch black. I kill my headlights at the same time the lights on the van go out. When Arya gets out and walks towards my car, I can only make her out because of the glint of moonlight against her dyed blond hair.

She climbs into the passenger seat and releases a long sigh. "Fancy seeing you here. How's it going?"

"I've been better."

Arya laughs. "Have you? This isn't the best night of your life?"

It feels strange to laugh, considering... well, everything.

"No," I rasp. "The best night of my life remains the night I walked into your clinic."

Arya's smile slips away. But her eyes are still bright, still sparkling.

Then the van's headlights come back on and the moment is broken.

To my surprise, the van starts to move. I go to wrench my own car into drive, but Arya lays a hand over mine on top of the gear shifter.

"It's okay, Dima."

"Like fuck it is! My son is in there, in case you forgot."

Arya turns my face with her other hand so I have to look at her. "Lukas is going to stay with Ernestine and June for a bit."

"No," I say flatly. "Hell no."

Quick as lightning, she reaches over and yanks the keys out of the ignition. My car groans and dies. "I wasn't asking, Dima. It's not safe for him right now. We don't even know what's going to happen next. Who is going to come for us. He's better off with Ernestine while we figure it out."

I bite back a frustrated grunt and slump into my seat.

I know she's right—an infant would only complicate things. But that doesn't make it any harder to watch the van drive away in the rearview mirror.

Then I become aware of Arya's gentle breathing next to me. I turn to look at her once more.

"So you're with me then."

She shrugs. "I guess so."

"Didn't think that would be your first choice."

Arya hesitates for a minute and then shakes her head. "Fun, upbeat guy like you—what's not to love?"

"Very funny."

"Nothing's funny anymore." She sobers up. "You're my son's father, Dima. I can't hate you. I can't fear you. Don't get me wrong—I do hate you a lot of the time and you're definitely scary. But… that's no way to live."

I tilt my head and look at her. I wish I knew how to describe what she meant to me. Is she a thorn in my side? An angel I don't deserve? I don't fucking know.

But despite all the dark, fucked-up shit we've been through together…

I'm glad she's here.

I reach across the front seat and gather Arya's hand inside of mine. Her fingers are cold. I lift them to my mouth and press a delicate kiss into her knuckles. She watches me, her green eyes unreadable in the dark.

Then she blinks and pulls her hand away. "What's your plan now? What's next?"

The plan is to fuck you senseless, I say in my head. But I know it's not the time for that now. It'll have to wait. My cock is not pleased about it, but oh well. It'll have to wait, too.

"I think the only plan I have is to go see my brother."

"Ilyasov?"

I nod. "I fucked up this hit. Bad. I don't see a way to fix it now that Ennio is dead."

"Maybe killing the son will be enough for him," she suggests. "If he just wanted revenge, killing the man's kid is a surefire way to do it."

"I doubt Ilyasov will see it that way. Still, I have to go talk to him."

"He's your brother. Surely he'll understand."

I scoff. "Spoken like someone who doesn't know my brother."

Arya lays a hand on my arm again. I barely resist the urge to pull her across the car into my lap. God knows I could use an outlet for some of this tension right about now. But sex would only make things more complicated than they need to be.

"We've got a long drive. You sure you want to come?"

In response, Arya reaches up and grabs her seatbelt, strapping it in place. Then she looks at me. "Well, what're we waiting for?"

She looks… well, maybe not happy. But she doesn't look like she's in a waking nightmare.

It'll have to suffice.

I point the car towards Chicago and drive for a while. When my eyes start to close, I pull over to sleep at a rest stop for a few hours. Arya curls up like a cat in the back seat, using one of my jackets like a blanket. I lay my seat back as far as it will go and try to stretch my legs out as best as I can.

It's not comfortable in the slightest. Still, I manage to doze off to the even sound of Arya's breathing and the smell of her shampoo.

When I wake up, I start driving again. The sun is dipping low in the sky before we finally start seeing signs for Chicago.

"I can't wait until this shit is over," I grumble. "Making this drive too many times is going to kill me."

"You think there's a real chance that will happen?"

"That this will kill me?" I ask. "If the terrible drivers here are anything to go by, neither of us is long for this world."

"No, I mean—" Arya swallows nervously. "You think your brother can make it so we won't be on the run anymore?"

I grip the wheel and stare straight ahead at the road. I've tried not to think about seeing my brother too much since we left. Because every time I do, I can't help but feel I'm wasting my time.

"I think my brother has the power to give me what I need," I say diplomatically.

"That doesn't answer my question."

"No, it doesn't," I admit. "Because your question is a tough one to answer. With a lot of history."

"So, tell me. And don't say, 'It's a long story.' We still have another few hours before we get there and I've been doing all the talking. It's your turn to fill in the silence."

No one has ever had the audacity to talk to me the way Arya does. It should infuriate me. I should threaten to backhand her for even thinking about giving me a command.

But I can't bring myself to care when it's her.

I like that she talks to me like a person. That I feel, for a minute, like the title 'Don' fades away. I'm not in charge of the life and death of men anymore. I'm not a titan, not a kingpin.

I'm just Dima.

Maybe that's why I tell her the story.

"Ilyasov is my older brother," I begin. "My parent's firstborn son."

"But you're the one who took over after your father?" she asks.

"Astute," I say with a humorless smile. "That is the crux of our problems, yes. My brother was irresponsible. Unprepared. He didn't mature as quickly as he should have and he wasn't ready to be a good leader in the way I was. He wasn't ready to work for what he wanted."

"So your father rewarded you."

"At my brother's expense."

Arya turns to me, eyebrows furrowed.

"I thought at the time it was the right thing to do. Ilyasov was doing lots of bad shit in his younger days. Drugs. Drinking. Partying with dangerous people. I believed he'd ruin the Bratva if he was handed the keys. That he'd run it right into the ground. If he had taken over, his problems would have only gotten worse. I've seen it happen a hundred times. Men get money and power and their vices eat them alive. My brother wouldn't have survived the year. So I told my father about what Ilyasov did when he thought no one was looking."

"Does your brother know you did that?"

I shake my head. "I've never told him. I don't plan to. It wouldn't have changed anything, anyway. My father already knew. He just wanted to test me and see if I'd tell him the truth."

"Well then, it seems to me, if your brother should be mad at anyone, it should be your father. Your father chose you over him. It wasn't your doing."

"Ilyasov expected more loyalty from me. I think, in his perfect world, I would have refused my father on principle and left the family with him. Maybe we'd be running his mafia together or something like that. I don't know, but he didn't expect me to accept the position over him. Not after I spent the previous eighteen years at his side night and day. We were best friends… until we weren't."

Arya clicks her tongue. "I'm so sorry. That's sad."

"It's fine. You had it worse than I did."

Arya shrugs. "Things like that are hard to quantify. No two traumas are the same."

Arya may be right, but trauma or not, I put my shit behind me and did what I had to do. It isn't my fault Ilyasov couldn't do that, too.

So if he decides to hold that over me and stop me from protecting my family, he's got another thing coming.

15

ARYA

Dima's brother's house is on a tree-lined street close to the river. It's oddly picturesque. Oddly peaceful.

"This is where a big mafia boss lives?" I ask, eyebrows raised.

"It was our parent's second home," Dima says. "Ilyasov didn't get the Bratva, but he got the house. It was a consolation prize, I guess."

"One hell of an expensive consolation prize," I mumble.

Dima called Ilyasov twenty minutes ago to tell him we were back in town. If the elder Romanoff was surprised, he didn't express it on the phone. I could hear the conversation quietly through the speaker.

He simply told Dima to come over. "You know the place," he'd said.

It's weird to see it now and picture it as the Romanoff family home. Dima spent time here as a child. Slept in the bedrooms, played in the yard, ran up and down the sidewalks with his brother at his side.

Bizarre to think of him as young and carefree.

As we stand at the front gate, waiting to be buzzed in, I wonder if there are photos of him as a baby somewhere in the house. I can't even imagine what Dima was like as an infant. It's easier to think that he just sprang up from the earth, huge and fully formed.

Then the door opens and an older, more weathered, far more tattooed version of Dima is standing in front of me.

"Little brother, to what do I owe the unexpected pleasure?" Ilyasov asks. His eyes shift to me. "And you brought your woman. I've heard a lot about you."

Something in his tone makes me shudder. Not just the fact that it's a bold-faced lie, either. Something about the man himself.

Ilyasov leads us down a hallway, past a grand staircase, and into a sitting room with double doors, large windows, and a very pregnant woman sitting on a sectional sofa.

Dima seems taken aback by the woman. But he hides it quickly. "Vera, it's nice to see you."

The woman rubs her belly dramatically and rolls her eyes. "There's a lot more of me to see, isn't there?"

"Did I not mention that last time we spoke?" Ilyasov asks. "Vera is pregnant. With twins."

"Oh my goodness," I say before I can help myself. "Poor thing."

Vera laughs, tossing her platinum blond hair over her shoulder. "Thank you. Only women know to sympathize with me. Men always offer their congratulations."

"Carrying one was hard enough. I can't even imagine two."

Ilyasov looks at Dima and gestures to the adjoining room. I can spy a well-stocked bar glistening in the corner. "Let's talk, *sobrat*." The two men leave.

I watch as they go. There's a weird tension in the air I can't quite put my finger on. Maybe I'm just on edge being separated from Lukas.

I remind myself why we're here. *So we can end all this shit and be safe.*

Even if I can't bring myself to fully believe that, Dima does. I try my best to follow along—for his sake.

Once we're alone, I gesture to Vera's round belly. "How far along are you?"

"Thirty-two weeks," she says. "Another month before I'm full-term. I waver between being excited and dreading it."

"I know what you mean. Aside from the aches and pains, the constant peeing, and the heartburn, pregnancy is nice. It's a lot nicer than labor."

"And having a newborn, I imagine," Vera says. "I hear they are rather demanding."

"Do you have any other children?"

Vera shakes her head. "These are our first. I've been anxious to start a family for a while now, but Ilyasov has been so busy building his empire."

Vera says it so casually. As though she's discussing her husband's small business instead of a criminal enterprise. I wonder how much she knows. How much she's seen. How much she's done herself.

"And you aren't worried about what his 'empire' will mean for your children?" As soon as the question is out of my mouth, I realize I've overstepped. "I'm sorry. I didn't mean for it to sound that way. I shouldn't have—"

Vera leans forward and lays a manicured hand on my knee. "Don't trouble yourself. It's a good question."

"No, it's not. I shouldn't pry."

"It's only prying if I'm not willing to open up about it," she says. "And I am more than willing. Ilyasov's activities are a unique challenge for a relationship and a family, but every family has its... challenges, don't they?"

I think about my own family. As always, it makes me shudder. Like remembering a night terror—it feels distant and vague, but you can never forget how you felt in the midst of it.

"I suppose. But most families struggle with divorce or cancer or financial issues. Not... this."

"Ilyasov cares for me. He protects me. And nothing will change once 'me' becomes 'us.'"

She sounds supremely confident. And maybe a little naïve?

Or maybe I'm just jaded.

I don't know which, but I can't help but look around at the couple's lavish home and growing family and wonder if something like this isn't possible for me and Dima.

In my mind, I imagined us living in a bunker, staying away from windows and hiding indoors. But that doesn't seem to be how Ilyasov and Vera operate. They flaunt their wealth, their power, like there's not a care in the world.

I want that sense of security for myself.

I've spent my whole life without it.

Vera excuses herself to use the restroom, complaining about the babies using her bladder as a trampoline. I sit back on the sofa and pretend I'm not listening in on Dima's conversation with his brother.

"...There is room for you to stay here. Both of you."

"Awfully generous of you, Ilya. Especially last minute. Sure there's not a catch in your offer?"

"What is family for if not to house strays?"

Dima growls. It's not quite a laugh, but not quite a threat, either. There's still something happening here that I can't figure out.

"So what happens now?" he asks.

"You tell me."

"What does that mean?"

"It means you're in charge of your own fate now, Dima. The deal is off."

I freeze. This is not good. This is not good at all.

"What the fuck are you talking about, Ilya? I killed a D'Onofrio. Giorgio's heir. That must count for something."

"If only there were silver medals for hitmen. Unfortunately, there's not. Either you killed the target or you didn't. Did you?"

"Be reasonable," Dima snarls. "I risked my life to do what you asked even after you changed the terms of our deal in the first place. Now, you are going to abandon your brother?"

"I'm not abandoning my brother. You are here in my home as my guest. We are closer than ever, brother. I'm abandoning a failed business deal. It is nothing personal. As always, your emotions are getting the best of you."

"How is this not personal?" Dima snaps. "You are threatening my entire life's work. Our family's legacy. And for what? A sick taste of long-desired vengeance? An *I told you so*? You're better than this, Ilyasov."

"It appears I'm not."

Even sitting all the way across the room, the tension is thick. Vera, however, breezes back into the room as if it's two brothers bickering, rather than two mob bosses on the brink of ripping each other's throats out. "Come on, boys. Let's not fight already. We've only been together an hour."

"Dima and I haven't fought in ten years, *zolotse*," Ilyasov croons. "Just discussing."

"Well, let's discuss something lighter then. How about over dinner? I'm craving seafood. What if we get a family-size order of the lobster alfredo from that place you like?"

"Fabulous idea."

∼

Half an hour later, we're walking into the formal dining room. The walls painted a dark green with gold-plated orbs hanging above the long table.

I manage to hold Dima back for a moment. "Is everything okay?"

"Fine," he says, looking furious. "We'll talk tonight."

16

ARYA

Vera is exhausted not long after dinner. She and Ilyasov retire to their room, which is on the top floor of the house, leaving the rest of the mansion to Dima and myself.

"Make yourself at home. Explore, eat, be merry," Vera says, winking suggestively as she heads up the stairs. "We sleep with white noise, so you won't bother us, no matter what you choose to do!"

When they leave, I turn to Dima. "Vera is a character."

"She's one of a kind," Dima agrees. "That's why Ilyasov picked her. That, and she refused to marry him at first. He has always wanted what he can't have."

We wander into the guest room. It's really more of a suite, complete with a sitting room and luxurious master bath. The mahogany bed is huge and loaded down with pillows and blankets. Through a door to the left is a massive bathroom with a double standing shower, a jacuzzi tub, and double sinks.

After the accommodations I've grown used to the last few weeks, I'm in heaven. I flop onto the bed.

"My God, I could die on this mattress. It is so soft."

"Guess I'm sleeping on the floor then."

"You don't like soft mattresses?"

"Soft things make the men who use them soft."

I wrinkle my nose. "That's the dumbest thing I've ever heard. Do you dry off after a shower with a brick?"

I realize all at once I've never seen his home. Not his real one, anyway.

"I forgot the safe house isn't where you usually live."

"My normal place is bigger than this," he says, looking around. "And less... traditional."

"What's wrong with traditional?"

In response, Dima picks up a corner of the floral comforter and holds it out like it's disgusting, as if that explains it all.

I laugh. "Please don't tell me your house is all black and white and straight lines."

"Do you really think I'm that predictable, Arya?" He stands up and peels his shirt off, tossing it on the floor.

I'm momentarily distracted by his tanned skin and rippling muscles to remember what we're talking about.

"What is it then?"

"Just black and straight lines. No white."

I laugh and chuck a pillow at this head. He blocks it away and laughs along with me. "You'll see it one day," he mumbles.

The thought is a strange one. "Maybe I'll help you brighten the place up. Put some art on the walls."

"I've got art," he replies defensively. "Plenty of it. Expensive shit."

"Dima Romanoff is an appreciator of the arts?" I feign a gasp, still fighting to draw my eyes away from the artwork of his body. "Why, I'm shocked. I never would have suspected it. I assume it's all bloody battle scenes and oils of naked women."

"Not too far off," he chuckles. He lays back on the bed, his hands tucked behind his head. "My mother loved art. She was constantly bringing home new paintings and commissioning new pieces. It drove my father mad."

"He didn't like art?"

"He didn't like her making decisions without him," he explains bitterly. "My father liked to be in control of everyone and everything. Including his family. But my mother was never one to be tamed. She fought back."

"How?"

"By spending his money and sleeping with other men."

It shocks me to hear a son speak so freely about his mother's sex life, but Dima seems unfazed. I suppose he's had a long time to process the information.

"She would leave in the middle of the day without telling him or anyone else where she was going. It would always cause a massive fight, but she never stopped doing it."

"What did your father do?"

"Had her followed. Locked her inside. Tracked her movements." Dima shrugs. "The usual."

"That doesn't sound like 'the usual' to me. It sounds horrible. They were supposed to love and trust each other."

Dima rolls onto his side, his head propped on his hand. "For a long time, I didn't know the difference. My parents' marriage was all I knew. The only measure I had for love."

"That was control. Not love."

He nods. "I know that now. I also know love can be a weapon. You can use it to protect your partner or tear them down. My parents used it to make each other weaker."

I consider his words for a moment. "That's actually kinda beautiful."

Dima smirks. "Thanks. Saw it on a bumper sticker."

I roll my eyes. "Can you be serious for two seconds?"

He gestures to me. "The floor is yours."

"Thanks," I sniffle dramatically. Then my voice drops a bit. "People so often think of love as a force for good, but it can be used for bad. It can be wielded like a weapon against the people who feel it."

"Is that what it was like for you and your asshole ex?"

"Jorik?" I ask, surprised Dima is mentioning him at all. "God, no. I didn't love him. Well, maybe I thought I did once. But that all changed when I found out what kind of person he really was. He let power corrupt him. He didn't care how many people died so long as he made a profit. It was disgusting."

Dima nods, unsurprised. "A man's vices will eat him alive in this world. If you serve something before you're rich and powerful, you'll serve it all the more later. Sometimes until it kills you."

I twist the comforter between my fingers, playing with the material nervously. "And what do you serve, Dima?"

He doesn't answer for so long that I finally look up. Dima is staring past me at the wall, deep in thought.

Finally, he turns back to me, his icy blue eyes clear. "Loyalty. Honesty."

I flinch. The lies I've told him linger between us, unspoken and foul.

I reach out and touch his hand with mine. His skin is warm and the contact sends a jolt through my arm. "I see that. You embody those things. You're loyal to your Bratva, even when they've turned away from you. You're loyal to your friends and your family."

"And am I loyal to you?" he asks, turning his hand over and squeezing my fingers. "That's all I really care about. You and Lukas. That's who I serve now."

His vulnerability is touching and more than a little surprising.

I swallow and decide—for once in my life—to be honest. "I've been with someone who valued his business over his fiancée. Jorik cared more about his power and influence and money than he ever cared about me. I've seen power corrupt people. I don't want that happening to me. More importantly, I don't want it happening to Lukas."

"That doesn't answer my question," Dima says.

I give him a small smile. "No, it doesn't, but it's because the answer is complicated."

"Break it down for me."

"I think you want to be loyal to me, Dima. I believe you've been honest with me and I appreciate that more than you can know, but—"

"But what?"

"But," I continue, needing to get this all out while I can, "I'm afraid that won't matter. Because I have to be loyal to Lukas now. He doesn't have a voice, so I have to speak up for him. I have to be the one who makes sure he is safe. He can never be safe here."

"Look at Vera," Dima suggests. "Bringing twins into this world."

I don't know if Dima heard our conversation earlier or not, but that thought has been in my mind all night. Vera seemed to think Ilyasov was worth the potential risk to her children.

I don't know if I could ever agree.

"I made the mistake once of leaving you both behind," Dima continues. His breath is warm on my skin. "I won't do it again. There's a place for you in my world. And if there isn't already, we'll make one. We'll carve one out."

What Dima is saying sounds like a dream. But it's a dream I wouldn't mind falling into.

Is there a world where I could have everything? Where we could be together and Lukas could be safe?

Where Dima gets what he wants?

Where I get what I want?

Dima rises onto his hands and knees and slides across the bed towards me.

I feel like prey being stalked by a predator. But instead of running or fighting, I lie back and let Dima crawl over me. I let him pin my wrists to the bed. To knock my thighs apart with his knee.

My chest is heaving, straining against the deep V of my t-shirt, as Dima lowers his head and presses a kiss to the top of my cleavage.

"We can have everything, Arya," he says. "Starting right now."

Looking up at Dima, feeling his warmth around me, is like being intoxicated. My belly feels warm and my thoughts are muddled. I'm not longer worried about what I should or shouldn't do, what is right or what isn't.

All I can think about is what will feel good. What will make me happy.

And right now, the answer to that is him.

My wrists are still pinned to the bed, but I strain against his hold and sit up to kiss him. Immediately, Dima drives me back down to the mattress, teasing me away from him.

His knee slides higher between my legs. I grind myself over him like an animal in heat, desperate and needy.

Dima unbuttons my pants. My free hand immediately slides into his hair. I curl my fingers through his locks as he rips my jeans down and tosses them into the pile with his shirt.

I'm conscious of the fact I slept in a car and haven't had a real shower in God only knows how long—but only for a second. As soon as Dima pushes my panties aside and curls a finger against my center, I'm barely conscious of anything.

I spread my legs and beg him for more. I'm moaning with every caress. Every thrust.

"You're so wet," he whispers, sliding a second finger inside of me and curling against my insides until my toes curl.

"I had a sex dream about you last night," I admit breathlessly. "All of my sex dreams are about you. All of them."

Dima stops suddenly and crawls over me, his blue eyes nearly eaten away by the black of his pupil. "Describe it to me."

I miss him inside of me already.

I want it again. I want more.

"What?" I ask, lost in lust.

"Tell me your dream," he says, "any dream. Let me make it real."

My entire body comes alive at his words. At this man, this sex god, hovering over me, asking if he can make my fantasies come true.

Suddenly, my hesitation and nervousness is gone. The hunger inside of me has taken over.

I want this. I want him.

When I don't answer, he leans back and slides out of his jeans. His eyes stay locked on mine as he watches me pull my shirt over my head, slide my panties down my legs, and unsnap my bra.

When I'm before him, naked, Dima bites his knuckle and shakes his head. "Holy fuck. You're a goddamn dream, Arya."

I smile and shake my head. "No, that comes later. First, we play."

Something between a laugh and a growl escapes Dima. He reaches for me and, to my surprise, flips me over with one huge hand onto my stomach. He spreads my thighs apart again.

"Stay like that," he orders in a husk rasp. "Bite the pillow if you need to scream."

Then he descends over me. His body blankets mine with heat and scent and weight, pressing me down. All I can smell is him.

Dima slides his hard cock between my ass cheeks.

"Tell me your dream, Arya."

Rather than tell him, I show him.

I lift my hips slightly, elevating my body off the bed just high enough that Dima's hand can slide around to my center. His finger circles over me readily. Warmth floods from my head to my toes.

I shimmy my hips so I can grind against his hand and stroke his cock with my ass at the same time.

Dima growls and rubs my clit faster. Just when my body starts to crest, when I feel myself reaching the tipping point, I lift my hips higher, grab his length, and press him to my entrance.

He slides in without hesitation. He doesn't stop until he's as deep inside of me as possible. Our hips meet flush.

I've never been fuller.

I cry out, grateful Vera informed us about her white noise machine. I'd hate to ruin my dream come true with muffled cries.

"Fuck me," I beg, reaching back to grab his thighs with my hands. "Hard."

"Don't fucking move," he barks. Dima grips my hips and slams into me again and again. Each thrust presses me into the mattress.

The force of his fucking is enough to make my back curl, to make me arch my hips even more in an effort to give him better, deeper access.

"Right there," I moan. "Please."

His finger finds my center again. My orgasm is instantaneous. My body clenches around him hard as Dima moans through my convulsing. "You're so tight. Fuck."

I push my hips back against him to meet each savage thrust. "Come inside me," I beg.

Dima's fingers dig into my flesh as he starts to roar. "Arya…"

Before he can finish, I slide off of him and collapse on my belly. Dima slides his aching length between my ass again and it only takes two thrusts before I feel him empty himself on my lower back.

I like being marked by him.

I like smelling like Dima, tasting him, feeling him inside and outside of me.

A desperate thought crosses my mind: can I live without this for the rest of my life?

And the answer is just as instantaneous. Just as troubling.

I don't fucking know.

17

DIMA

Arya is still asleep when I crawl out of bed.

It's late. Just before three in the morning, judging by the old grandfather clock in the hall. I pad silently out into the main living space.

Somehow, I'm not surprised when I see Ilyasov.

He's sitting in the reading nook by the window, smoking a cigarette. Shirtless, so the faint moonlight trickling in catches the gold chain around his neck and illuminates his endless tattoos.

He exhales a cloud of smoke into the night and then speaks without looking at me. "I had a feeling you'd be joining me."

"Cut the spooky shit, Ilya," I snap. I walk over to him and lean against the wall.

He fixes me with a lazy glance, then goes back to smoking his cigarette. "Couldn't sleep?"

"I should be asking you the same question."

"I never sleep anymore, brother. If I do, it's with one eye open. You never know when the people you love will betray you. You know that better than anyone, don't you?"

I grit my teeth. "Are you talking about our ancient past or my recent past?"

He chuckles. "You tell me."

I crack my knuckles and lapse into silence. Ilyasov was all smiles when Arya and I arrived. The consummate, brotherly host.

Now, he's returned to the way he was when I first saw in him in Chicago, what feels like a lifetime ago.

Jagged. Haunted. Grim.

It doesn't bode well for me.

He leans back against the wall as he stubs out his cigarette. "So, *sobrat*, have you considered your next move?"

"That depends. Are you reneging on our deal again?"

He shakes his head in dismay. "I'm not the one who broke the deal, Dima. I asked for a man to be taken out. You killed his son instead. I fail to see where I made a mistake."

"Because I already killed the first man you wanted dead."

"We've done this before, Dima. We've had this argument. I don't like wasting my time going around in circles."

"You say that, and yet it feels like we spend a lot of time talking about shit from a decade ago, brother dear."

Ilyasov turns those dark eyes up at me. "Some things shouldn't be forgotten."

I'm getting frustrated already—which I'm sure is the point. Ilyasov has loved holding this power dynamic over my head since the second I waltzed into his office and asked for an army.

I'm very fucking sick of it.

"You asked for Giorgio D'Onofrio's head. I can still give you that. The deal isn't dead."

Ilyasov raises his brows. "Giorgio will be on high alert now. It will be even more difficult to reach him now than it would have been before. I'm not sure you have the resources necessary to carry out a hit like that."

"No, but you do." Ilyasov opens his mouth to argue, but I cut him off before he can. "I'm not asking for your army right away. What I am asking for is your help. You have ways of finding out information that I don't have access to right now. Look into where Giorgio may be hiding."

He tilts his head back and forth like he's weighing it. "I could do that."

"But will you?"

Ilyasov hesitates for a moment. Then a slow smile spreads across his face. "Brother, I already have."

My heart jumps into my throat. Suddenly, I'm wide awake. "Where is he?"

"Hiding out in one of his New York casinos that's closed for renovation."

"Holed up like a fucking rat in a sewer," I mutter. "How many people are there with him?"

My mind is already moving through the process of figuring out how I'm going to get inside. *How many men are on guard? What are the security measures? Can I get to him on my own?*

I broke into his inner sanctum once before. Even with extra protection in place, I'm confident I can do it again.

"Not many people know he's there, even within his own organization. Giorgio doesn't want anyone turning him over for a softer punishment if the police take them in. Can't be too careful in our line of work, can you?"

"Hell fucking yes." I clap my hands and stand up. "This is what we needed. I have to get to him before he moves."

Ilyasov sighs. "Are you sure this is worth it, Dima?"

"What the hell does that mean?"

He holds up his hands as if in surrender. "I'm just saying… you could die, no? Zotov and the Albanians have driven your Bratva halfway into the ground. Are you sure reclaiming it is worth your life? Wouldn't it be easier to just start over with your pretty girlfriend upstairs?"

Fuck, how many people are going to ask me that?

I look my brother square in the face, trying to make sure he'll hear me. "Would you give up your Bratva for anything?"

He doesn't say anything, but I can see the answer written on his face.

"That's what I thought," I say. "You and me, we come from the same family. We were raised by the same father. Whether we want to admit it or not, power and control is important to us. We'd both rather die than let someone steal it from us."

"You're not wrong," Ilyasov admits. "But that doesn't mean the way we feel is right, either. Maybe it would be better to let it go and live than to die trying."

I shake my head. "I'd never be able to look in the mirror again if I let people take everything my family has built, everything I've built, away from me. I'd be a coward."

Ilyasov nods and shrugs. "Fine. I figured as much. It's your funeral."

"No," I fire back. "It's just business."

"It's always just business," Ilyasov agrees. "Nothing more. Nothing less."

Arya is showered and getting dressed when I come back up to the room.

"Good news. Ilyasov has a connection to a private jet we can take back to New York City. No more fucking driving."

"Are we leaving right now?" she asks, buttoning her jeans and straightening her shirt.

"The plane can be ready in an hour, which is about how long it will take us to get to the airport. The sooner we get there, the sooner I can get to work."

Arya sits on the edge of the bed. "So you talked to Ilyasov? Did he change his mind about helping?"

"No, but he found Giorgio D'Onofrio's location. Now, I can finish the hit."

Her face falls. Her forehead wrinkles and she looks down at her lap, her fingers tapping together nervously.

I walk over and kneel down in front of her. "Everything will be fine. It won't be like last time. Giorgio's staying in an abandoned casino and he's so paranoid about being caught by the police that he doesn't have very many people with him. He thinks he is well hidden. It'll be easier than ever to take him out."

She chews on her lip. "Okay, good. I'm happy for you."

"You could have fooled me." I grab her chin and tip her face up to mine. Her green eyes are wide and worried.

"If this is what you want, I'm happy for you," she says. "I'm glad the trip here was worth it for you."

I lean back, frowning at her. "Why do you keep saying it like that? 'For *you*, what *you* want.' This is for us, Arya. For you and me and Lukas. It's for all of us."

Her lower lip catches between her teeth as she chews on it. "That's sweet of you, but I already told you what I have planned for me and Lukas."

Her words take me so much by surprise that I have to stand up and back away. "What do you mean? We talked last night. We solved this."

"Dima." Arya's voice breaks on my name. She takes a shaking breath. "I know you believe that and I know that is what you would try to do. You've always done your best to take care of me and Lukas, but—"

"No." I wave away her words. "Period. That's it. I've done my best, Arya. You trust me, don't you?"

"I trust you, but I don't trust them." She gestures past me towards the windows. "All those people out there who want to hurt you, who care more about money and power than they do human lives—I don't trust them. And I never will."

"Fuck that. We talked last night. We—"

"We said goodbye," she finishes. "Maybe last night was the perfect way for us to end it. It's kind of like coming full circle in a way, isn't it?"

No. Hell no. My anger bubbles up in my chest.

"Is that all this is to you? We fucked a few times, had a kid, now we call it quits, no big deal?"

"I'm not saying it's no big deal! I'm just saying it might be time for this to be over. Life would be easier for you if you didn't have to worry about us."

"Don't pretend you're doing me a favor," I growl. "I'm not doing this for you? Well, you sure as fuck aren't doing anything for me."

"Dima, that's not what I—"

"If last night was goodbye, then what's your plan now?"

"I already told you," she says quietly. "I had someone make me some fake passports. They'll be ready to pick up today."

I stare at her in utter disbelief. "So you think I shouldn't get a say in whether my son is in my life or not."

"Are you even listening to me? You do get a say!" Arya seethes. "If you want him to be in your life, then you have to make your life less dangerous. That's my condition. It's not crazy."

Staring at Arya, I hardly recognize her. Her face is set, determined. She has made up her mind. There's nothing I can do to change it.

Which means I have a choice: do I break her into submission? Or do I let her go?

Anger boils inside of me. I feel like I could breathe fire.

I open my mouth to say something. What to say, I don't know, but I have to say *something.* Anything.

Before I can, there's a knock at the door.

"Hello?" It's Vera. "I hear you two lovebirds are leaving. Say goodbye before you go, okay?"

Arya takes the out and hurries towards the door, pulling it open and disappearing into the hallway.

Leaving me in the room alone—with nothing but my anger, my sins…

And one hell of a fucking choice to make.

18

DIMA

Ilyasov accompanies us on the flight from Chicago to New York.

I'm not sure who I want to talk to less—him or Arya. She and I haven't spoken since we left Chicago. Hell, she'll barely even look at me. As soon as she got on the plane, she put on the headphones that were sitting in her seat and stared straight ahead at the screen in front of her.

Two hours later, the plane lands.

Arya hesitates at the bottom of the stairs. The wind is whipping across the runway, sending her hair flying out behind her. She gathers it in her hand and holds it over her shoulder.

"I'm going to take a cab," she says. "I've talked to Ernestine and given her the number for my new phone. I wrote it down for you, too, in case… in case you need it."

Like me, Ilyasov has a stash of burners sitting at the ready in a hall closet. He let Arya use one.

"I'm sure I'll see you later," she says. Her voice wavers like she isn't sure at all.

"Yeah, I'm sure." I offer a dismissive wave. Arya walks over to the waiting cart, climbs on, and is whisked away towards the hangar.

Once she's gone, the anger that has been bubbling just beneath the surface since back in Chicago erupts with a vengeance. I whirl around and throw one savage elbow into the handrail of the plane stairs. It bends with a metallic shriek beneath the blow.

"*Suka!*" I roar in Russian.

Behind me, Ilyasov lets out a long, low whistle. "That was brutal. Heart-wrenching, truly."

"Shut the fuck up."

"No, I mean it. I'm sorry. But I'm sure she'll come around."

"Are you now?"

He shrugs. "No, but you're upset, and I want to help."

I let out a bitter, humorless chuckle. "Since when?"

He narrows his eyes at me. "You're here in the city because I told you where Giorgio is and because I flew you here on a jet on my own dime. Don't come at me like—"

"You're right. You've helped a lot."

I hate saying those words. My life is starting to feel like one big fucking charity case. I'm ready to get back to my old life. Whether Arya wants to be part of it or not. I'm ready for my orders to be carried out. I'm ready for my enemies to fall at my feet.

Mostly, I'm ready for murder.

Ilyasov has two cars waiting in front of the airport, both under his name.

"Why two?"

"You think I came here just for you?" he asks, eyebrow raised. "Remember, I don't do altruism. I have some business to attend here, so I thought it was a convenient time to take care of it. Especially before the babies come."

My phone buzzes. A desperate, pitiful part of me hopes it's Arya. I squash that instinct at once as I answer.

"Where you at, man?" Gennady's voice comes over the phone.

"In the city. Plane just landed."

"You flew?" He sounds worried.

"Private. Ilyasov set it up."

Gennady makes an interesting humming sound in the back of his throat. I can't tell what it means, but I don't care.

"Listen, I'm here to finish the job. Right now."

There's a long pause. "You mean the D'Onofrio hit? How do you know where he's at? His name is plastered on headlines all over the place. The police are looking for him because of the murder of his son."

"Ilyasov has a tip on his location."

"Shit, I dunno about all that, Dima. I'm sure your brother's info is good, but you don't want to put your nose in this business right now. If you do, this whole thing could be turned around on you. You want to deal with cops on top of everything else we've got going right now?"

"I'm not going to get tangled up in it. I'll finish the job and be out of there before anyone knows any different."

"But what if you're not?" Gennady presses. "What if something goes wrong? Right now, you got away with it. You are in the clear. Don't do something that will cause you more trouble than it's worth."

"I'd go through any amount of trouble to get my Bratva back."

Gennady sighs. "That isn't what I mean. I mean, don't get yourself killed being reckless. You don't even have a plan."

"Listen, I didn't call to get your permission. Maybe you've forgotten who I am the last couple months, but I'm still the calling the shots."

"What does Arya say?" he asks suddenly. "Have you told her what you're planning?"

Gennady is bringing Arya up to try and make me more rational. To try and remind me what I have to lose. Unfortunately, he doesn't know I've already let her go.

"She told me to do whatever was best for me. So that's what I'm doing."

There's a long pause. "Did something happen with you two? Where is she?"

"Gone. But this has nothing to do with her. I'm going to get my Bratva back and this is the way to do it. I just thought you should know."

I hang up before Gennady can say anything else. I don't need to rehash the events of the day with him. This isn't therapy.

It's war.

"Your second isn't on board?" Ilyasov asks, leaning against a stone pillar in front of the airport with a cigarette hanging out of his mouth.

"My second is always on board. I'm the one in charge."

Ilyasov shrugs. "I don't blame him. This is a crazy plan."

"The fuck are you talking about? It was your idea."

"No." Ilyasov wags his finger. "I told you where Giorgio was hiding out. You're the one who decided to break in on your own and kill him. It's a suicide mission."

I stare at my brother, blinking in disbelief. "You flew me here on a private jet to go on a suicide mission?"

"I flew you home," he corrects. "What you choose to do now is your business."

"Except it isn't my business. It's yours. You're the one who wants Giorgio dead."

"And you're the one who agreed to the deal. That makes it your business."

I hold out my hand. "Where's the key for the car?"

Ilyasov hesitates, his lips twisting to one side. "I don't want to part on poor terms, brother. It is not good luck."

"We're as good as we've ever been. Where are the keys?"

He digs into his pocket and tosses me the keys. "I know you think I'm a cold son of a bitch, but I do want to help you out."

Fucking sure he does.

"I'll pass."

He purses his lips, thinking. "At least let me check in on your son for you. Let me take him and whoever the hell is watching him to a safehouse. They'll be secure there. You won't have to worry."

My instinct is to dismiss the offer out of hand, but it's actually not a bad idea. I'd be much more focused on my task if I knew for a fact Lukas was safe. Plus, if he's at a Romanoff safehouse, I'll at least get to hold him one last time—before I lose both him and his mother forever.

"Fine," I grit. "Yeah, that makes sense. They're holed up in a hotel somewhere, but a safehouse would be much more comfortable."

"Great. Text me the address. I'll take care of it."

"I'll let them know you're coming," I say as I'm pulling out my phone to text Ernestine the new plans.

Ilyasov throws a small black bag into his car and then turns around, arms folded over the top of the door. "Can I do anything for you? A different gun? More ammo?"

I shake my head. "I'm good. I have all I need."

"So be it. A word of advice, brother: move slowly, pay attention, and don't make any rash decisions. That's how you end up dead."

"Since when are you the worried big brother?" I ask with a bitter laugh.

"Since now, I suppose." Ilyasov shrugs and shakes his head. "We share the same blood, do we not?"

I shrug. "Don't go soft, Ilyasov. Love is a weapon, remember?"

"Father drilled it into our heads. How could I forget?"

Ilyasov gets into his car and I get into mine. We follow each other out of the airport.

Then, as we get onto the highway, he peels off, speeding away and disappearing into the road ahead.

And just like that, I'm alone again.

19

ARYA

I almost call a cab, but when I realize how far I have to go, I realize renting a car is cheaper.

I don't like the idea of having a paper trail with my name on them, but soon enough, Arya George won't be my name anymore.

As soon as I pick up the documents from Arnie at the pier, I'll be someone else. Lukas will be, too. And Ernestine. And June. We'll all be able to leave our messy pasts behind.

How long have I wished I could be someone else? Live another life?

After I left Jorik, I desperately wanted to start over. To be normal for once. Someone with two normal, alive, non-addicted parents. Someone with a support system. With a normal asshole ex-boyfriend, not a wanted criminal and mass murderer.

Then, for a brief minute there, I liked being me.

I had a beautiful son and a man who, while not perfect, was kind. To me. To Lukas.

Dima is still kind—deep down. But there's darkness in him that he can't shake. I don't know how to deal with all of that.

So I'm leaving it behind and wiping the slate clean. I have no other choice.

I grab the keys, get in the car, and start the drive to Atlantic City. So close to the finish line. So close to a new beginning.

∼

My new phone buzzes in the center console of the rental when I'm almost there. I pick up instantly. Only Dima and Ernestine have the number.

"Did you make it to New York okay?"

I pull the phone away from my ear and stare at the screen as if there might be caller ID. There isn't.

"I'm sorry, who is this?"

A tinkling laugh on the other end of the phone. "Sorry. It's Vera. Ilyasov left everyone's number in case I needed anything."

"Oh, okay. Sorry. Do you, uh… do you need anything?"

"Company," she says at once in a faux-pouty voice. "I'm bored here all alone. And I liked having a woman around I could talk to. I wish you could have stayed longer."

"Oh. Right. Me, too," I lie.

"Also, I have to admit something," Vera says. "Ilyasov just called and told me things with you and Dima are on the rocks."

"Did Dima tell him that?" I can't imagine Dima opening up about his feelings with anyone, let alone his brother, but what do I know.

"Ilyasov is perceptive. And I'm nosy," she says with a laugh. "I just wanted to ask what happened overnight to change things. I like the two of you together."

I don't owe this stranger any explanation, but at the same time, I can't deny that it is nice to have another woman to talk to.

I used to have Brigitte, but she betrayed me, and we all know how that ended. All things considered, that put a serious damper on my female friendships.

But Vera understands what I'm going through better than anyone. She knows what it's like to love a violent man.

"Nothing changed. Old problems just resurfaced," I admit. "It's the same fight we've been having for a while."

"Oh no. I'm sorry. Are you okay?"

"I will be," I say with as much confidence as I can muster.

Truthfully, I feel broken over my decision. I tried to put on my best face and be strong, but I'm not entirely sure I'm doing the right thing.

"How did you know Ilyasov was worth the risk?" I blurt, the words tumbling out before I can stop them. "You said that he is worth the risk, but I just wonder how you knew?"

"Oh, well..." She clicks her tongue as she thinks. "I don't really know. I just... knew. I love Ilyasov. I knew I loved him from the second I met him, and with how much awfulness there is in the world, it seemed stupid to give that up."

"Yeah, but so much of that bad shit is part of *his* life. *His* world."

"You're right," she says. "It is. And admittedly, it's gotten harder over the years as his business has grown and he has become more powerful. Sometimes he gets blinded by the work and loses track of what's important. But then he comes home at night and loves me. What more could I ever ask for?"

Power corrupts people. I watched it happen with Jorik. I don't want to see it happen with Dima, too.

Since I've known him, he has been a don without a Bratva. Homeless. Wandering. How much will things change when and if he regains control of his Bratva? Will I even recognize him anymore? Will he even want me anymore? Or our son?

The questions are too painful to really consider. It's easier to leave knowing Dima doesn't want me to go.

But realizing that there may come a day when he doesn't care at all? That hurts more than anything.

"Love is always worth the risk," Vera says. "That's my advice."

"Right," I mumble. "Yeah. Thanks, Vera."

"Anytime."

I thank her for her call and her help—though I think she helped in a way she didn't intend—and park in a garage across from the pier.

I didn't call Arnie to tell him I was coming, but he's always at work. Plus, he told me to come today. He should be expecting me.

When I pull back the striped tent curtain and step inside, it's darker than usual. The windows are still closed since the crew is setting up for the day's events. Animals are being walked through their routines and two clowns argue back and forth.

No one seems to notice me as I walk around the edge of the tent to the staff hallway. The door is unlocked, so I let myself in.

Arnie's office is straight ahead. The door is open. When I walk into the hallway, he looks up and waves me in.

"I've been expecting you." His voice isn't as warm as it was before, but I chalk it up to my strange mood and move into his office.

"Sorry I didn't call. I just got off a plane. I was out of town and... things got crazy."

"Things got crazy on my end, too," he says. He leans back in his chair and grabs a pocket knife from his desk. He flips open the blade and begins sliding it underneath his nails, digging dirt out from underneath them.

I frown. "Is everything okay? Were you able to secure the papers?"

"I was."

I sigh, relieved. "Okay, good."

Arnie doesn't say anything. I realize now that his strange tone of voice was not just my interpretation. Something is definitely wrong.

And I didn't bring a damn thing to protect myself. No gun, no knife, no pepper spray.

When will I learn that no one can be trusted? Anyone can turn on me at any moment? When will I finally understand to always expect the worst?

My heart begins to race. I take a deep breath, trying to stay calm. Just because Arnie is acting strange doesn't mean he wants to hurt me.

Relax, Arya.

"What's going on?" I ask finally. "Is everything okay?"

"You lied to me darling," Arnie says, his Brooklyn accent thick as he flicks the knife blade under his thumbnail.

"About what?"

"Let me rephrase. You didn't tell me the whole truth."

My heart is a jackhammer now. I don't have a backup plan. If Arnie doesn't follow through and tries to back out of the arrangement, I don't have anywhere to go.

"I'm not sure I know what you mean."

Arnie leans forward and points the knife at me. Then he seems to realize what he's doing all at once and drops it on his cluttered desk, pointing with his finger instead. "You are asking me to hide the child of the don of the Romanoff Bratva. You don't think that's information I needed to know?"

Oh, shit. I bite my lip. "…You didn't ask."

He barks out a humorless laugh. "Little lady, I've survived to this ripe old age because I stay out of people's shit. But keeping a don from his child, his heir, is not staying out of shit. It's diving headfirst into it."

"Dima knows I'm here," I argue. "I'm not sneaking away. I told him that I planned to get new documents and leave the country. You aren't doing anything sneaky."

Arnie presses his thin lips together. "I don't like this. Not one bit. When I thought I was doing you a favor, sure, it was fine. But now? Shit, Arya. I don't want to get myself in hot water. Especially since I'm doing this for free. Some risks are worth the reward, but what's the reward here?"

"It's not for free. You told me you underpaid me when I sold you the engagement ring. You said this made you even."

He tips his head to the side, eyes sad. "I exaggerated. It didn't quite cover the costs, but I figured there was no harm. But now? People are looking for you, girl. Powerful people. Powerful people who, if they find out I helped you, will come to me looking for you."

"And you won't know anything! It was just a business deal as far as you knew. That's what you say."

I can feel this slipping away from me. I don't know how to get it back. The cash I snuck from Dima's stash is dangerously low. I gave a lot of it to Ernestine to take care of Lukas, spent a good portion of the rest on the rental car, and now I have enough for maybe a movie ticket in my back pocket.

Point is, I'm broke and desperate. Desperate enough to do anything to make sure this deal goes through.

"I wish it was that simple. But I don't think the kinds of people after you are going to listen to my explanations. If I don't have the information they want, the show is over. Forever." He slides his thumb across his neck to emphasize his point.

"I didn't tell Dima where I was going to get the passports. He doesn't know your name or where you work. How would anyone find out?"

"How does anyone find out anything?" he counters, shaking his head. "I'm sorry, Arya, but—"

Before he can finish, I lunge forward and grab the pocket knife from where it lays on the table. I hold it out, point pressed against Arnie's neck.

I hate this. Hate doing this. Hate being this person.

But desperate times call for desperate measures, I guess.

His eyes bulge and he swallows several times, his skin brushing against the point of the blade.

"Arnie, please don't make me do something I don't want to do."

"That knife isn't sharp enough for any real damage."

"You're right. It's so dull that it won't slice your neck, but where I'm pointing the blade? That's your carotid artery. The blade is dull, but all I need is the point of this knife and one good thrust. You'll bleed out in less than a minute."

A shiver moves through Arnie. I make sure to keep my knife pointed exactly where it needs to be.

"Then just don't do it," he growls. "Kill me now or kill me later, I'm dead all the same. Either you kill me to get your documents or I get killed because I gave them to you. There's no difference."

If I felt at all that Arnie was right, I'd consider walking out and finding another way.

But I know Dima won't come for him. And no one else would be that desperate to find me that they'd hunt him down.

Once I'm gone and out of Dima's life, Zotov won't care about me anymore. Arnie will be safe and well. So if I have to hold a knife to his neck to get what I want, then so be it.

"You aren't going to die, Arnie. Neither now nor later—unless you go back on our deal. If you do, I'll kill you and search through every piece of paper in this office until I find what I'm looking for."

Arnie narrows his eyes at me, sizing me up. "You're a nice girl. You wouldn't do it."

I press the point a bit harder against his neck, my knuckles white from gripping the handle so tight. "Do you know how many nice girls have done horrible things to protect their children? I'm not a nice girl right now, Arnie. I'm a desperate mother to a baby boy who needs me. You have no idea what I'm capable of."

My voice sounds unrecognizable to my own ears. I see the shift in Arnie's posture. The way he sits up a bit higher and leans further back in his seat.

He's frightened of me.

Good.

"Give me what I came for and I'll leave," I say. "You'll never see me again."

He stares at me for a second. Blinking. Thinking.

Then, finally, he lifts his hands in surrender and nods. "I'll do it. Get the knife away from my whatever artery and I'll do it."

I step back but keep the knife raised, reminding him I'm ready and willing to use it. But Arnie doesn't seem to need the encouragement. He turns around, grabs an unmarked envelope from the shelf behind him, and flops it down on his desk.

"Your basic 'Witness Protection' package is all there, okay? And I also included the birth certificate your friend had me make about six months ago. She paid for it but never picked it up."

I'm about to pick up the folder when I register what he's said. "What birth certificate? Which friend?"

"Brigitte. She called me and wanted a birth certificate made. I didn't pay close attention to the details because she paid me in cash, but she said she was going to adopt a baby and wanted some official paperwork to keep people from asking questions."

My stomach bottoms out. Goosebumps break out all across my skin. I feel faint.

I know Brigitte betrayed me. I've known it for months now, but that doesn't make her callousness any easier to take.

Six months ago, he said.

Four months before I even had Lukas, Brigitte was planning to take him from me. She was planning to forge documents and make herself his mom. She probably would have done it, too, if I hadn't killed her.

"I'll make sure she gets it," I mumble. My fingers feel like ice cubes around the folder.

With the folder in my hands, Arnie looks torn. There's a desperation in his eyes I've seen in wild animals before—when they're cornered.

He doesn't want me to leave with this folder.

I hold up the knife. "I won't say a word about where I got any of this stuff from, Arnie. I won't tell a soul, okay? You're going to be fine."

He sinks down in his chair, his face white. "No, darling. I won't be."

I back out of the room and hurry out of the carnival.

The air feels stagnant and hot. It's not until I get outside in the ocean breeze that I feel like I can breathe. But even then, there's a vise grip around my chest.

There's a lesson I've been slow to learn, but it's finally starting to sink in.

No one can be trusted.

I am the only person I can depend on.

20

DIMA

The first time I tried to kill Giorgio, I spent countless hours planning every detail of the hit—only for everything to go to hell. This time, I'm not going to overthink it.

Giorgio is expecting someone is out to get him. He is expecting a sly operation. Something covert. Secretive.

He doesn't know I'm willing to steamroll through the doors and slaughter every single guard and ally he has just to get to him.

He's expecting an assassination. Not a motherfucking massacre.

The casino still has neon lights hanging above the front doors and wrapped around the circular wings of the building, but they are all dark. Yellow caution tape and orange construction cones litter the parking lot and the front entrance. Building permits hang in the papered-over windows.

The place looks deserted.

Only I know it's not.

I park my car in the empty lot next door and approach the building from the side. Usually, I'd ask Gennady to get me the building plans or blueprints, but there isn't time.

I have a handgun in my hand, extra ammo in my pocket, and a bulletproof vest on underneath my shirt. It won't save me against a headshot, but it will give me a fighting chance against anything else.

With a space this big, there are plenty of exit doors dotting the entire perimeter of the property. I select one that is tucked away between two large shrubs and shaded by a tree. I try the handle, just to see if my luck has turned around, but it's locked.

So I kneel down and get to work. It's been years since I've picked a lock, but it's an art you never really unlearn. Like riding a bike.

I slide a pick into the keyhole and shimmy it gently, my ear pressed to the door, tongue between my teeth. It takes a few minutes of working to hear the first tumbler fall.

But as I go, the work gets easier. The tumblers give way faster and faster until finally, I try the handle again.

This time, it turns.

The hallway inside is dark. I stand inside the door for a minute, listening as my eyes adjust. The carpet has been ripped up, revealing the subfloor beneath, and half of the light fixtures on the wall have been ripped out.

I don't hear any movement inside, but it's a big building. Giorgio could be anywhere. One step in. Still nothing. I pick up speed, moving down the corridor on silent feet.

When I reach the end of the hallway, I hear a door slam closed.

Someone is close.

The hallway ends in a 'T'. I can take a left, a right, or, as a third option, walk straight through the door in front of me.

Going left or right will take me down more hallways towards staff rooms, I assume. The door ahead will likely lead into the casino proper. It will also take me closer to where I believe I heard the banging noise.

So, with my gun ready, I slowly push the door in front of me open and move into a massive room.

There are roulette stations and card tables along the edges of the room. Some of them are draped in drop clothes like misshapen ghosts. Chairs are stacked, legs pointed at the ceiling like spikes, and every third light is on, casting the casino in a dim kind of haze.

I keep to the shadows. Delve deeper. Still nothing makes a sound.

Then I spot motion.

I duck down and peek around a table in time to see someone walk casually around the bar and sit down in one of the barstools.

The man seems to struggle to lift himself into the stool, moving slowly. With the light above him turned on, I can see his hair is graying and his hands are shaky around a glass of amber liquid.

It's Giorgio D'Onofrio.

After weeks of shitty luck, I can't believe this turn in my fortunes. He's sitting in front of me, back turned, alone. It seems too good to be true.

I almost stand up, but that thought sticks in my mind.

It is too good to be true.

Giorgio isn't expecting anyone to know he is at this casino, but he wouldn't be sitting in an empty room alone. A man like him would always have a guard nearby. Especially if he expected to be murdered.

Something is wrong.

Rather than rushing forward to shoot him like I planned, I stay put, frozen with indecision.

Do I take a chance and try to take him out? Or do I leave the way I came?

I've been powered on adrenaline and anger for so much of the last twelve hours, and now it's all gone down the drain. The only thing I can think about is that I've made a terrible mistake.

"Come on out, Dima. We know you're there."

I close my eyes for a moment at the sudden voice. My worst fears confirmed.

It's a fucking set-up.

I stand up, gun in my hand, and see another figure has emerged at the end of the bar.

Zotov Stepanov.

After so many weeks of chasing after him, it feels like I'm staring at a ghost.

"Put your gun down and come over here," he says. "It's been a long time." Zotov talks with the confidence of a much older, much more powerful man. He sure as fuck hasn't earned it.

I scowl when I see him. He's wearing a double-breasted suit like he's fucking Al Capone. I can't express how much I want to shoot him between the eyes.

I have my gun. I could do it.

But I'm certain he has backup. No doubt there are men hidden around the perimeter of the room, guns trained on me.

I can't take a shot at him unless I'm ready for people to take shots at me.

And I'm not quite ready to go down in a blaze of glory.

"Come on," Zotov urges. "Come on out."

I grit my teeth and move forward. "I'm going to hold onto my gun, thanks."

Zotov nods. "I'd expect nothing less. If it makes you feel more comfortable, then go ahead. Though I'd caution you against using it."

"Oh, you would? And why would I give a single fuck what you have to say?"

I'm hoping I can goad Zotov into revealing his hand. How many men are in this building? How many guns? Do I have any fucking chance?

Giorgio spins around in his stool, sagging eyes fixed on me. "Because you killed my son and I'd be more than happy to watch you become target practice."

"Easy," Zotov warns the old man. "We're getting to that."

"My son isn't an item on your goddamn agenda," he snaps.

"No, I took care of that already," I deadpan. I take pleasure in how Giorgio flinches—even though, deep in my own chest, I feel an echo of that pain.

A father who's lost his son. The agony must be horrific.

Zotov tuts. "Dima, that is in very poor taste."

"I came here to kill him," I say, gesturing at Giorgio, "and I very much plan to kill you, too. I think good taste is behind us, Zotov. Particularly once you put a target on my infant son's back."

He shrugs. "Leverage is leverage, okay? You know that. It's just business."

"Goddamn it," I growl. "I'm so fucking tired of hearing that. Business can be personal. When your business involves harming my child, that's personal. When your business involves ripping away my family's legacy, that's very fucking personal."

"Still," Zotov demurs, "I'm not doing it because I dislike you. Or your son. I'm sure he's a lovely little boy. I'm doing it because I want power and you have it. Well, you *had* it. Now, I do."

"Do you want to get to the point?" I snap. "What are you doing here? If you're going to kill me, do it before you literally bore me to death. Or, better yet…" I raise my gun and step towards him, tired of waiting for the inevitable. "… I'll just kill you right now."

Zotov claps his hands. "You're right. Time to get to the point. Would you mind taking out your phone and calling the number of the elderly woman with whom you left your son?"

I freeze. I don't react, but I go perfectly still, trying to work through what this means.

Zotov knows I left Lukas with Ernestine.

How?

I tell myself it doesn't mean anything. It's a bluff.

But it's never a bluff. Not really.

This is bad.

"Whenever you're ready," he urges. "Take your time."

I don't lower the gun, but I use my other hand to reach into my pocket and pull out my phone. Ernestine's number is programmed as the first setting. I hit the button and wait.

"Arya?" Ernestine's voice is high-pitched and panicked. She is breathless and I can hear murmuring in the background behind her.

"No, it's Dima. What's going on?"

She exhales loudly. "I don't know. I don't know. They knocked on the door and then, I don't know what happened. June is gone."

"June? What did they do with her?"

"I don't know." Her voice breaks. "They won't tell me anything."

"Who won't?"

"I don't know!" she cries. "I don't know anything. Lukas and I are being held somewhere. June is gone. I don't... I don't know what's happening. You have to do—"

Before she can finish, the line goes dead.

And my body goes cold.

"See?" Zotov asks. "Aren't you glad you didn't act rashly? If you had killed me, your son would have been in serious danger."

"Where is he? What do you want?"

"Me? What do I want?" He tips his head up, lips pursed. "Ultimate power, endless money, beautiful women. The usual. I suppose I'm not very original in that regard."

"And what does my son have to do with any of that?"

He smiles at me. "I can't have any of those things if I'm dead. Holding onto your son ensures you don't make a poor decision."

I grit my teeth. "Why not just kill me? If you have the man power to kidnap my son, why not just have someone end it all now? You don't need to bother with him. Let him go. Let them both go and we'll settle this ourselves."

Zotov folds his hands behind his back and looks over at Giorgio. "Look, Giorgio. I told you he'd come around. We are already moving on to negotiations."

I want nothing more than to choke the life out of this smug son of a bitch.

But if I kill him, Lukas could be hurt. June could be hurt. Ernestine could be hurt. Arya could be hurt.

I lower my gun to keep myself from doing anything reckless.

As soon as I do, Zotov pulls out a gun of his own.

"Unfortunately," he says, "the only thing I really want is your head on a silver fucking platter."

21

ARYA
AN HOUR EARLIER

I told Ernestine to meet me at the outlet mall. Fifteen minutes later, she hasn't texted back nor shown up.

They are probably napping. Her phone is on silent. That's all.

It's hard not to assume the worst immediately.

They're dead.

They've been kidnapped.

They're dangling off the edge of a cliff somewhere while Zotov laughs in their face.

I have to remind myself to breathe. To just drink this ridiculous orange slushie I bought and stay calm.

It's strange to watch normal families stroll by, pushing babies and holding bags of new clothes. It feels like I'm in a twilight zone. Like it's another world altogether—because these people can't possibly be living in the same world as me. How can they exist so peacefully in a world where mafias fight wars and bad men with big guns slap you across the face hours after you gave birth? How can my world and their world be one and the same?

But it is the same.

What I've finally come to learn—which took way longer than it should have—is that there's no escaping this nasty universe I was born into. Once you're tangled up in it, you never get out. Like a fly in the corner of a spider's web, you may be forgotten for a while. But the spider will come for you eventually.

And it'll come hungry.

I hear a small cry behind me. My thoughts turn immediately to Lukas. I spin around, looking for him and Ernestine and June.

But they aren't there. Instead, I see a small boy, no older than three, clinging to the arm of the bench behind me. He's looking around with wide, panicked eyes.

"Hi there," I say gently. "Are you lost, sweetie?"

The boy blinks at me. His brown eyes are brimming with tears as he nods.

I grab his hand. "Come on, honey. Let's find your mom and dad. Do you know where they are?"

He shakes his head, either incapable of speaking or too nervous to talk to a stranger.

I scoop him up as I scan the crowd for anyone searching frantically. By now, the boy's parents probably realize he is missing and are beginning the search. But I don't see anything or anyone who looks concerned.

"Maybe we'll take you to a security station," I murmur.

Not far down the sidewalk, I see a sign with a blue flashing light on top designating the security office. I'm moving towards it, navigating the crowd, when the boy suddenly squirms in my grasp.

He's a small kid, but the sudden shift of weight still jostles me. I have to squeeze him tightly around the waist to keep from losing him.

"Whoa, what is it?" I yelp. At the same time the boy yells, "Mama!"

I hear a woman cry out in relief. "Oh, thank God!"

I spin around. A dark-haired woman with a top bun is running towards me, arms outstretched.

"Are you his mom?" I ask.

"Yes," she gasps, clutching at her chest. "I was waiting in line at the coffee shop and he was in the stroller, but after I ordered, I looked down and he was gone. He just learned to undo the straps and I didn't notice him walk away. Oh God. I can't believe I did that."

"I found him on a bench not far from there. You would have found him sooner, but I was taking him to the security office."

"That's where I was headed," she says, reaching out to take the boy from me. "Thank you so much for helping him. I feel so stupid for letting this happen. I can't believe he was out of my sight for even a second."

Motherly guilt claws at my heart. I think of what Lukas has been through already in his short life. I was supposed to protect him. I was supposed to keep him safe.

The problem is that the scars he bears from what's happened to us are invisible. Maybe they'll matter down the line; maybe they won't. Either way, I won't know until it's far too late.

And if something does turn out to be wrong… it'll be all my fault.

I mumble goodbye to the woman and leave. When I get back to my seat, my slushie is gone. Someone must have thrown it in the trash. I sink down on the bench and pull out my phone to call Ernestine again.

She doesn't answer.

Panic rises up inside of me, but I do my best to push it down. She'll be here soon.

I lean back on the bench, trying to regulate my breathing, but I can feel my heartrate increasing. My palms are sweaty and my head is starting to pound.

I close my eyes. Trying to ground myself. To remind myself where I'm at, that I'm safe, that Lukas is safe. But it's getting more difficult to swallow and the back of my neck is prickling like someone is standing over my shoulder.

Then I turn around to see that someone is in fact standing over my shoulder.

I scream. People turn to me, shocked by my outburst. I take in a breath to scream again—and then I realize I recognize this creep.

"Gennady?" I reel back from him. "What are you doing here?"

His brows are pinched together. "Holy hell. What's wrong with you? Are you okay?"

"What are you doing here?" I repeat. "What do you want?"

He holds up his hands innocently. "Don't be mad, but Dima helped me set up a cloning app on Ernestine's phone so I'd know where she was and who she was talking to. I saw the text you sent her, which is how I knew where to find you."

I'm not mad. That's actually a good idea. Another layer of security to protect Lukas.

"Okay, we'll circle back on that. Why are you looking for me?"

Gennady looks at me from under lowered brows, his expression grim. "Because I think Dima is about to ruin his life."

I call Dima for the third time, but he doesn't answer.

Gennady is still talking. "... He told me he was going after Giorgio, but I assumed he had a plan. Or back-up. Or something."

Ernestine still isn't answering. I send her another text, letting her know there is an emergency and I had to leave. That we'll meet later.

"He's not thinking clearly," Gennady says. "I tried to talk to him earlier, but he didn't sound like himself. Honestly, he sounded like he was heading to a suicide mission."

My heart clenches. *This is my fault.*

I told him Lukas and I were leaving for good. I told him to do whatever he thought was best for himself. I didn't really listen or try to understand what he had planned. I just wished him luck and turned my back.

"He can't already be inside, can he? We've only been in town a couple of hours. I mean, he spent days canvassing the last hit."

Gennady shakes his head. "We aren't working with a rational Dima right now. He's acting on impulse, which is not good, to say the least."

"Do you know where he's at?"

"I have the address," he says. "I did some quick research before I came to find you."

I glance over at him, noting the firm clench of his jaw and his white knuckles. He's nervous. "Why did you come to get me? I'm not exactly a trained fighter."

"No, but you're the person Dima cares about most in this world. Aside from Lukas, if there's any chance at all to stop him, it's going to be you."

I ignore the pang in my chest. I know Dima cares about me. He has made that perfectly clear. Still, it doesn't ease my conscience at all to hear someone else say it.

Vera's words play in my mind. *Love is always worth the risk.*

This thing between me and Dima, it's love. I know it is.

So this is worth it. It has to be.

When Gennady pulls into the parking lot, he curses under his breath. "That has to be Dima's car. It's a black rental with tinted windows."

I remember seeing the cars sitting in front of the airport when I left. There were two of them. One for Dima, one for Ilyasov.

"It's his," I confirm.

Gennady curses again when we pull up alongside the car. "He's already inside. Shit, shit, shit."

"Okay, so we go in and get him?"

Gennady turns to me, eyes wide. "You say that like it will be easy. There are men with guns in there, Arya."

"Do we have guns?"

Gennady takes a deep breath and then angles around to reach into the backseat. He comes back with two handguns. "Of course we do. But still, I want to make sure you understand there is a chance we don't come out of there. I can't have you backing out once we're in. If we go in, you have to be ready for whatever we may face. Are you sure you want to do this?"

Love is always worth the risk.

I hold out my hand. "Just give me the gun and tell me what to do."

Gennady's expression blurs between admiration and an eyeroll. But he hands me the gun and we step outside.

"There aren't any other cars here. I don't see any sign of active patrols."

"What signs?"

Gennady points at the freshly-turned dirt that has been turned up during the renovation. "No tracks and no footprints on the concrete. If Giorgio has guards here, they're all inside."

"Dima said there wouldn't be very many guards here. Giorgio wants to keep his location quiet."

"Let's hope he's right."

Gennady goes straight for a side door between two large bushes with an overhanging tree. When he turns the handle, it opens immediately.

"That's lucky," I say.

He shakes his head. "No. That's Dima. He picked the lock."

I follow him inside. The hallway is dark and it takes my eyes a moment to adjust, but Gennady doesn't seem bothered by it. He charges full steam ahead, gun drawn. I do my best to keep up.

At the "T" in the hallway, Gennady stops and presses his ear to the door. "I hear voices."

"Should we go in?"

He shakes his head. "Let's find another door. Dima probably went in this way. We want to come in behind Giorgio, not behind Dima."

I'm glad Gennady is here. At least one of us should know what we're doing. I probably would have walked through the first door I saw and ended up with a bullet between the eyes.

I still might, I suppose. I haven't had much time to process this truly insane turn of events.

The hallway wraps in a circle around what I guess is the main casino room. We move cautiously through it, ready to fire at anyone who appears.

But no one does. It's silent as the grave.

"Either they're all in that room with Dima or no one is keeping watch," Gennady says, shaking his head. "It's bizarre. I've never seen anything like it."

I'm not sure if that's a good thing or a bad thing. But as we keep walking, I start to wonder if we aren't going to make a full circle around the premises. Gennady halts and points to a door.

"We're on the opposite side. This is where we're going in."

He presses his ear to the door again, but doesn't say whether he hears anything or not. Then, slowly, he pushes the door open.

It's incredible to me how slyly he moves. Gennady is not a small man by any means, but he manages to slide between a small crack in the door without making a noise.

I do my best to follow suit. As soon as I make it through, he grabs the door and drops it gently back into the frame without a sound.

We're in.

But we aren't alone.

Most of the overhead lights are turned off. The only ones on are in the center of the room, and even then, only every third light. It's dim, but I can see Dima standing on the far side of the room, facing two men I don't recognize.

Gennady pulls me behind a covered table and gestures to my gun, silently instructing me to be ready to use it.

I've been to a gun range before and I've fired a gun, but none of that means I'm comfortable with a weapon.

Gennady scans the room and then gestures for me to go one direction and him to move the other. We are going to circle around and attack the two men from each side. So long as there aren't other people hiding in this room, it's a good plan.

Keeping low and staying beneath the tables, I edge around the room. Dima is talking to the men, but I can hardly hear them over my own heavy breathing and the thunder of my heart.

Stay focused.

I move around until I'm at eight o'clock from the younger of the two men. Gennady is in the same position on the opposite side.

I don't know if Dima has seen us. I hope he has. I'd love to not be shot by the man I've come to save.

Gennady lifts a hand, waving once and then pointing a finger. At the same time, we rush from our hiding places, guns drawn. It happens so fast I don't even have time to be nervous.

"Don't do anything stupid!" Gennady yells. "I know that may be hard for you, Zotov."

Zotov?

The younger of the two men looks more annoyed than concerned. "Christ, do you two go anywhere without each other? My God."

"We shouldn't," Gennady says, throwing a sharp look at Dima.

I can't look at him yet. My hand is shaking on the weapon. I'm trying to convince myself I can do this.

I'm only a foot behind Zotov now, gun trained on his head. I should just pull the trigger. Be done with it. End him. End all of this.

"Arya," Dima says, voice soft. "Listen."

"Shut up," I snap at him. For a second, I was relieved Dima was still alive. Now, I'm livid. That he came here and risked his life this way. That he could be so reckless.

"No, listen to me," he begs.

I chance a look at him, eyes narrowed. "I mean it, Dima. Don't talk to me right now."

In the second I lose my focus, Zotov spins around with a flying elbow. At the same time, he grabs the handle of my gun and points it away from his face as I pull the trigger.

When I fire, the round goes straight into the floor.

"You should really listen to him," Zotov sneers, his breath hot on my face.

Gennady yells and another shot rings out. This time, it's from his gun.

Zotov ducks, dragging me down to the floor with him.

The old man shoots at Gennady, who dives behind a table for cover, and then turns and takes aim at Dima.

"This is for Ennio, you piece of shit!" he yells.

Zotov still has his hand on the gun, despite my thrashing. He looks over his shoulder to try and corral the old man. "Giorgio, don't lose your temper. Remember the plan!"

The plan. This was a set-up. They're working together.

But why? How? I don't know and I don't have the time to work it out.

The room is chaos and gunfire. While Zotov is distracted, I manage to bring my knee straight up into his crotch. He groans, doubling over and releasing my gun. Then, before I can even stumble back, he lifts his own weapon and shoots.

I don't feel anything as I scramble for the edge of the room, looking for a table to hide behind. I find somewhere and sink to the floor. My forehead is slicked with sweat, but when I go to wipe it off with my shirtsleeve, I feel something wrong.

There's a growing dark stain on my forearm. I pull back my sleeve.

That's when the pain starts.

I've been shot.

22

DIMA

Arya is hiding behind a table. Gennady and Giorgio are exchanging bullets with each other while Zotov tries to control his man.

This is my chance.

Zotov is distracted, so he doesn't notice me approaching him from behind. I stalk close enough to make my move, then I leap forward and press the muzzle of my gun against his temple.

"Drop the gun," I order. "Now."

"I've already warned you," Zotov says. "If anything happens to me, I have your son."

"And am I supposed to believe you're going to give Lukas back if I let you live?" I scoff. "Don't bullshit a bullshitter, Zotov. Drop your gun and call your man off of Gennady. Now."

Zotov hesitates for a moment and then drops his gun on the floor. "Enough!" His voice breaks. He sounds scared.

Good.

Giorgio stops and turns around. He considers aiming his gun at me, but as soon as he does, Gennady presses his gun to the old man's back.

"Game is up," Gennady says, walking Giorgio forward. "Drop your gun, old man."

Giorgio starts to raise his hands, but at the last second, he places his finger on the trigger and whirls around.

Gennady shoots him before he's even made it halfway through the turn. The elder D'Onofrio drops to the floor.

Dead before he lands.

Zotov curses. "Fucking sentimental old man."

He sounds like my father. Like Ilyasov, too. Part of me even thinks he's right. Sentiment is what gets you killed.

But it also gives you a reason to fight. Right now, that reason is everything. Lukas and Arya are my everything.

"He's a father grieving his son," I snarl in Zotov's ear. "It's amazing what a man will do when his son is in danger."

Zotov's hand starts to tremble. "Listen, Dima, I've just been following orders."

I laugh. "Fuck you, you sniveling fucking coward. Your back is against the wall and suddenly, you're innocent. What happened to how much you want power and control? Not so confident anymore?"

"I do want those things, but I don't have them yet. I mean, really, do you think I have the sway necessary to pull off this operation on my own?"

"No. That's why you partnered with the Albanians."

"I did," he admits with a shrug. "But someone else has been bankrolling this entire thing. They are the ones who set the plan in motion, who is really striving to take control. I'm a fucking pawn, *sobrat*."

Part of me wants to believe Zotov is talking out of his ass. He's just scared. He doesn't want me to kill him.

But then again, my thought since the beginning has been that Zotov doesn't make sense as the leader of this mutiny. How he got so many of my men to turn away from the Romanoff family line and my leadership never made sense.

"Who's the mastermind, then?"

Zotov takes a breath. "I don't want to say. You'll shoot me."

"I'll shoot you if you don't say, so you may as well speak up."

"Can I at least explain first?" he asks. "Just give me a chance to fucking explain."

"Get on with it. Clock's ticking."

"Think about it, Dima. Giorgio and I are here together. Why? Giorgio was a target you tried to take out. Who asked you to do that?"

I don't answer.

"You've been taking out leadership from the Albanians and the Italians alike," he continues. "You're taking out the biggest threats to your Bratva one at a time. Why?"

Because Ilyasov asked me to.

Ilyasov.

His name is seared into my brain like a red-hot brand. But I can't bring myself to say it. Zotov has to be the one to speak it out loud.

I press the gun harder against Zotov's temple and close my eyes. "Keep talking."

"It's your brother. He did all of this."

My teeth clench hard enough I think they'll crack. I told Ilyasov where Ernestine and Lukas were staying when we got into town. He told me where I could find Giorgio.

Both were a trap. A trap I fucking waltzed into. Willingly. Stupidly.

Because of goddamn fucking sentimentality. Because I still thought family loyalty meant something to him. I thought he still had a shred of humanity left in his heart.

I was wrong.

And it's about to cost me everything.

"But listen, I know his plans now," Zotov says. "Some of them, anyway. I can help you take things back from him. I can be an asset to you."

I pull back, though I keep my gun aimed at his stupid traitorous skull. "Spin around." He does so obediently. "You want to be loyal now? Fine. Tell me where my son is."

"What?" I hear Arya's voice behind me.

I wince. She doesn't know yet.

"What do you mean? Where is Lukas?" Arya is at my side in a second, clutching her arm with her other hand. I can see blood oozing between his fingers. "Who has him?"

"Ilyasov wanted him captured," Zotov blurts. "He knew it was the best way to be able to control Dima. That's the only reason I used him as blackmail. To save myself."

"That didn't work out very well, did it?" I wave my gun in front of him. "I guess Ilyasov didn't consider the fact that there's nothing for me to gain by following your orders."

"We'd gain our *son*," Arya cries. "You can't kill him."

I shake my head, but Gennady answers before I can. "No. No matter what, they aren't going to hand Lukas over. Whether Dima kills Zotov or not, they're going to keep him."

A sob breaks through Arya's lips. I want to reach out and pull her close to me. I want to tell I'm sorry for being so blinded. For not seeing what had been right in front of my face the entire time.

But I don't. Now is not the time.

Then a thought occurs to me.

"Are you alone here?" I ask.

Gennady answers before Zotov can. "Arya and I walked all through the hallways and we didn't see anyone. I didn't see any signs of patrols outside, either. I think they're alone."

I tilt my head to the side, a slight smirk pulling up the corner of my mouth. "Huh. That's interesting."

Zotov swallows. "Ilyasov thought Lukas would be enough to keep you in line. He told me it would work. He said—"

"Ilyasov says lots of things. Most of them are lies. I learned that the hard way." I point my gun at his forehead. "Unfortunately, I think you will, too."

"What do you mean?" Zotov's pupils are fully dilated, and I can see the thump of his pulse in his throat. "I told you I can help you overthrow him. I'm willing to help."

"I know you are. Because you're a fucking spineless coward."

He nods. "I understand why you're angry. But I swear, I'll be loyal to you now, Dima. I can help."

I run my tongue over my teeth. "Then tell me where my son is, Zotov."

Zotov hesitates. His eyes dart over to Arya and then towards a door on the far side of the room.

"Come on," I say, curling the fingers of my other hand. "Tell me where my son is. Then you can take me there and we'll get him together. That's how you can help."

He swallows. I can feel the trigger just a hair's breadth away from the pad of my finger.

"Where is he?!" Arya screams.

Zotov flinches. "I don't know," he admits, his shoulders slouching forward. "Ilyasov didn't tell me much. He is the one who arranged the pickup from the motel and he is the one who arranged where to keep them. I don't know anything."

"And do you know why?" I ask.

Zotov stares up at me, blinking. He looks so much younger now. So much weaker. I almost feel bad for him.

Almost.

"Because you are expendable." I enunciate each word. "Ilyasov sent me here because, either way, he would win."

It's clear Zotov doesn't understand what I'm saying, so I spell it out for him.

"Ilyasov wanted us to kill each other. He wanted every single person in this room to die and he set it up so he wouldn't have to pull a single trigger. The son of a bitch is smart. It runs in the family. I admit, I've been a bit slow on the uptake, but I'm getting it now. Either way, someone would get taken out. Ilyasov would clean up whoever was left. It's a smart plan, really."

Reality washes over the poor kid. He backs away from me only to bump into Gennady, who also has him on the business end of his gun.

"Then let's not give him what he wants," Zotov begs. "Let's team up and fight back. Let's take him out instead. That's real revenge. Right? Right?"

I clench my jaw "Eh, I don't know. To me, real revenge would be taking out every single person who came for me and reclaiming what's always been mine. It has a much more poetic ring to it."

Zotov opens his mouth, but I silence him before he can even speak.

BANG.

It's a clean shot. A bullet straight between the eyes. Just like I've imagined for the last few months.

But the part that comes next isn't what I imagined at all.

I don't feel complete. I don't feel satisfied.. Because for all he's done… for all he's taken… Zotov isn't the reason my life has turned upside down. He isn't the reason I'm without my son.

I understand now—that honor belongs to my brother.

That means he'll be the next one to die.

23

ARYA

We can't go back to the safehouse because Ilyasov knows where it is. We can't go find Ernestine and June because we don't know where they've been taken. It feels like we can't do anything or go anywhere without Ilyasov somehow finding out about it. I've never felt so trapped. Not even when I was a slave at Taras Kreshnik's house.

Dima finds a motel nearby and we rent a room just to have a private place to talk. And plan.

As soon as we get inside, Dima kicks over the table and breaks one of the cheap wooden legs. "Goddamn it!"

Usually, I'd stand up and lay a hand on his shoulder, try to comfort him. But this reaction seems appropriate. He fucked up. We all did.

"He is your brother, Dima. Of course you thought you could trust him." Gennady sits down in the armchair and buries his face in his hands.

"I was stupid."

"You're loyal," Gennady says. "You expect it from other people, too. It's a good thing… most of the time."

I stay quiet. I haven't been able to find the words to express much of anything. Not how I'm feeling about Lukas being gone. Again. Or how I feel about Ilyasov double-crossing Dima.

If I've had any major takeaway from the last couple months, it's that you can't trust anyone but yourself. Ever.

And just like that, I've found the words.

"No one can be trusted," I say. "Outside of this room, they are all the enemy. Every single one."

On cue, there's a knock on the door. We all look at one another, waiting to see who will move first.

Gennady gets up to answer. He stands up and moves towards the door, hand on his gun. "Who is it?"

"Hello?" The voice on the other side of the wood is small and weak. I recognize it instantly.

I rush forward and shove Gennady aside, throwing the door open.

June is standing in front of me. Her hair is in loose braids that are falling out, but she otherwise seems unhurt. Except for the tears in her eyes.

"Oh my God! June. What are you doing here?" I grab the girl by the shoulder and pull her inside, shutting the door behind her.

"They dropped me off," she mumbles.

Dima moves to the window and scans the parking lot. "I don't see anyone outside."

"They took my grandma," she says. "And Lukas. They knocked and said they were from the front desk, but when we answered, they pushed inside and grabbed us. I don't know where they're at."

"You didn't see your grandma or Lukas where you were?" I ask.

She shakes her head and her lower lip starts to tremble. "They wouldn't tell me where she was or if she's okay. I don't know what they want. They wouldn't talk to me and then they just put me in a car and brought me here."

I hug the girl and kiss her temple, smoothing my hands down her arms. She's shaking like a leaf.

"She could be wired," Dima says quietly. "Why else would they release her?"

Because they don't want to take care of a ten-year-old girl? She's not old enough to take care of the baby, and she's not very useful collateral, so that makes her expendable. Maybe they just let her go. Though even I have to admit, it seems unlikely.

Gennady agrees. "You have to check her."

I hate treating her like a criminal, but they're right. No one from outside this room can be trusted. Not even a small child.

"I'm sorry, honey, but I'm going to pat you down, okay? Just real quick."

June is trembling, but she nods and holds out her arms. I pat her down, feeling under her shirt and down her legs. I ask her if anyone attached anything to her or touched her at all and she insists they didn't.

"The only thing they gave me was this." She reaches into her pocket and pulls out a small slip of paper.

I take it from her.

The note is handwritten in a slanted hand. *Dvúm smertyám ne byvát, odnóy ne minovát.* "It's in another language," I say. "I can't read it."

Gennady plucks it out of my hand and scans it. His eyes widen before he hands it off to Dima. "It's for you."

Dima reads it and goes still. The volatile mood from a moment ago seems to disappear. He retreats within himself. Those dark eyes go stone cold.

"What is it? What does it say?" I ask, looking back and forth between the two men. "Is that why they sent her here? To deliver the note?"

Gennady is the one to speak. "It's a Russian proverb. It translates to something like, 'Two deaths will not happen, but one is inevitable.'"

I shake my head. "And what the hell does that mean?"

Dima drops the note on the desk and collapses on the edge of the bed. His hair is a sweaty mass of curls hanging around his ears and eyes. He runs a tanned hand through it. "It means people should be willing to take risks because they can't die twice."

I wrap an arm around June and sigh. "I need longer explanations. More words. What does that mean? What does that have to do with anything? Is Ilyasov saying you need to risk your life again by trying to fight him? Because that's a hard disagree from me."

Dima shakes his head. "It's the proverb my family has used to initiate the Romanoff Trials."

I wait for him to explain, but when he doesn't, I growl and circle my finger in the air. "What? More. Come on."

"The Romanoff Trials are a test that has been used for generations to decide which Romanoff heir should take over the Bratva. It's tradition, I guess. A nasty tradition."

"So Ilyasov wants to challenge you?" I ask. "After everything that has happened, he wants a one-on-one duel? That seems oddly gentlemanly of him."

"It's not quite that… straightforward," he sighs.

Before he can explain, Gennady interrupts. "It's the fucking rental car. The one Ilyasov gave you. It's got a tracker."

Dima growls in frustration. "Shit. I wasn't even thinking."

"We need to move, ASAP."

He nods. "We'll ditch the car here, steal a new one, and find somewhere else to hide out while we prepare."

"To participate in some kind of ancient fight to the death?" I ask, almost not believing the turn things have taken.

"I can't refuse. And I can't know what the outcome will be. But if I do win… it will end this fight for good."

"With Ilyasov," Gennady clarifies. "It will end things with Ilyasov. But whoever takes over the Romanoff Bratva, they are going to have to watch their back against the Albanians, the Italians, and God only knows who else. They'll be out for revenge."

"We're all out for revenge." I look around and shrug. "Tell them to join the party."

I know Dima wants to take out his brother on his own. If the Romanoff Trials are what they sound like, he will be the one fighting.

But I'm not going down without a fight, either. Ilyasov took my son from me. That isn't something I'll forgive or forget anytime soon.

I told Dima I didn't want to be part of this life. That I wanted to be normal. But maybe it's time for me to face the truth: I'm not normal.

The Arya George I am today was formed in combat. In blood and sweat and tears. And I will do whatever is necessary to make sure Dima is ready and able to reclaim what is his. To rain down vengeance on every single person who tried to hurt our family.

"It's going to be a rocky road, but I'm more than ready to fight or die trying." Dima looks around. "How about the two of you?"

Gennady stands up and clasps Dima's hand. "With you to the end, brother. Always."

I meet Dima's blue gray eyes. I love him. I know that without a doubt now. Maybe one day I'll even be brave enough to say it to his face.

For now, I just touch his shoulder. "I'm with you, Dima. Ilyasov fucked with the wrong mom."

24

DIMA

A FEW HOURS LATER

This is not how I imagined this going.

No Bratva. No backup.

Just me, my right-hand man, and the mother of my child.

We bound Arya's bullet wound with some ripped sheets from the hotel linen closet. She insisted she'd be fine. "It's nothing but a graze," she snaps. "Not all of us have to go kicking in clinic doors to find a doctor when we get a little scratch." She gives me a sassy glance.

"I thought you weren't a doctor?" I rumble.

She rolls her eyes and gives me the middle finger.

It's a strange, funny callback to the night I crash-landed in her world. But perhaps strangest of all is what we're doing now: hunting down my own brother.

I know I should have seen this coming. Should have trusted my gut where Ilyasov was concerned. And I did—right up until it mattered the most. At the crucial moment, I faltered. Believed in loyalty.

My son is missing as a result.

We're standing outside of a nondescript house. Sure enough, the rental car Ilya gave me had a tracker in it. We ditched the car and the tracker, but before we did, Gennady was able to work some of his magic and figure out where the tracker was being tracked from. The answer: right here.

"Fuck, this is a good door," Gennady hisses as he jimmies his lock pick in the handle.

Arya has been pacing on the top step, her hands tangled together nervously the way they have been so often the last few weeks. Finally, she growls, jumps off the porch, and grabs a rock from the landscaped garden next to the railing.

"Arya, what are you—"

Before I can finish, she pulls her arm back and lets the rock fly. Straight through the window.

The sound of glass shattering makes Gennady and me both wince, but the night remains calm and quiet. There's no alarm sounding inside. No footsteps. No movement.

"There," Arya says, walking through a bush to the window. She starts to break out the rest of the glass with her elbow. "I found a way in."

Gennady looks at me. I look at him. We both shrug and then follow after her.

"I'm loving the enthusiasm there, Arya," I deadpan. "But next time, ask me before you do anything stupid."

Arya turns to me. "I'm the one who got us inside. I think what you meant to say is, *Thank you.*"

Gennady boosts her through the window. He crawls in after her. I'm the last one inside.

The house is a rental, outfitted with bland furniture and dollar store paintings. It gives off a dentist's office vibe. But according to Gennady, it's where Ilyasov was last traced.

"It doesn't exactly look like a mafia headquarters," Gennady whispers. "Maybe I got it wrong."

I walk to the coffee table and pick up the frame sitting in the center of it. "No," I sigh, "you didn't." Arya and Gennady turn to me as I hold up the photo.

It's Lukas.

Arya runs towards it and plucks the frame out of my hands as if it's our actual son, not just a photograph. For a moment, I see the pain just under the surface.

But then she hides it away again.

"What does this mean?" she demands.

"Fuck if I know. But they were here." I take the frame back from her and study it, looking for a camera or a microphone. Anything Ilyasov might have hidden in it.

Then I notice the small piece of paper sticking out of the frame backing. I pop the frame open and a square of paper floats to the floor.

Arya lunges for it. "*'Trial One'*?" she reads. "What's that? Is that an address?"

"The Romanoff Trials have begun." Gennady sits down on the couch and pinches the bridge of his nose. "Goddammit. The fucker isn't here. Maybe he never was."

Arya is looking back and forth from me to Gennady. "Okay, but what in the hell is 'Trial One'? Anyone care to fill me in?"

"It's the first stage in the Romanoff Trials," I explain. "A task between the two men vying to be don. The challenge is to eliminate another mafia boss."

"For fuck's sake! Are you going to have to kill every mafioso in town?" Arya cries. "We don't have time for this shit!"

"She's right," Gennady says. "You've already killed Giorgio D'Onofrio."

"Jorik, too."

Gennady claps his hands once. "Great. Then we're done with number one. Let's get out of here and figure out what number two is."

"No!" Arya backs towards the door. Her face is white and her lips are pressed together into a straight line. "No, we can't leave yet. We haven't even looked. Lukas could still be here."

She spins around and rushes down the hallway. Part of me thinks I should follow her. Make sure she's safe. But deep down, I know Gennady is right. No one is here. The house is empty.

I slam the picture down on the coffee table. The glass shatters. Pieces of the frame splinter and fall to the floor.

And a small plastic piece with a red light falls, too. I pick it up and hold it out to Gennady, but I already know what it is.

"The tracker," he confirms.

Ilyasov lured us here. Because he's a showman above all. He couldn't just leave behind the family Bratva when I was made don over him. Who knows how long he's been planning this shit? It's intricate. Orchestrated. He's got a ten-year head start on his vengeance.

I can hear Arya moving around upstairs, searching every single room, opening every single cabinet.

Ilyasov couldn't just go after me, either. He had to go after my family.

Arya didn't ask for this. For any of it. But that doesn't matter to a man like him. Ilyasov wants to destroy me. That means destroying her, too.

It makes my blood curdle. He can fuck with me all he wants. I'm fair game.

But my child and his mother? It's a bridge too far.

"I'll kill him," I say, uttering the words under my breath. An oath to myself.

Gennady's hand claps on my shoulder. "And I'll help. But for now, we should go."

"I know," I agree. "The house is empty, but that doesn't mean it's safe. I'll get Arya."

I take the stairs two at a time and find Arya standing in the hallway, staring into the bathroom, her arms hanging limply at her side.

"We should go."

She jumps at the sound of my voice. I see that familiar mask slam down over her features. I caught her in a private, vulnerable moment. A moment she should be able to share with me.

But she won't. Can't. Refuses to let me in.

If it was up to her, she and Lukas would probably be on a plane already. Headed to a new life, far from me and the shit I bring to the table. Instead, she's searching an empty house for our infant son, wondering if she'll ever see him again.

"We're going to find him," I say softly. "Ilyasov won't hurt him."

Her jaw tightens like she wants to say something. But then just she brushes past me and down the stairs.

Gennady unlocks the front door and opens it, ushering Arya out. "Let's get the fuck out of here before the police show up."

The street is quiet. Just a series of row houses, cars parked all along the curb in front of us. Gennady parked the car around the corner, so I'm moving that way when Arya stops and grabs my wrist, pulling me back.

"We have to go," I insist, pulling her forward.

"Stop," she says. There's something in the tone of her voice that catches my attention.

She's staring at a black car in front of us. It's not noteworthy in anyway—except the tinted window is partially rolled down…

And someone is sitting inside.

It's dark and the streetlight is positioned in a way where it's casting more shadow in the car than light, so I can't see who it is.

I pull Arya behind me and reach for the gun on my hip. "Wait here."

"Dima…" She doesn't try to stop me or warn me. Just says my name.

I move slowly to the car. What could it be? Another trap? Another taunt? A car bomb?

I stop suddenly, remembering the car bomb that first sent me running all those months ago. The one that put me on a collision course with Arya I never could've seen coming.

It seems unlike Ilyasov to recycle plans, but it's also a real possibility. I have to be careful.

I edge towards the car slowly, squinting as I try to see through the crack in the window. The car isn't running, but I can hear the sound of a late night radio DJ talking through the speakers.

"Hello?"

No one answers. I'm hesitant to touch the handle.

I stretch onto my toes and peek through the crack. That's when I see a person slumped over in the passenger seat.

A woman.

A woman I recognize.

"Ernestine?"

I barely get the name out before Arya is running past me to fling open the door.

I wrap my arms around her waist and yank her back as fast as I can, but her hand is already on the handle. The door opens. I whip us both around, preparing for a blast that doesn't come.

"Goddammit, Arya!" I snarl. "That could have been a car bomb. It would have blown this whole block sky high. What in the fuck were you thinking?"

"I was thinking that my friend might be sitting dead in a car and that my son might be in there, too!" she yells. She pushes past me and kneels down next to Ernestine. Gingerly, she presses her fingers to the woman's neck and then sighs. "She has a pulse."

At that moment, Ernestine stirs. Her eyes flutter and she mutters something incoherent.

"We have to get her out of the car. What if it's still a bomb?" Arya asks.

Gennady makes a lap around the car, kneeling down to look underneath it. "I don't see anything, but it is weird the keys are still in it. We should touch as little as possible."

I grab Arya by the shoulders and forcibly remove her from the car. She fights for a moment, but as soon as she realizes we are helping Ernestine, she relaxes.

I scoop the old woman up, carry her to our new car, and lay her in the back seat. Arya sits next to her and smooths down her hair.

"Ernestine, can you hear me?"

The sound of Arya's voice seems to rouse the woman. She blinks hard, trying to open her eyes.

"Are you okay?" Arya asks. "What happened?"

It takes a few moments, but Ernestine finds her voice. "They... drugged me. Took Lu... Lu... Lukas."

Arya's shoulders fall in obvious disappointment. "Who did?"

"I don't... I don't know. A large man. He had... a strange name." Her words are garbled and quiet, but I can hear her well enough to recognize what she's trying to say. "Il... Il... Ilyas or—"

"Ilyasov," I finish for her grimly.

She tries to turn her head to look at me, but she's still too weak. She sinks down into Arya's lap with a nod. "Yes, that's it. Ilyasov took Lukas. They're gone."

25

ARYA

As soon as we get to the new hotel, Ernestine wants to be in a room alone with June. The rest of us—Gennady, Dima, and myself—get a different room.

I'm proud of June for doing so good on her own. We left her alone with strict instructions while we went to investigate the tracker beacon. But they both break out in tears when they're reunited.

I think Ernestine is badly rattled by everything that's happened. If anyone can understand that feeling, it's me.

"Fuck the Trials!" I say as soon as we shut the door. "I don't give a damn about the Bratva or any of it. We need to find Lukas. That's the priority."

"Obviously that's the priority, Arya," Dima snaps. "Lukas has always been the priority."

"Not always," I mutter. "Not for you."

The look on Dima's face is murderous, but he doesn't say whatever he's thinking.

He's been doing that a lot lately—staying quiet. He doesn't seem to know what to say to me or to anyone. And that breaks my heart in a whole new way.

I sigh and drop down on the bed, slowly unwrapping the bandage around my arm. The blood has only soaked through half of the layers, which is a good sign. It should heal up on its own without stitches.

"I'm just saying, we need to focus on finding out where Ilyasov is and getting Lukas back. We can't be worried about the Trials right now."

"They are one and the same. If I win, then—"

"Then your brother still has our son and absolutely no reason to give him back," I finish. "Lukas is blackmail. A final chip Ilyasov plans to play in case all else fails. We need him back with us now."

Dima's jaw shifts back and forth, his teeth grating together. "You're not wrong, but I still think it will pay to play his game at least a little bit. If I disregard everything—"

"We've been unknowingly playing his game for weeks! How many men did you kill on his call? How much time did we waste helping him take over your Bratva?"

"If I disregard everything," Dima continues as though I never interrupted, "Ilyasov may think I don't plan to follow protocol, and he may pull the Lukas card way earlier than he would have otherwise. We don't want that. We want Lukas to be safe."

The Lukas card. As if my baby is nothing more than a pawn in this sick game.

This is what I wanted to avoid. This is what I wanted to escape from.

"We don't even know if he's safe now," I say. "He could already be—"

Dima stands up, head shaking violently. "Shut up!"

I freeze at Dima's outburst.

"Just… don't," he says, softening. "Don't. Lukas is fine. My brother is a lot of things, but he isn't—"

I can't believe what I'm hearing. "A murderer? I beg to differ. A liar? Again, he has a track record. We can't trust a single thing he says. If he tells us he has Lukas with him, we should assume the exact opposite. If he says Lukas is alive…"

"He wouldn't kill his own fam—" Dima seems to stop himself and take a deep breath. "He wouldn't kill a baby."

"How do you know that? You didn't think he was capable of betraying you. How do you know he isn't capable of hurting a child? Why should I trust you? Why did you ever trust him?"

Gennady sits up now, and I had almost forgotten he was in the room. "Arya, come on. Dima is trying. He—"

Dima holds up his hand. Gennady goes silent immediately. When he turns back to me, his expression is blank. "You barely know my brother. I grew up with him."

"That's what's blinding you!"

"No, *YOU* blinded me!" he roars.

The carefully curated mask cracks in half. I can see Dima's rage now. His desperation to find Lukas. His frustration with me. With his brother. Every emotion he's been bottling up and pushing down.

It's like staring straight into the sun.

He takes a rattling breath. And then another. And another.

"What in the hell does that mean?" I bite out quietly.

Gennady stands up and hitches a thumb over his shoulder. "I think I'll head out for some ice."

Dima waits until his second-in-command is out the door before he looks back at me. "Everything I did for Ilyasov was because I wanted to get my Bratva back—for *you*."

"Bullshit. I told you to leave it! I asked you to abandon everything and leave with me. How was this for me?"

"For your protection," he says. "And Lukas's. I knew the only way I'd be able to protect either of you was with my Bratva, so I did what my brother demanded, no matter how dangerous. If anything blinded me, it wasn't my love for my brother. It was my love for you."

In another situation, maybe his admission would be sweet.

But right now, it feels like a slap in the face.

Love is a weapon, he's said before. Does he think I'm the one pulling the trigger?

"Great. So it's all my fault that Lukas is gone. Makes total sense that I'm the one to blame." I cross my arms over my chest tightly, trying to hold my chest together so my heart doesn't come jumping out. "Even though I said again and again I wanted my son out of this life. Even though I was making moves to get us both out of the country. Glad we cleared that up."

Dima growls. "It's not your fault."

"It doesn't sound like you really believe that."

"It's not," he says again. "It's not. But… look, I see Ilyasov very clearly now. More clearly than I ever have. You can trust me."

Blood is dripping down my arm. I sit down on the bed and grab a new roll of bandages. "Okay, so then where is he? If you know him so well, where has he taken Lukas?"

"I said I know his personality. I'm not a fucking mind-reader."

I want to scream. My son is missing, my arm has a hole in it, and I'm so fucking tired it takes actual effort to keep my eyes from rolling back in my skull.

"What's your best guess?" I ask. "What would *you* do?"

Dima recoils. "I wouldn't take a baby, for starters."

"Well, Ilyasov did, so why don't we all just play Make Believe for a little bit, eh?" I snap.

He clenches his jaw. "I think he is still in New York. We should stay here and keep looking. Keep playing Ilya's game."

"Why wouldn't he go home to Chicago?" I counter. "It would make a lot more sense. Clearly, he has been able to control things from a distance so far. I don't know why he'd stay here and risk playing this game on your turf."

Dima shakes his head. "His goal has always been to get back to New York City and run the Bratva here. Now that Zotov is dead and his plan is in motion, the members who defected will be even more willing to support him. It wouldn't look good if he fled the city. It would make him look scared. He doesn't want that."

This is Dima's world. He understands the mind of a don better than almost anyone.

But I understand something else that's key here: the mind of a don's partner.

"Vera will want him to be home. She's pregnant with his sons. Due any day now."

"Vera isn't calling the shots."

I lower my chin and raise a brow. "The wife is always calling the shots, Dima."

He rolls his eyes. "Going back to Chicago is a waste of time. There's no way he'd go back to his house where I could easily find him. He'll be hiding out here in the city."

"Okay, fine, then you stay here and look. I'll go back to Chicago."

Dima was about to say something, but he stops, his mouth hanging open, and stares at me. "You can't be serious."

"If we both think we're right, we might as well pursue every avenue."

"We should stick together."

"Why?" I ask with a bitter laugh. "You clearly don't value my opinion and according to you, I'm a distraction."

His hands fist at his sides. "That isn't what I meant."

"Maybe you'd think more clearly if I went somewhere else. And I know I'd feel better if I could actually contribute to the search. I can't just sit here in this room and listen to you plan for these Trials when my baby is out there."

"He's my son, too."

"Then you should be thrilled we'll be able to cover more ground this way." I tie off the end of my bandage and pull my sleeve down over the bulk. "This is a win-win."

Dima shakes his head and then turns on his heel and storms into the bathroom. "It feels like a loss to me."

∽

Gennady slips into the room sometime later, after Dima and I are already lying in bed.

I can tell by the sound of Dima's breathing that he isn't asleep. Despite how exhausted my body feels, my own mind is racing.

Blaming Dima for all of this isn't fair. If it wasn't for him, I'd still be a sex slave in Taras Kreshnik's house.

Or worse, I'd be dead and Lukas would still be with Brigitte.

Without Dima, my life would still be shit. But I just don't know who else to blame.

If I blame myself, I'll fall apart. Lukas needs me too much for that. So blaming Dima is the easiest option.

It's not fair, but nothing in life is fair right now. Then again, nothing has been fair for a long, long time.

26

DIMA

I call a meeting less than an hour after Arya leaves for Chicago.

"The main order of business is going to be restoring the Romanoff name. Everything Zotov did must be undone," I say to the gathered group of my inner circle.

It should feel odd being in front of them after so long. But it doesn't. This is where I fucking belong.

"We've already cut ties with the Albanians," Eduard Vinogradov says. He is one of my lieutenants and, according to Gennady, remained completely loyal throughout the mutiny. "Though that wasn't much of a choice. After you killed Jorik, they became suspicious of our motives."

"Then the fentanyl is gone from our supply?"

He nods. "Nearly. We have a few more storehouses we are clearing out."

"Make sure it's done by the end of the week."

"Yes, Don Dima. And sir…" He hesitates, then meets my eyes. "It goes without saying that it's good to have you back. But there are some… structural issues we should clear up. For your sake and for ours."

I cross my arms. "Which would be?"

"Much was said about your abilities as a leader while you were away. By Zotov and others—at the direction of your brother, I'm sure."

"They weren't exactly going to sing my praises."

"Perhaps not. But the main argument was about your conviction to the Bratva. Your dedication."

I bark out a laugh. "I risked my life to get back here, Eduard. I crawled through fucking hell to reclaim what's mine."

"We all know what you've done and we all respect it. But your… motivations have been called into question. Namely, where it concerns Aryana Georgeovich."

"Arya," I correct in a menacing growl. "She's not Albanian anymore. Not in any way that matters."

"Perhaps not," Eduard says with a shrug, "but many within the Bratva, on both sides of the divide, are worried about whether she has softened you."

I glance around the room. It's hard to get a feel for the others. If they agree. If they think I'm weak.

Time to remind them of who the fuck I am.

"I killed Jorik Bogdanovich. Giorgio and Ennio D'Onofrio. Zotov Stepanov. I slaughtered countless numbers of their men along with them." I glare from man to man. "Have you all forgotten who Dima Romanoff is? Have you forgotten what I'm fucking capable of?"

Eduard sighs. "No one has forgotten your pedigree, *patsan*. But that doesn't mean every Bratva man is willing to throw their lot back in with yours right away. Some are saying they want their trust to be earned."

"Whose trust?" I demand. "Yours?"

Eduard lifts one shoulder in a shrug. "Everyone's. The Bratva is on shaky ground right now. We are fighting on all fronts. Including on the inside. All of these adversaries have to be dealt with and the men want to make sure you are the right person to do that. The Trials would go a long way to prove you're the right leader for the job."

"How did you know about the Trials?" I demand, glancing to Gennady. He shakes his head, indicating to me that he never told.

"Ilyasov relayed the message to everyone," he explains. "He informed us he had challenged you and that the winner would take control of the Romanoff Bratva. It seems like a fair way to—"

"*Fair?*" I spit. "'Fair' was being chosen by my father for the job. 'Fair' was me dedicating years of my life to expanding our territory, maintaining alliances, eliminating enemies. The only thing not 'fair' about this entire situation is my men turning their backs on me to support the brother who lost in the first place. Ilyasov is a spoiled child throwing a temper tantrum."

"That may be, but—"

"I'm not fucking finished," I snarl. "That all being said, I am more than willing to engage in Ilyasov's ridiculous game to prove to any doubters once and for all that the Bratva is mine and mine alone."

When I'm done speaking, the room is silent for a long time. I look each man in the eye to test his mettle.

To see who needs convincing.

Who needs intimidating.

Who needs eliminating.

Then Eduard nods. "That is all we ask. Bravery and loyalty."

I press my knuckles into the surface of the table. "I've always been loyal to the Bratva."

"And no one else?" he inquires. "Ilyasov may have convinced some of the men that you are more easily manipulated by Aryana—er, Arya—than you ought to be. That she and the baby have pulled your focus and your loyalty from what truly matters."

I wait for a long time before I reply. When I do, I'm vibrating with fury.

At my full height, I tower over the seated men. My eyes burn a hole in each of them. "That is going too fucking far, Eduard—and any of you who agree with him. I'll say this only once: the next man who claims Arya and my son have weakened me will not draw another breath. The Bratva is bigger than all of us. But none of you are bigger than your don. I'm back now, gentlemen. Start acting like it."

A wave of shocked discomfort moves through the room. Even Gennady scratches nervously at the back of his head before giving me an encouraging smile that looks more like a wince.

A few months ago, my word was enough to silence discussion on an issue. My opinion was enough for any man in any room to nod in agreement.

It wasn't because they were afraid—but because they trusted me.

Now, because of Ilyasov, that trust is gone. They doubt me. Only blood can fix that.

Ilyasov's blood.

27

ARYA

Dima might be right. Maybe Ilyasov is still in New York City.

That doesn't mean Lukas is.

To me, it seems most likely that Ilyasov would shove Lukas off on someone else to take care of. He is busy trying to overthrow his brother. I can't imagine he wants to take care of a needy baby while trying to organize Bratva business.

I'm betting he'd leave that to Vera.

As soon as I get to Chicago, I go to Ilyasov's house. Dima said he'd never be stupid enough to go back there, but I hope he's wrong.

When I pull up to the house, though, it's clear by the shuttered windows that Dima was right and no one is home. Still, I get out and walk around the perimeter of the property.

Every single window is closed tight. Blinds drawn, curtains closed, shutters locked. If anyone is inside, they are walking around in absolute darkness.

I pull out my new burner and dial Vera's number. The number rings and rings and rings, but I have a hard time hanging up even when I know she isn't answering.

Where is my son? I want to scream. *What have you done with my baby?*

If I could just talk to her, I could convince her to end all this madness.

But she doesn't.

Onto Plan B.

After stopping at a pizza place to fuel up, I nab a copy of the yellow pages from the restaurant's ancient-looking payphone and begin calling pediatricians.

The phone book is old, so half of the places I call are no longer in business or the number is disconnected. Even the clinics I do get in touch with are unwilling to help me.

"If you aren't calling for an appointment for yourself or your child, I'm afraid I can't help you," one receptionist says. "I am not allowed to give you information about other patients."

"But the patient I'm asking about is my child," I explain. "He has been kidnapped and I'm trying to find him, but—"

"I'd suggest calling the police. I can't help you." It's clear by the woman's voice she thinks I'm deranged. I'm sure I sound like it.

Still, I keep calling.

I sit on a bench along the street for several hours, asking anyone who will pick up the phone if they've seen a heavily pregnant woman with a two-month old—the image can't be an easy one to forget.

No one can tell me anything.

Then I reach the M's in my search, and my finger stops on one of the names in the list—the Malone Family Practice. The advertisement is a square, listing the names of the doctors in the clinic.

And my heart lights up. There's a name missing from this list. A name I know well. Or well enough, at least.

I rip the page out of the phone book and run to the bus stop.

Lauren Malone was my lab partner in our cadaver lab at Cornell. We were on the same pre-med track before I switched my focus to being a veterinarian and she went the pediatric route.

It's been years since we spoke. But it'll be enough—I hope.

It has to be.

~

The Malone Famaily Practice office is a modest space in the center of a long strip mall. But the inside is clean and modern.

The receptionist behind the desk gives me a wide smile as I walk in. "Your name?" she asks, fingers poised over the keyboard.

"Arya George—but I don't have an appointment."

The woman's smile falters. "Oh, I'm sorry, dear. We don't take walk-ins."

"I'm actually not here for an appointment. I just need to speak with Dr. Malone. Dr. Lauren Malone, that is." I smile. "She and I are old friends. I just got back into town."

The receptionist looks to be my age, but the crown of her hair is teased up high, and she's wearing a floral button-down I'd associate with someone double her age. It may just be her work attire, but I get the sense the woman is a strict rule follower.

She gives me an exaggerated pout. "I'm sorry, but if you want to speak with Dr. Malone, you'll have to reach out to her yourself. I'm supposed to make medical appointments. Anything else is outside the scope of my duties."

"I'd love to call her, but I actually lost her phone number. Which is why I came here." I flash a saccharine smile. "If you could just leave her a message, I would appreciate it."

"Ma'am, I'm sorry, but I can't. I don't schedule Dr. Malone's social calendar, therefore I—"

"Social calendar?" A woman with long blonde hair and a white doctor's coat comes out of a back hallway, a stethoscope around her neck. "You can't be talking about me. I haven't had one of those in years." She looks over at me with a blank, friendly expression. "Did I hear you say you were here to see me?"

The receptionist looks smug that Dr. Malone doesn't remember me.

I never expected her to. I just need to talk with her.

"Hi. Yes, I did. I know you may not remember me, but we actually went to school together. We had biology together. My name is—"

"Aryana!" Lauren snaps her fingers. "Of course. I knew there was something familiar about your face. Yes. Come on back to my office."

I thank the receptionist for her help on my way past her desk, but she gives me little more than a flippant wave and an eye roll.

If only she knew why I was really here.

Dr. Malone's office is bright and clean. "You became a veterinarian, right?" she says as we step in. "I knew you left pre-med, but I got so bogged down with coursework I couldn't keep up."

"Same. It's hard to have friends when you're becoming a doctor," I laugh. "Yes, I was a vet."

She frowns. "Was?"

"It's a long story, but I'm not practicing right now. I've had some… personal issues come up."

Lauren purses her lips. "I'm sorry to hear that. Is that why you're here to see me today? I'm a pediatrician primarily, but of course, I'd be happy to recommend you to one of the other doctors here. My dad just retired, but my mom is still practicing. And my younger brother just joined the practice two years ago. It's a family affair, if you didn't know."

"Actually, it's not medical. Well, not for me. It's about my son."

Her brow furrows and she leans forward slightly, hands clasped in front of her. "I see. And what is wrong with him?"

"Nothing—that I know of." I see the confusion cross her face and take a deep breath. "This is coming out in a jumble and I'm going to sound crazy, but bear with me for a second here. Essentially, my son has been... kidnapped."

Her eyes widen in horror. "Have you called the police? I'm not sure how I can—"

"I can't call the police. The man who took him has connections everywhere, including police officers. I have to do this on my own."

She blinks, like she needs a second to digest that. I wonder if I'm about to get thrown out of here. I bet the bitchy receptionist would love to see that.

"Who is he?" she asks finally.

"He's the leader of a mafia here in Chicago."

She gasps and claps a hand over her mouth. "Oh my God. Aryana, I'm so sorry."

"It's Arya now," I correct. "And thank you. I came here because my son is still young. He hasn't been to a doctor yet, and I'm wondering if the man's wife has maybe tried to have him seen by a pediatrician. I've called around, but no one will give me any information."

"It would be a HIPAA violation for them to tell you anything. Even telling me is a violation," she says. "But…"

"But what?" I press hopefully.

She gnaws at her lip. "Well, as doctors, we talk. When the matter is important enough. I may be able to ask around for you."

For the first time in days, my heart soars. "Could you really? I don't want to get you involved in this, but I don't know where else to turn. I'm desperate."

She nods. "I'm sure. I'd prefer if you didn't mention my name to anyone. Ever. But I can help. I can try, at least."

"Thank you." I reach out and grab her hands with both of mine. "The woman he's most likely to be with is heavily pregnant with twins—due any day. And Lukas is only two months old."

"Do you have a picture?"

The question is so normal. What new mother doesn't have a picture of her child? A million pictures, even?

But suddenly, I realize I don't have a single picture of me with Lukas. Anywhere.

My face heats up. "I actually don't. Not on me. No."

"I have a printer," she says helpfully, hitching a thumb over her shoulder. "If you send me one, I can print it out."

My face must be bright red by now. "I don't have any pictures of him. I lost my phone and there's no back-up, and—"

Lauren senses my embarrassment and gives me a kind smile. "It's okay. I understand."

She's lying, but still, I'm grateful.

"He hasn't had any of his vaccinations. He hasn't even had a check-up." I shake my head. "It's been a crazy couple of months. We had to flee the hospital where he was born."

Lauren gasps and claps a hand over her mouth. "That was you?!"

I frown. "Huh?"

"The woman and child who fled from a hospital in New York City under gunfire. No one was able to confirm any details like your name or the baby's name—probably because the mob wiped it all clean—but I saw that story."

"Oh. Yeah, that was me." I let out a long breath and drop my face in my hands. "I don't know how my life has come to this point. I swear, I was a normal person a few months ago."

Lauren lays a hand on my arm and squeezes. "What is normal, right?"

"Normal is wanting to protect your child from the evil in the world," I blurt. "In that regard, I'm the most normal mom there is. It's all I want."

She wrinkles her nose in a smile. "There is good in the world, too, Arya. I'll get the word around. If you leave me your number, I'll call you if I hear back."

Tears well in the backs of my eyes, but I blink them away. "Thank you."

As I walk out, I remember something Ernestine told me the day we met.

Accept kindness. It's the only way we can make it through this world.

Maybe she's right. Maybe there's still some hope for a happy ending.

28

DIMA

Being back in my mansion is strange. I thought I'd be returning here as a conqueror. The world at my feet once more.

Instead... well, it's not quite that.

I wander from room to room, wondering what's missing. Everything is exactly the way I left it, so how can something be out of place?

Then I realize what it is.

Arya should be here.

The thought rises unbidden in my mind, but once it's there, it sticks. She wanted to go to Chicago. After everything I've put her through, I didn't want to stop her. Still, I wish she had stayed. I fucking hate the way we left things.

I reach for my phone on the end table and punch in Arya's new number. She answers right away.

"Did you find him?" She's breathless, excited, and my heart sinks.

"No. I was just calling to see how things were going."

It's a dumb question. She would have called me right away, of course. But maybe she's not the only one hoping for a miracle.

"I have a doctor friend who is willing to ask around and see if anyone has seen Lukas or Vera. But otherwise, nothing." She hesitates. "You may have been right. I'm not sure if Lukas is going to be here."

"We don't know anything yet. We just have to give it time."

"Every second is another second Lukas is without us. I can't… I can't take it anymore, Dima. I'm missing his life. I'm barely his mother anymore. Do you know I realized today I don't have a single picture with Lukas? I never took one."

She's starting to spiral downward. To fall to pieces. "Enough, Arya. You can't take the blame for this. It'll destroy you."

"I guess you're right."

There's another long pause. All I can hear is Arya's breathing on the other end of the line. Quiet and even. Finally, she speaks. "I miss you."

Every part of me aches for her. Heart. Head. Dick. This isn't how things should be. And if I have my way, it won't last much longer.

"I miss you, too. I'm sorry things have been so… I don't even know what to call it. I'm just sorry."

She doesn't tell me it's okay. Because it isn't. But she says the next best thing.

"I'm going to fly back tomorrow. Now that I have someone here looking out for Lukas, I don't think there's any point in me still being here. Whether Ilyasov is here or not, I won't find him on my own. And I don't know what I'd do if I did."

"Good. I want you here with me."

"Dare I say you're worried about me, Dima?" I hear a smile in her voice. It's been so long since I've heard anything but sorrow.

"Me? Never."

There's a low sound deep in her throat. "I wish you could take care of me."

My cock rises to attention. I recognize the tone in her voice. "Then lay back and let me."

Arya giggles. "Right now?"

"Right fucking now, Arya."

I hear her shift around on the other end of the phone and then she pauses, her breathing quick.

"I'll palm your breasts and flick your nipples until they're hard."

"They're already hard," she whispers.

"Then I'll slide my hand across your hips and cup your center. Find that needy clit of yours. Drag my fingertip across it slowly."

She exhales. "I'm so sensitive."

I slide my hand inside my own jeans. I'm already hard and throbbing.

"I'll take it slow, then," I assure her. "I'll stroke you a few more times before my fingers slip inside of your panties to feel how wet you are."

"So wet," she gasps.

I pump my hand once, imagining the precum beading on the tip of my cock is instead Arya's wetness. My breathing hitches.

"I'll drag up to your clit and circle two fingers around your center quickly, until you start to squirm. To beg."

I can hear her breathing growing rougher, little gasps escaping. What I wouldn't give to see her face. I massage myself, thrusting with my hips, sliding myself into my fist agonizingly slowly.

"Are you squirming? Does it feel good?"

"Yes, Dima. So good."

"Then I'll curl my finger inside of you."

"Oh, God," she breathes, exhaling loudly. "Can I put in another one?"

Fuck. My cock twitches at her need. At how badly I wish I was with her. To do this in person.

"Slow," I order. "Don't you dare rush it. Make it last."

She moans. "I'm going to come soon. Do you want me to come?"

"Not yet. Keep going."

I can hear the pace of her thrusting. She gasps each time. I match her pace, sliding my hand up and down my length.

"More," she gasps. "Please, God, let me do more."

"Slide another finger in."

There's a brief pause and then a groan of relief. "I'm so tight."

"Keep it slow."

"I want more," she whimpers, voice soft.

I bite my lower lip. "Put in another finger, *krasavitsa*."

"Oh, God," she groans. "It barely fits. I'm too tight."

"Go slow." Heat is building low in my belly. "Don't rush it."

"I wish it was your hand," she moans. "It feels so good. I wish it was you."

I can't wait. Part of me wants to drag this out, to force her to hold off for as long as possible, to spend as much time in this moment as possible.

But my balls are bursting. Hearing Arya on the verge of pleasure, wishing she was with me—it's enough to push me over the edge by itself.

"Fuck yourself. Come for me now," I order. On this end of the phone, I'm thrusting myself into my own hand and quickly losing control. "Come with me."

"I'm… I'm… I'm coming," she squeaks. "Oh, God, Dima…"

I'm coming, too. A few more jerks, a spasm of the hips, and then I spill myself onto the bed with a primal roar.

We both go quiet for a few minutes.

"My men think you've made me weak," I rasp finally to fill in the silence. "They're wrong. They're dead fucking wrong. I'll see you tomorrow, Arya."

"I'll see you tomorrow," she sighs. "Goodnight."

I pad into the bathroom and clean myself up. I haven't had phone sex since I was a horny teenager hiding in my bedroom. Bursting with desires I didn't know how to tame. That's how Arya makes me feel now. Despite everything else we've been through, that hasn't changed.

She makes me want her more than I've ever wanted anything.

I'm walking back into the bedroom to strip the bedding off the sheets when I hear a noise coming from the doorway.

I spin around…

And almost don't believe what I'm seeing.

"Ilyasov."

My brother is standing in the doorway. He smiles. "I would have come in sooner, but you sounded… busy."

I reach for the gun that's usually on my hip, but it's gone. It's on top of the dresser. I glance at it desperately.

Ilyasov tracks my gaze. "No need to kill me, brother. I didn't see anything. I left when I realized where the conversation was headed. Privacy and all that."

"I could kill you for much more than eavesdropping."

He lifts a shoulder in a half-shrug. "I suppose, but killing me wouldn't bring your son back to you or win you the respect of your men. After all, killing me before you've even completed the first Trial would make it look like you were too afraid to compete."

"I already completed the first Trial several times over. You know that."

He purses his lips. "The points you score before the game starts don't count, Dima. You know that."

My heart sinks, but I do my best not to let it show on my face. "Why are you doing this, Ilyasov? Any of it? Why challenge me and take my son? Why now?"

"Because I want what belongs to me," he says simply. "My birthright."

"That's not what you said when Father died."

"We both said a lot of things when Father died. Only some of them were true."

I stare at him. "I thought after all we've been through—after everything we've done together—we were better than this. Closer than this."

Ilyasov snorts. "Idiot. I'll never understand why Father chose you in the end. You're a fucking fool. Even now, you don't see what's happening right in front of your face."

He smiles at me for a beat and then looks around the room as though he's assessing the place to see if he'd like living here.

Then he turns to go. Before walking through the door, however, he stops and turns back.

"By the way, I killed the Irish don."

"Bullshit."

He raises an eyebrow. "I thought you might say that. I left the head on your kitchen table for proof." He chuckles low, then starts to whistle as he struts away. "You better catch up, Dima!" Ilyasov calls over his shoulder. "Clock's ticking."

29

ARYA

There's a car waiting for me at the airport when I arrive. The driver doesn't say a word to me as he helps me into the backseat and drives through the city streets. After so many betrayals, I can't help but be nervous about where I'm being taken. I worry it's a trap or a trick. Something Ilyasov set up to capture me.

But then the car pulls through a wrought iron gate and stops in front of a two-story white house with pillars along the front, jutting balconies, and massive windows.

Dima is standing in front.

He opens my door and pulls me in for a kiss as soon as I'm standing. His hand curls around my lower back, pulling me against him, and his other hand rakes through my hair.

"I'm glad you're back," he murmurs against my lips.

"I sense that," I tease, poking a finger into his rock-hard abs. "Anything interesting happen while I was away?"

Immediately, the smile slips from his face.

My stomach twists. "What? What is it?"

He tips his head towards the house. "Come inside. We'll talk."

The house is huge. And somehow, even more grand inside than it looked outside. The ceilings are high with matching windows that let in long shafts of daylight. Dark wood floors and rich, jewel-toned walls make me feel like I'm in a palace. Technically, I might be.

"Is this *your* house?"

"My family's. Passed down to me. I redesigned it a few years ago."

The place is a dream. Antique furniture and portraits give the mansion a sense of history, but modern light fixtures and touches keep it present.

It's nothing like I imagined.

"Is it safe to be here?"

Again, I notice Dima's body tense. Something happened that he isn't telling me.

He sets my bag aside in one of the many rooms and then leads me further down the hall to an office.

"This is an office conversation?" I ask.

He sits down behind a wide, wooden desk. "If we went into the bedroom, I was afraid I'd get… distracted."

What we did on the phone last night flashes in my mind. I can feel the memory burning in my cheeks. I push the thought away and sit down opposite him, hands folded in my lap.

"What's going on, Dima? You're frightening me."

"I'm glad you're back," he murmurs again. "You were gone forever."

"It was only a couple days."

"Well, it felt like forever."

I laugh nervously. "For a change, I agree with you. But going was useful. We have someone in Chicago looking out for Lukas, which makes me feel better. Still, it feels good to be together again. Safer."

His smile tenses around the edges. I've had enough of the secrets. "Okay, come on, Dima. What in the hell is going on? What happened?"

If it had something to do with Lukas, he would have told me. I know that. Still, the gears of my imagination begin to turn.

"It's not Lukas," he says as though reading my mind. "I still don't know where he is and we haven't heard anything."

"Okay, so what is it?"

He sighs. "Ilyasov was here last night."

If it was possible for my eyes to shoot out of my head the way they do in cartoons, they would have. I'm stunned. I don't even know what to say.

"He walked in like he owned the place. I had security change all of the locks and alarm systems this morning." He leans back in his chair and shakes his head. "He was listening in on our phone call."

"Fucking pervert," I seethe. "What did he want? What did he say?"

Dima shrugs. "He wanted to rattle me. He wanted to show me that he can get in this house, that he knows where I am, that he is already one Trial ahead of me."

I frown. "He already finished Trial Two?"

"No. He claims the people I've already killed don't count because the Romanoff Trials hadn't been initiated yet. I have to kill another don."

My shoulders sag forward under the weight of all of this shit. "Fuck."

"Yeah."

There's a frustrated pause between us.

And then Dima's fist slams down on the table. The lamp on the corner rattles off and explodes on the ground. Dima doesn't even seem to notice the damage. He shoves himself up out of his chair and paces across the room.

"I know this is all him fucking showboating. If Ilyasov was truly confident he'd win, he wouldn't bother trying to get in my head. We both grew up in this house. He and I learned all of the secret passageways in and out. All of the windows that can be shimmied loose, all of the trellises that can be scaled. My parents never thought one of our own would betray us this way, so how am I supposed to keep him out?"

"Let him in," I say, throwing up my hands. "Let him walk through the front door—and when he gets here, put a bullet between his eyes. Done."

Dima shakes his head. "The men who remained loyal to me are shaky at best. They need to see me as a genuine leader. They need to know I'm strong enough to defend my family name and them. I can't just kill Ilyasov. I have to destroy him."

He makes a sickening amount of sense. But God, I wish he didn't.

"Plus, we still don't know where Lukas is. If I kill him, there's no reason for anyone to ever give him back to us."

"And you think if you win, he'll just hand him over?" I ask.

"I hope it doesn't come to that," he says. "But if I reclaim my role as don, I'll have enough power to find Lukas myself or strong-arm Ilyasov into returning him. If we can't find Lukas ourselves, that's our best chance."

Again, I know he's right, but I wish he wasn't. I wish there was an easier, more simple answer.

Too much hangs in the balance.

"Look." Dima leans forward across the desk, resting on his elbows, blue gray eyes focused on mine. "I know I've fucked up with you too many times. But when it comes to this situation, I know I'm making the right call. I'm sure of it. Going through the Trials is the only way to ensure Ilyasov is out of the picture forever. My men will trust me soon enough. I just need you to trust me, too."

Dima's face is flat, but I can see the turbulent emotions beneath it.

I nod shakily. "I trust you, Dima. Of course I do. Even when I haven't, I have. I know that doesn't make sense, but it's the only way I know how to put it."

Obvious relief crosses his face. "Thank you."

"And I've fucked up, too," I admit. "I shouldn't have trusted Brigitte. When we first parted ways in Chicago, I'd only known you a few days, but I felt in my gut that I wanted to stay with you. I didn't want to leave. And I ignored that feeling. That was my fault."

"She was your best friend. You couldn't have known."

I reach across the desk and lay my hand over his. "And he was your brother. You couldn't have known."

He gives me a tight, sad smile. "We both fucked up. We lost our son twice to people who we thought loved us. What are the odds?"

The pang of Lukas's absence hurts. It never seems to lessen or soften with time. Every time I think about it, my breath is stolen away by the pain.

"Pretty good, apparently." He drops back down into his chair and runs a hand down his face. He hasn't shaved in a few days. His stubble is dark and thicker than usual. I can't say I don't mind the rugged caveman look.

"What's next?"

"Killing a don," he growls. "But hell if I know how I'm going to do that. After all the recent assassinations, everyone is laying low. They don't know what's going on, but they know it's bad. Everyone is underground right now."

Suddenly, I realize I might not be so useless after all. "So you need to know where a boss might spend his down time?"

Dima frowns. "Explain."

"Okay, so when I was talking to—" Arnie Fleishman's name almost rolls off my tongue, but I stop myself before it can. I made a promise to him that I wouldn't mention his involvement to anyone. I intend to keep my word. "Well, I was talking to someone who has good information. It seemed useless at the time, but he mentioned that the leader of the Aryan Brotherhood had a mistress."

"That's not as helpful as you think it is," Dima says, sagging down in his chair. "I'd love to take out Richard Solomon, but I'd need an address."

"And I have one. Sort of."

"Go on."

"Well, what my… contact said? It jogged my memory. Something I'd forgotten about altogether. When I was dating Jorik, he and Richard Solomon were acquaintances. They shared drugs on the cheap, and one time, Jorik called Richard about a pickup. We ended up outside of the Kingsroot Apartments."

"I know where those are," Dima says.

"Jorik asked Richard when he moved, and he said he hadn't. It was his girl's place, and he made a crack about how it was his, though, since he paid for it. Can't promise they're still there, of course—it's been years. But you never know…"

Dima twists his lips to the side, thinking.

"I know it's not the most to go on, but—"

"No, it's not," he says. "But it's a place to start. Better than I had before."

"Okay," I mutter.

He's halfway to storming out of the room—to call Gennady or his lieutenants or something, I'm sure—when he pauses and whirls back around to face me.

"Thank you, Arya," he says awkwardly.

I can't help laughing. "You're not very good at that," I tease.

"At what?"

"Being grateful."

He pauses for a moment. Then, without changing his expression, he takes one huge step to close the distance between us. He bends down, palms the back of my head in one huge hand, and presses me with a fierce kiss.

His tongue parts my lips. Greedy. Hot. Aggressive.

And just when I reach up to touch his hair, he pulls away.

"I'm better with my hands than my words," he murmurs.

I laugh again, although I'm suddenly several degrees hotter and my thighs are tingling. "I'll say so."

"But I mean it. Thank you."

"You're welcome," I whisper.

Then he's gone, whisking out of the room and leaving me with his touch on my skin and words I've never heard from him before surging through my heart.

Another man will die soon. I'll be a part of it, just like I was a part of Jorik's death, and Zotov's, and Ennio's, and Giorgio's.

And my son is still gone. Snatched away yet again by people who want to hurt me.

All that shit is horrible and I'll spend the rest of my life thinking about it.

But right here? Right now?

Things feel like they're almost okay.

30

DIMA

It takes Gennady half an hour to confirm Richard Solomon's mistress still lives in the Kingsroot Apartments.

"Do you have the unit number?" I ask.

He nods. "Eduard had a few guys rough up the building's manager. He gave it up real quick. No one saw Richard there, though. No idea when he'll be by."

"I'm not in the mood for a long stakeout. The sooner we get this over with, the sooner I get my Bratva back."

Gennady claps me on the back. "Then I'll leave you to it. Good luck."

Arya offered to come with me, too—to keep me company—but I don't want her anywhere near this scene. If anything goes wrong, I don't want to have to worry about her being caught in the crosshairs.

This job is for me and me alone.

For the first time in almost an hour, I see movement further up the street. A black car parks at the end of the street and a figure climbs out. I'm too far away to tell if it's a man or a woman, but the person walks with their head down and a hood up.

After sitting for so long, it seems worth checking out. But I don't want to spook whoever it is, so I wait until they pass by where I'm parked on the opposite side of the street before I climb out and move towards the building.

The person stops and buzzes in. I try to run after him and catch the door before it locks, but I miss.

"Shit."

There are fifty buttons that correspond with all of the apartments. I press every single one except for number 34. Someone else in this damned building has to be expecting a guest.

A few people call back. "Hello? Who is it?"

But eventually, someone buzzes me in without even checking to see who it is. I open the door and step into the small entryway.

A wall of small mailboxes line the left wall and a set of stairs beckons at the far side of the room. I can hear someone's footsteps climbing them. I begin to go after them.

I take the stairs two at a time, but slowly and silently. I don't want to draw any attention to myself or alert the man to the fact that someone is on his ass.

We reach the fourth floor. A sign notes that this is where Units 31 through 40 await.

The man above me opens the door from the stairwell and slips out. That's a good sign.

"Go to 34, *mudak*," I growl under my breath. That's the number Gennady gave me. "Go knock on that goddamn door."

I step out onto the fourth floor just in time to see the man whisk around the corner. I race down and then peer around carefully.

He's stopped outside of Unit 34.

He pulls down his hood to reveal a bald head—and a swastika tattooed along his scalp. It's him alright, no doubts about it.

"Got you, motherfucker," I whisper.

The door opens a little, though not far enough for me to see who is on the other side. He steps inside.

I pull out the master key my men snatched off the building manager. Delicately, I slide it into the lock. Once it's in, I pause to gather my composure. To remember why I'm here.

You're doing this for you, croons a selfish voice in my mind.

I shake my head. That's wrong. Maybe the old Dima would've been doing this for himself. But I'm not the same man I once was.

I'm doing this for my family now. For Arya. For Lukas.

I pull up my hood and a bandana to cover the lower half of my face, take a deep breath, and twist the key in the lock. At the same time, I shove my shoulder into the door. It flies open with a bang and I surge in gun-first.

I don't have to look hard. Richard Solomon is fucking his mistress on the kitchen counter.

He's only been inside the apartment for ninety seconds at most, but the woman is already sitting on the counter with her legs wrapped around his waist. Her shirt is off, fake tits exposed, and Richard has a double handful of ass.

"Who the fuck are you?" he asks, struggling to make himself decent.

It's a dumb question. And it doesn't matter, because he won't be alive long enough to hear the answer.

The woman hurries to cover herself. I don't give a shit what she looks like, though. I only care if Richard is breathing.

Up close and in good lighting, I recognize Richard from the photograph Gennady found online. It was a previous mugshot, before he had the under-eye tattoos I see now—an A and a B in old-school Latin script under each eye.

"A" for Aryan.

"B" for Brotherhood.

Piece of shit would deserve his death even if the Trials weren't a thing.

I raise my gun and take the killing shot. I almost feel bad how easy it is to kill the bastard.

He falls flat to the floor. His girlfriend screams, but I don't have time for her. I bend down and rifle through Richard's pocket until I find his wallet. His ID is tucked beneath a clear flap at the front. I remove it, dip the corner in the spreading pool of his blood, and then bow to his mistress.

"Have a nice evening, ma'am."

In response, she screams again. I don't stick around to see if anyone rushes out of their apartment to aid her. I got what I needed.

One down.

Now, it's time for Trial number two.

31

ARYA

It's hard to relax while Dima is gone.

Gennady assures me Dima has it under control. "He'll be back soon. This is an easy hit. Don't worry."

But I do worry. Of course, I do. And when my phone rings, I lunge for it across the bed, answering the call before I even check who is calling.

"Dima?" I ask, breathless.

"Lauren, actually," a female voice says. "Dr. Malone. Is this Arya?"

My heart can't seem to decide whether it should sink or swell with hope. "Lauren. Hi. Sorry. I was expecting another call."

She chuckles. "That's okay. I'll be brief. I just wanted to call and let you know that a local pediatrician called me today with some possible information about your son."

"Have they found him?" I jump off the bed and immediately begin pacing across the carpet in my bare feet.

I just got back from Chicago, but I'll drive there overnight if someone has found Lukas. Hell, I'll run there, shoes or no shoes.

The ache to know where Lukas is, to hold him and squeeze him close, to keep him warm, is almost overwhelming. It feels like I'm walking around without one of my limbs.

"I'm not sure," she says. "I called around to all of the doctors I have a good working relationship with. No one had seen or heard anything suspicious. But then tonight, a doctor my father has known for years called me. He works at a free children's clinic twice a week, and today, he was at the clinic when a couple came in with a small baby."

"What did he say? Who were they with? Was it Lukas? Did—"

"He didn't mention much about the baby, but he actually knows the couple. They've been to see one of his colleagues before. A fertility specialist. The guy said the woman wasn't pregnant during that visit, and then bang, suddenly he sees her with a two-month-old in her arms. The math doesn't check out."

I'm trying not to get too hopeful. Trying not to be too excited. I've experienced enough disappointment to know the dangers of that. But it's hard. After no news for far too long… this is *something*. Finally.

I'm not done with the questions, though. "Did they give names?" I ask. "Did she have long blonde hair? Was he a—"

She cuts me off. "No names, but he told me the couple are as plain as a couple can be. He's a tall, thin man with glasses and a bald spot, and she is mousy—brown hair, petite little thing. The way he described them, they didn't sound anything like the couple you told me about."

That doesn't mean anything, I tell myself. I know Ilyasov is in New York City, so maybe he put Lukas in someone else's care. Maybe someone else in his Bratva is watching over him.

But it could also be a false lead that will take me to a dead end and a broken heart.

Breathe, Arya. You can't fall to pieces just yet.

"Did the doctor ask them any questions?"

"He was nervous to tell me too much, but he did talk to them a little bit. The baby hadn't been seen by a doctor yet, and when he asked why, they didn't want to give him a clear answer."

"He didn't ask where they got the baby?"

"It's not a very common question on the intake forms, I'm afraid," Lauren said. "He couldn't even mention that he had seen them at the fertility doctor's office without potentially violating their privacy. The only thing he could tell me is that the baby had darker hair than either of the parents. And they were acting weird."

"That's all?" I groan and then clear my throat. "I mean, thank you for calling. You've been so helpful and I really appreciate you—"

"Your kid is missing. I get it," she says. "Well, I can imagine, at least. I did manage to get one more piece of information out of him that could help you out. But you have to swear you will never tell where you got—"

"Cross my heart and hope to die."

Lauren sighs. "He memorized the address they gave. He was hesitant to even give it to me, and I repeat, you have to swear you will never tell a soul. I could be sued for this. They'd take my license away."

"I swear on my grave and my mother's grave. On my son's life. I swear on everything I will never tell a soul."

There is a brief hesitation, and then she asks whether I have a pen and paper. Lauren reads the address out, and I write it down.

"Thank you so much, Lauren." I clutch the address against my chest. "There are no words for how grateful I am for your help. Thank you, thank you, thank you."

"Of course. I hope you find your son."

As soon as I hang up the phone, I rush down the hall to the guest room where Gennady is staying. I knock on his door and then push my way without waiting for him to answer it.

"You're supposed to knock and then wait," he mumbles. "I could've been indecent."

"Well, sounds like we both dodged a bullet. I need you to look up an address for me."

"So much for pleasantries. I slept okay, thanks for asking. Where'd you learn your manners—from Dima?"

"Focus. An address, Gennady."

He sighs. "Right now?"

"It's not even eleven PM," I argue. "Plus, Dima left you here to help me."

"Yeah, in case anyone broke in and tried to hurt you. Not with chores."

"It's not a chore. It's about Lukas."

Gennady's eyes narrow. Suddenly, he's wide awake. "What do you mean? What did you find out?"

Briefly, I fill him in on what I did while I was in Chicago and the doctor I talked to. I tell him about the call I just had with Lauren and then hand him the piece of paper with the address on it. "She gave me this address, but it's all the information I have. For all I know, it's a fake or it's owned by Ilyasov or... shoot, I don't know. Can you just look into it?"

He plucks the paper out of my hand and moves quickly out of the room. I follow him, walking down the hallway, across the entryway, and into a security room lined with dozens of computer screens. Gennady sits down, pulls up a screen, and begins typing.

I've always laughed at the scenes in movies when people type insanely fast on keyboards and pull up top secret information in a second. But that's what it feels like watching Gennady. He barely even pauses to think about what he's going to do—he just does it, moving so quickly I could swear he has an extra few arms.

Within two minutes, he has all the information I could want.

"Nick and Jody Watkins," he reads out, pointing at a screen with two photographs on it. "They were married seven years ago. No criminal histories. They live at the address you gave me. Bought the house last year. Could've gotten a better rate on the mortgage, but hey…"

I lean down and study the pictures. They look like passport photos.

Nick Watkins has small glasses and a receding hairline that dips back just above each of his temples. Jody Watkins is round-faced with light brown hair and pink cheeks. Both exactly as the doctor described them.

"That's them," I say, feeling suddenly weak-kneed. "Those are the people who have my son."

"They aren't listed as parents on any public birth records." Gennady scrolls down the page, studying each line. "It doesn't show they have any children at all. But if you ask me, they don't look like the type who would kidnap a child."

I wish I could disagree, but Gennady is right. Just like the doctor said, these people are unassuming. The last two people you'd suspect of something like this.

What the fuck does that mean?

"They had been going to a fertility doctor to try and have a family. That's what the doctor said, anyway."

"It worries me. Something's not adding up here."

I shrug. "I don't know anything else, but I sure as hell intend to find out. How soon can I get back to Chicago?"

"What do I look like, a travel agent?" Gennady scoffs. "I had to book your last flight and arrange the car to pick you up. I'm tired of this assistant kind of shit. I'm supposed to be a lieutenant. A spy."

"Well, use your skills to spy a good deal on a flight," I retort.

Gennady sighs and mutters under his breath as he walks away. "Not even married yet and already acting like a queen. I better get a fat bonus this year."

A queen. The idea is… not entirely unappealing.

And not just any queen, but Dima Romanoff's queen. The queen of the most powerful Bratva in New York City.

Almost as if my body could register his nearness, not a second after I think of him, the front door opens.

Dima calls my name. "Arya, where are you?"

The tension that had been in my shoulders for the last few hours dissipates. I run out of the room and towards the sound of his voice.

Towards my king.

32

DIMA

It's a short flight—just a couple of hours—and Gennady didn't spring for first class, that bastard. Arya's knee is bouncing like a jackrabbit and it's vibrating both of our seats.

I lay a hand on her thigh. "Everything will be okay."

She looks over. "I know."

"Are you nervous?"

She shakes her head. "Not at all. Why?"

I tap the magazine in her hands. "Your magazine is upside down and you've been on the same page for twenty minutes."

Her cheeks flush as she shoves the Sky Mall in the back of the seat in front of her. "Fine. Yes. I just don't want to be disappointed."

I squeeze her knee and then smooth my hand up her thigh. "No matter what happens today, we will find Lukas. One way or the other. I promise."

She lets out a shaky breath and nods, but it's not convincing.

I lean across the arm rest and press my lips to her ear. "Do I need to help you relax?"

She shivers but grins. "How do you plan on doing that?"

My hand moves higher on her thigh, inching towards the warmth between her legs. "I have a few ideas."

Arya's eyes widen. She swats my hand away and looks across the narrow aisle to see if anyone saw. The elderly couple seated next to us are both asleep, mouths wide open. The man looks seconds away from losing his dentures.

"I don't think anyone would notice if I just…" I drag my finger up and run it across the seam in the center of her leggings.

Arya lets out a tiny squeak and sits up, squeezing her legs together. "Dima, no. We will never find Lukas if we're in jail."

I tip my head back towards the bathroom at the back of the plane. "Let's go get some privacy then."

"Flight attendants pay attention to that kind of stuff. And it's a daytime flight. Everyone except the old people are awake."

"It sounds like you've thought about this a bit."

Again, her face flushes. She bites her lower lip. "It might've crossed my mind once or twice."

"Then let's—"

"Dima!" Arya widens her eyes and wags a finger. "No, sir. Keep it in your pants."

I sigh and look out the window, pretending to be disappointed. But my hand stays on her knee. A minute ticks past.

Then I slide it up her thigh again.

To the crease in her hip.

Another minute.

Then more motion. This time, up to the warmth between her legs.

I hear a soft, husky breath escape from her lips. She doesn't move. Doesn't say a word. Not even as I find the waistband of her leggings and sneak my hand inside.

I hiss when I realize she's not wearing any panties. I look at her—but she's looking straight ahead. As if this is fine as long as we don't make eye contact.

I chuckle. Then I slide one finger along her slit.

She's absolutely dripping wet. My finger is soaked immediately. As I watch, her lips part, then clamp back together again.

"You're already on the edge, aren't you, *krasavitsa*?" I mutter to Arya, who still refuses to look back at me. I lean closer and brush my lips against the rim of her earlobe. "You're doing everything you can not to come like my beautiful little whore in front of everyone on this damn plane."

She's squirming imperceptibly. Damn near vibrating. Her hands are clamped tight on the armrests.

Between her thighs, I find her clit and rub slow circles, again and again and again. Each one brings her closer and closer to shattering completely.

I laugh again, low and dangerous. "They don't know what's happening to you. They don't know I'm ruining you one touch at a time. This is our little secret, Arya."

"Dima..." she chokes out. Her hand flies from the armrest and clamps onto my forearm, clinging to me for dear life.

"Say stop and I'll stop. Just one little word. You can do that, can't you?" I tease. "All you have to do to make this end..."

She's vibrating even faster now. I swear the seat is shaking. My cock is an iron rod in my pants.

But this isn't about me. This is about bringing this little hellcat to the peak—and then shoving her right off it into the fucking abyss below.

"But you aren't going to do that. No, no, no. Because you are my little whore. You are my *krasavitsa*. So when I tell you to come, you come. Are you ready?"

I'm stroking faster and faster now. One finger plunging in and out of her relentlessly. The other circling her clit. Her fingers are digging into my arm.

"Dima…" she whimpers again. "I'm going to…"

"Not until I tell you to," I hiss. "Tell me you're ready. Beg for it."

"Please, God," she says at once in the tiniest whisper. "Please let me come."

I lean closer. Drag my lips down from her ear to the base of her throat and nip lightly. She's bucking her hips against my palm, needy and desperate.

Then I raise my mouth to her ear again. I'm driving hard into her now with three fingers and she's so soaked that I slide in and out effortlessly. She's clenching over and over and I know that she's right there, so fucking close to coming all over my hand.

Which makes it all the more delicious when I make my next move.

I press my lips to her ear one more time and whisper, "No."

Then I draw my hand out and don't say a word to her for the rest of the flight.

A rental car is waiting when we get to the airport. We don't have any luggage, so we climb inside, enter in the address, and start driving.

Arya is quiet, but I don't try to distract her now. She needs time to think. To prepare for whatever we may find.

The lead is flimsy, at best. A strange couple with a surprise two-month-old? It isn't exactly a smoking gun. But it's the best we've got.

The GPS tells us we're within a few minutes of our destination. Arya sits forward in her seat. She looks out the window, studying every face that we pass. I can feel nervous tension rolling off of her.

"Listen to me, Arya."

"I'm not in the mood for a lecture, Dima." She's a little pissed at me after my stunt on the plane. The nerves aren't helping, either.

"All the more reason to listen," I insist. "We are here to scope out what's going on, okay? We won't be using any unnecessary violence. Nothing that could hurt Lukas."

Arya nods. Her shoulders relax.

"We will watch the house for a bit, see what we can see. If there's an opportunity to go inside and snoop around, we'll take it. And if the baby is Lukas…"

Honestly, I hadn't truly considered the possibility until now. It's… a lot.

"If it's Lukas…?" Arya presses.

I park the car in a spot across from a tall, narrow home just across the street and look at Arya. "If it's Lukas, then we'll take him home. By any means necessary."

Her eyes go glassy for a moment, but she blinks back the emotion. "Okay. It's a plan."

And we wait.

I'm planning to watch the house for at least an hour before I make any alternative plans. Maybe if there's no movement in that time frame, we will knock on the door or try to see if anyone is inside.

We only have to wait fifteen minutes.

Arya gasps and points towards the house. "The door opened! They're coming out."

The woman Arya showed me in the photo last night—short and stout with brown hair—comes out of the house with a small child cradled against her chest. The balding man behind her is carrying a stroller.

Both adults have big, wide smiles. They laugh when the husband struggles setting up the stroller, and the woman lowers the baby inside—just slowly enough that we get a good, long look at the baby.

Arya's voice breaks when she speaks. "That's Lukas. That's my boy."

I feel the same tug in my chest. One glimpse was all it took for me to recognize my *malyshka*.

It's a struggle not to jump out of the car, gun down the two people who have my son, and grab him.

"There are too many neighbors," Arya says, reading my mind. "We can't take him right now."

I nod in agreement.

"So what do we do?" she asks.

The couple starts pushing the stroller down the sidewalk and around the corner, happy and clueless as can be. As soon as they're out of sight, I turn off the engine.

"Let's get inside before they come back."

Casually, Arya and I walk across the street and up the steps to the house. To my surprise, the door is open.

"They didn't even lock it behind them." I shake my head, dumbfounded.

"Do you think they're working for Ilyasov?" Arya asks.

I usher Arya inside. "Let's find out."

The house is clean and tidy. There's a baby blue rug in the entryway, pale yellow walls, and purple pillows on the floral-printed couch.

"It looks like my grandmother's house. Do you think they really live here?"

"Do you think any rental company would be out of touch enough to decorate their house like this?" I ask, lifting up the edge of a white lace doily.

Every room is more of the same. Kitschy signs in the dining room with the words *"Live, Laugh, Eat!"* and *"Home is where the cat is"* hang on the walls.

Also on the walls? Family photographs. All of them are conveniently baby-less. There aren't even any photos of the woman pregnant.

It's all the proof I need. If I wasn't entirely sure that I recognized Lukas out front, I'm positive now. Whoever these motherfuckers are, they stole my son.

Arya heads upstairs to poke around while I stay on the first floor and look for an office.

I find a craft room spilling with baskets of yarn and a media space with a television and a leather loveseat with a "Man Cave" sign above the door. But no office.

The most I can find is a metal document box in a hallway closet, but it doesn't even have a lock on it. I slide the latch over and instantly, I'm met with the couple's financial records, medical history, and Social Security numbers.

How could Ilyasov work with someone this incompetent? These people don't know the first thing about security.

Still, even after rifling through their private papers, I can't find anything that connects them to Ilyasov. No strange payments from shell companies or contracts. Nothing at all beyond the ordinary.

They seem… normal.

I run my hands along the closet floor searching for a false bottom, but it's just an ordinary closet. It doesn't make sense. None of this does.

"Did you find anything?" I call up the stairs.

Arya comes out of a door with a stuffed animal held to her chest. Her face is red and angry, her green eyes fierce.

"I found a nursery. They have the name 'Matt' stitched on a teddy bear in the crib. Matt? Fucking *Matt?*" She hurls the bear down the stairs. "These fucking people are monsters. They took someone else's child without a second thought, and now they rename him and act like he's theirs. I could kill them. I could—"

I take the stairs two at a time and grab Arya by the shoulders gently, pulling her against my chest. "We have to be smart about this. Any slip-up could be an advantage to my brother. We have to be careful."

"Fuck being careful," she sobs, shaking her head. "This guy is as bad as Ilyasov—maybe even worse. Ilyasov kidnapped our son, but Nick Watkins decided to take him in and lie to him his entire life about where he came from. It's sick."

"I haven't found anything yet that shows they are working with Ilyasov. I'm looking, but—"

"Look around!" Arya says, throwing her arms wide, gesturing to the house. "Here's the proof. They have our son, Dima."

"We can't confront them without all of the facts. I should go check and see if they are on their way back. We don't want to be caught in here if—"

Just then, the handle on the front door rattles.

A second later, the door opens. Nick and Jody Watkins walk into their home, holding our son.

I clamp a hand over Arya's mouth and press her against the shadows along the hallway wall.

It looks like that confrontation is going to happen sooner than I planned.

33

ARYA

Shit. They're home.

Lukas is home.

I strain forward to try and see down the stairs, but Dima presses me against the wall harder and shakes his head.

"I can't believe it's so beautiful today!" Jody is saying. "I'm glad we got out and enjoyed the weather while we could. Huh, Matt? Wasn't that fun?" she asks in a motherly sing-song voice.

I want to rip her vocal chords out.

"He loves the fresh air," Nick says. "I thought he'd fall asleep, but he was alert and looking around the whole time."

"It's because he's so smart. Aren't you, Matty? So smart," Jody croons. "Let's go get changed for dinner."

Dima shimmies us down the hallway wall and pushes me through the nursery door.

I hear footsteps on the stairs. I am going to be in the same room as my son in a matter of seconds. My heart is pounding against my rib cage and I'm shaking. But I try to stand firm.

Dima positions himself between me and the door. When Jody walks in, she doesn't even see us at first. She heads straight for the changing station.

Once she sets Lukas down, Dima speaks. "Why do you have our son?"

Jody screams. I hear something clatter to the floor downstairs. A few seconds later, Nick is in the room, too.

"Jody, what is it—" He looks over, and his face goes white. Bedsheet white. I've never seen anything quite like it.

"Wh-what d-do you want?" he stammers, backing up towards his wife and Lukas. He stretches an arm out in front of them protectively. "We don't have much money, but we'll give you everything we have. Just don't hurt us."

Jody picks up Lukas from the changing table and cradles him against her, turning her body to shield him. "Please. We have a baby."

"My baby!" I don't mean to scream, but it comes out that way.

Lukas starts to fuss. My heart aches. Is he crying because he recognizes my voice or because I've scared him? Does he even know me well enough to recognize my voice?

I lower my voice and step around Dima. "Give me my baby back and we won't hurt you."

Nick steps in front of his wife. "Now, listen, I don't know what you are playing at, but—"

"I'm not sure what you think you're playing at!" I cry. "You can't kidnap other people's babies and expect to get away with it."

"Kidnap? We did no such thing."

"Well, your wife sure as hell didn't give birth to him. Considering he came out of my body, I can attest to that."

The couple look at each other, speaking in a silent language I don't understand.

Dima pulls his gun out of his holster and keeps it pointed at the floor. "I don't want to hurt anyone. Don't make me."

He's being calmer than he would be normally. With Lukas in the room, neither of us want this to escalate. Jody and Nick don't seem to want that, either.

They seem to be…protecting Lukas. Trying to shield him from us. They certainly don't look like they ever expected this to happen.

"We just want you out of our house. Whatever it takes to make that happen. Just please leave," Nick says. "Take whatever you want and leave. We'll give you anything."

"I want my son!"

"Except him," Jody says, laying her hand over Lukas's head. He's crying louder now.

"We aren't leaving here without our son," Dima intones. "Hand him over. Now."

Nick holds up his hands in surrender. "Listen, I think there's a misunderstanding here. My wife didn't give birth to Matt, but—"

"Lukas," I correct, eyes narrowed. "His name is Lukas."

"My wife didn't give birth to him," Nick says, "but he is ours. We adopted him."

Dima snorts. "From where? The black market. You can't buy a baby."

"We didn't buy him! We found him."

That gives me pause. Dima, too, apparently. He pulls back his chin slightly, brows furrowed. "You *found* him?"

"At our church," Jody adds. "He was abandoned. Left there by someone. Our church is a safe haven for unwanted children."

My jaw clenches. "He isn't unwanted. I wanted him. I *want* him."

Jody looks to her husband. "Nick, do something!"

"Don't talk to him!" I snap. "Talk to me. I'm his mother. You need to explain yourself."

I feel unhinged and I'm sure I look it, too, but my son is mere feet away from me and I can't touch him and it's tearing me apart.

"This baby was a gift from God," Jody says, tears brimming in her eyes. "We've been trying to start a family for years and we were running out of options. We had just broached the topic of adoption and then we got the call from our pastor that a baby had been left on the doorstep. A man walked up to the church, dropped off the car seat, and walked away."

"That's *my* baby he dropped off."

Nick runs a hand through his thinning hair. "Have you called the police? How did you even find us?"

"The police can't help us. We had to track him down ourselves."

Jody lays a protective hand over Lukas's head. "I can't hand my son over to you just because you say so. We don't know anything about you. You broke into our house. You seem like criminals."

She isn't too far off, though I doubt that would earn us any points.

"We aren't here to ask," Dima growls. He lifts his hand just high enough to remind them of the gun he's holding.

Jody and Nick pull closer together. For the first time, Lukas turns to look at me. His neck is still wobbly, and Jody has to hold him steady with her hand. But my baby boy is looking at me and when he does, my heart cracks and melts and dribbles down my rib cage.

All of the emotions I've been holding onto funnel into the only emotion that truly matters: a mother's love.

"Hi, baby boy," I coo, wagging my fingers at him. "I love you."

Jody turns him away from me, but that little look from Lukas is enough to ground me.

"Listen, I can tell you whatever you want to know," I say, voice soft. "I can tell you about the birthmark he has on his thigh that's shaped like a four-pointed star. I can tell you that he reaches for every mirror he sees. When he smiles, the right side of his mouth goes up first and then the left."

"None of that means anything," Nick snaps.

Dima steps forward—but before he can, Jody lays a hand on Nick's arm. She shakes her head.

"You're not listening to this, are you? It's crazy!" Nick isn't a big man, but the angrier he gets, the more space he seems to consume.

"He had a blanket that I haven't seen since he was taken. A blue one with a yellow duck stitched in the corner. Did he have that when you found him?"

Jody gasps and then looks at her husband. "She knows things about him, Nick. How would she know that?"

"Anyone could have told her! Maybe whoever dropped him off told her! Maybe it's a plan."

"A plan for what?" she asks. "Why would someone go to these lengths to abandon a baby and then steal him back? It doesn't make sense."

Her logic seems to hit Nick hard. His shoulders sag, but his face is still contorted in anger. "He's our son. Ours. We took him in and he's ours. If we call the police, they'd side with us over these... these... these *home invaders*. He was abandoned."

"He was kidnapped," Dima corrects. "You only had him because someone took him from us. I'm asking politely—one more time before I change my tone—for you to hand him back to his mother."

Jody's lips purse and after a quick squeeze of her husband's hand, she steps towards where Dima and I stand.

"Jo…" Nick sighs mournfully.

But Jody keeps coming. I step forward, meeting her in the middle of the room.

Gingerly, I reach out and brush Lukas's hair. He turns to me at once. I wiggle my nose and make a little face at him—one he loves—and he giggles. He reaches for me. He touches my cheek.

At the brush of contact, the tears that have been welling in my eyes finally break through the floodgates and pour down. I swipe them away, but they are falling too fast to stop.

He remembers me. This isn't too broken to be fixed.

This can be saved. All of us can.

Jody releases him to me, shifting his weight onto my hip, and I clutch him to my body like my life depends on it. I kiss his round cheek and his nose and his hair. I bury my face against his little body and feel his heart beat.

Dima moves next to me, his gun now holstered, and holds us both.

"He has your nose," Jody whispers, her voice breaking. She nods to Dima. "And your… well, not quite a smile."

My chest is bursting with gratitude and relief, but I hurt for the Watkins. They didn't deserve this pain.

I called them monsters, but they are angels. Especially now that they've returned Lukas to me.

The next few minutes are a blur. I apologize several times before we leave for breaking into their house. Jody is more forgiving than any normal person would be.

She sends us home with a few of the things they'd bought for Lukas. Little outfits, a favorite toy, and the blanket he was wrapped in when they first saw him.

Jody kisses Lukas on the cheek as we leave, tears streaming down her own cheeks. She waves from the porch as we drive away.

34

DIMA

On the flight home, Arya won't let go of Lukas. But even in her arms, he's unsettled. Anxious. Squirmy and upset.

"Maybe he doesn't remember me," she says softly. "Maybe he misses Jody and Nick. Or Brigitte."

I grip her shoulder. "He's just not used to the pressure change in his ears."

"Maybe, but..." She shakes her head. "I can't help but wonder if we did the right thing."

I snap my attention to her. "What do you mean?"

"I mean... I don't know. I'm glad Lukas is with us. It's all I wanted. I'm ecstatic. But is it... is it what's best for him? Am I what's best for him?"

Tears prick at the corner of Arya's eyes. I reach over and slide Lukas out of her arms and settle him in the crook of my arm. He looks up at me with a puzzled expression. When I put a bottle in his mouth, he's so busy trying to figure out what's going on and where Arya went that he opens his mouth and begins to eat.

After a few seconds, his eyes flutter, and soon, they are closed. He's relaxed.

"Being with his parents is what's best for him," I say firmly. I reach out and grab Arya's hand with mine. "Being with us is what matters."

Arya doesn't respond, but she squeezes my hand back. That'll have to be enough.

Lukas finishes his bottle and drifts off to sleep. Arya lays her head on my shoulder. And for one blissful minute, I can let myself forget everything going on tens of thousands of feet below. I can let myself believe that we have our son and life will be perfect now. Uncomplicated.

Of course, that isn't true. Ilyasov is waiting down below. And the Trials. And an unknown future.

All that shit must be on Arya's mind, as well.

"What's the next stage?" she asks, sitting up and turning towards me. "What happens when we land?"

"I have to kill or corrupt a police officer."

Her eyes widen. "You can't kill a police officer."

"Then I'll have to corrupt one," I say. "Or find one bad enough that he's earned his death."

She chews on her lower lip. I know she doesn't like the idea. I already have more blood on my hands than she's comfortable with. And if my guess is right, there will be a lot more before these Trials are over.

Ilyasov will make sure of that.

∼

We land at LaGuardia well after it's dark, but Gennady is waiting for us out front with a car. He goes gaga the second he sees Lukas.

"He's so cute. Is this the first time I'm meeting him? Oh my God, it is. Hello, I'm Uncle Gennady."

"Have you heard anything from Ilyasov while we were gone? Has he made any moves?"

Gennady's smile falters and he tips his head towards the car. "I'll explain on the road."

I frown, but we all make our way into our seats. "What happened?" I ask when everyone is settled.

"I think Ilyasov met with some of your men."

"My men?" I ask, not fully comprehending what he said.

He nods. "Some of the inner circle sat down and listened to him. I wasn't invited, but—"

"Is this a fucking joke?"

"It was to satiate him. To make him think he had their ear," Gennady says. "That's what Eduard told me."

I shake my head. "It was to make sure they can seamlessly transition to his leadership if I fail. Fucking traitors. Fucking cowards. Fucking—"

Gennady nods. "I get it. We have to keep our plans close to the vest. I don't think any of them are actively betraying you—they don't want to upset either you or Ilyasov—but still, it's best that they not know any more than they have to. Whatever you need, I'll help you."

I clap a hand on his shoulder. "Thank you, *sobrat*."

My phone buzzes when I switch it on from airplane mode. And again. And again. Message after message after message from members of the Bratva, all with the same link.

I click it.

"Fuck!" I skim the headline and then read the article out loud to Gennady.

"'Two officers with the New York Police Department were found gunned down and left for dead in their patrol car. There is no apparent motive for the shooting. The officers were on break, eating their lunch when the attack occurred. Names of the victims have not been released and the dashcam footage from the car is still under review. The only evidence released to the press at the time of print is the number '2' painted on the hood of the car in blue spray paint. Anyone with any information should contact the NYPD or the tip line—"

I trail off.

"That was him? Ilyasov killed two cops?" Arya asks.

I wish I could hide this from her. I wish I could give her just a few hours of bliss with our son. But in my life, a few minutes is all you get. Sometimes, not even that long.

"Yes. Ilyasov completed the second trial. He killed two officers today."

Her green eyes fill with worry. "What are you going to do?"

"Killing a cop is the easiest option," Gennady says. "That's why Ilyasov did it. It's faster."

"But riskier. Especially now that Ilyasov has killed two so brazenly. The NYPD will be out for revenge. Up in arms."

Gennady groans. "So corruption, then? That takes time. The men won't like it."

"Well, the men won't know what I have planned until it's done. We don't speak a word of this to anyone. They'll hear about it once it's finished."

"Once what's finished?"

"My plan," I say simply. "What? You don't think I have one?"

Gennady sighs, knowing I won't say another word until I'm ready. Not to him or anyone else in the Bratva.

I'm the only one I can trust.

35

DIMA

I walk into the law office in a suit.

While on the run, I wore whatever I could find in a box store—sweatpants, ill-fitted jeans, cheap t-shirts. But this is a capital-S *Suit*. It's tailored perfectly, fits like a glove, made from the finest material with the finest craftsmanship.

I look like myself.

I look like a fucking don.

The receptionist behind the front desk thinks so, too. When I walk in, she does a double take and gives me a suggestive smile.

"Do you have an appointment, sir? You must be a new client. I've never seen you before." Her lipstick is faded where it's come into contact with her coffee mug too many times, but she purses her lips and bats her curled eyelashes at me.

"I'm here to see Kurt Vaughn. I don't have an appointment. But he'll know who I am."

Without taking her eyes from my face, the receptionist picks up her phone and taps in an extension. "Mr. Vaughn, someone is here to see you—Yes, I know, but he said—Yes. Okay, I'll tell him."

She drops the phone down and shrugs. "I'm sorry, but he is busy right now. Perhaps you can make an appointment and come back another day?"

I shake my head. "Call him back and tell him my name."

Her eyebrows lift. "And what is your name?"

"Dima Romanoff."

Suddenly, her smile flattens. She stares at me in shock as she calls the lawyer again.

He must be annoyed because he starts talking before she can even explain. She sighs. "I know, sir, but Dima Romanoff is here to see you—Yes, right now. He's in the office. Yes. Okay."

The receptionist stands up and smooths a hand down her pencil skirt. "Follow me, Mr. Romanoff. Mr. Vaughn will see you now."

"How nice of him to accommodate me," I drawl.

I'm shown back to the office in the corner of the main room. Kurt Vaughn's name is spelled on a background of foggy glass. I can see the rough shape of his silhouette moving around inside before the receptionist opens the door and ushers me inside.

The office is wooden and filled with leather-bound books that've no doubt never been touched. It looks like he ordered the *Big Impressive Lawyer* Starter Kit.

"Mr. Romanoff, what a pleasure," Vaughn lies. "Please sit down."

He's a good-looking middle-aged man. Good-looking in the way that expensive, morally dubious defense attorneys like him always look: lots of Botox, perfectly coiffed hair with a bright sheen in it, a smile like the cat that just ate the canary.

I don't trust him as far as I can throw him. But then again, I'm not here to trust him.

I'm here to destroy him.

Vaughn folds his hands on the desk in front of him and leans forward. "To what do I owe the pleasure?"

I give him a curt smile. "A little legal dilemma, I'm afraid."

"For an upstanding citizen like you, Mr. Romanoff? Color me surprised." He chuckles casually at his own joke, like we're old buddies. But I see the fear in his eyes. He's searching my face, trying to figure out what the hell a man like me is doing coming to see a man like him.

He'll find out soon. And he won't like it one bit.

"It happens to the best of us," I sigh. "And the worst."

"Right," Vaughn says, a little uncertain of my tone. "Well, you came to the right place. I'll absolutely help you out. First, we will want to—"

"Actually, it's not me who needs helping," I interrupt. "Not quite."

Vaughn lays down the pen he just picked up to scribble notes. "Oh. Of course. What did you have in mind…?"

"There was a case not too far from here a few years back. I think you might remember something about it. Does the name 'D'Onofrio' jog your memory?"

All at once, the man's forehead starts to bead up with sweat. He can sense the jaws of the trap I'm laying beginning to close around him.

But it's too late to escape. It's been too late since the second he let me set foot in his office.

"Oh—uh, I mean, well, I can't say I have… Or rather, of course, everyone knows the name, but—"

I hold up a hand and he stops babbling. "It involved a woman named Maria D'Onofrio. Born in Calabria, Italy. Came to the United States as a young woman. Met a charming entrepreneur, got married, had two girls and a boy. The American Dream in a nutshell, isn't it?"

Vaughn swallows hard. His Adam's apple bobs in his throat. "Uh, I suppose so…"

I wag my finger in his face. "Wrong. The American fucking Nightmare, Kurt. She fell down a flight of stairs and broke her neck. Tragic ending for the poor woman."

His desk starts to shake from the force of his bouncing knee. He's paranoid and nervous and trying hard as hell not to lose his cool. But he's failing badly. "What does any of this have to do with me, Mr. Romanoff?"

"Oh, Kurt," I sigh. "It has everything to do with you. Before all this—" I wave my hand around to point out the fancy office we're sitting in— "pricey bullshit you've surrounded yourself with… Before the money, the private, wealthy clients… You were just a Deputy D.A. in Atlantic City, weren't you? Making shit money and doing shit work. I'm sure you had noble intentions when you started. But those didn't last long, did they?"

"Mr. Romanoff…"

"Shut the fuck up," I growl. "Just sit there and listen. I'll tell you when to fucking talk."

I lean forward and rest two huge hands on the edge of his desk. Vaughn eyes them like they're murder weapons. I suppose, in a way, they are.

"Do you know what I heard recently, Mr. Vaughn?" I continue. "I heard that you knew a little something about what actually happened to Mrs. D'Onofrio. And I heard that Mr. D'Onofrio—that would be Giorgio D'Onofrio, the man whose name almost made you shit yourself a minute ago—gave you quite a bit of money to keep some of those details out of the official record."

Kurt frowns. He's desperate to salvage the situation. To find some way out.

It's a waste of effort.

"That's hearsay, Mr. Romanoff. Gossip. My mother called it the devil's telephone."

I shake my head and grin wickedly. "Giorgio shoved his wife down the stairs because she wanted to leave him. You covered it up. You're as bad as he is, Kurt. You're going to burn in hell for it when your time comes. And you might burn in this life, too. That all depends on what you choose to do next."

Vaughn tugs at the collar of his shirt. He's sweating through it now and fidgeting relentlessly.

"Those are damning accusations you're making—"

"I know damn well what I'm doing, you piece of shit. Listen to me: I know exactly what kind of man you are. You're careful. Cunning. And when someone like Giorgio D'Onofrio offers you that kind of money to do that kind of thing, you wouldn't accept without keeping some kind of safety measure, would you?"

The pens in the desk are rattling now from the force of Vaughn's trembling. He's starting to understand what's at stake here.

"Mr. Romanoff," Vaughn rasps, "I believe you are talking about blackmail, and I can assure you I do not have any."

I click my tongue. "I know you have what I'm looking for. I'd love for you to give it to me willingly, to help me out. I want our relationship to remain civil. But of course, like you, I've learned a few tricks over the years to ensure I get the outcome I want."

"There's nothing to give you, I swear!" Kurt gasps. "I really don't know what you're looking for, but I don't think I have it. I can't produce something that does not exist."

Before he can blink, I lunge across his desk, wrap my fingers around his wrist, and pin his hand to the table. In the same motion, I free the knife from my pocket.

"How long do you think it would take you to learn to type with only nine fingers?" I muse as I press the blade to the first knuckle of his middle finger. I slide it over to his pointer finger. "Not too bad. But what about eight? That would be difficult, I think."

Kurt lets out a squeal and tries to pull his hand back, but my grip is too tight. "Please, Mr. Romanoff. Dima, please, for the love of God! I don't have what you're looking for!"

I release his hand and flop back down in my chair, enjoying the way the lawyer's chest is rising and falling rapidly. His cheeks are so red they are nearly purple.

"I can't stand that you're lying to me. But cutting off your fingers today would take so much time and this suit was far too expensive to get bloodstains in. Don't get me wrong—I'd do it, of course," I say, slipping out of my suit jacket and hanging it on the back of my chair. "But it would be so much less mess if you would just cooperate."

"Please..." he whimpers.

"I came here in good faith today, hoping you would be honest with me. Because if you're honest with me, then you won't have to be honest with the FBI."

The redness in Kurt's face fades to a sickly gray. "The FBI?"

I nod. "I have it on good authority that an agent is coming to your office today to speak with you about how you covered up Maria D'Onofrio's murder. Hence why I arrived without an appointment. There was no time for formalities."

The lawyer's mouth opens and closes several times without him saying anything. I think it might be the first time in history a lawyer has ever been speechless.

"They're coming today?" he squeaks.

I nod. "Any minute."

Right on cue, his phone rings.

"Jasmine, I'm in the middle of—An FBI agent?" he asks, looking towards the door as though he may be able to see through it. "O-o-okay, thank you. H-have them wait for me."

When he hangs up the phone, I notice the tremble in his hands.

I look down at my watch. "I'm cutting it close, aren't I? So, what will it be, Mr. Vaughn? I doubt I have the time to cut off your fingers now that a federal agent is in the building. But I am happy to take a rain check."

Vaughn looks from me to the door and back again before he violently pushes his chair away from his desk, unlocks the largest bottom drawer, and then removes a fake bottom.

Beneath it is a manila envelope and a disc in a clear plastic case. Kurt pulls the items out and slides them across the desk to me.

He starts to explain without meeting my eyes. "All the proof is in there. The original coroner's report before we had it doctored. The record of the wire transfer from Giorgio D'Onofrio to my account. I'm sorry—oh God, I'm so fucking sorry," he sobs.

"You're just sorry you got caught, you fucking *mudak*," I snarl. "You weren't sorry when you were dumping an innocent woman's body into the river and helping her husband get away with murder."

He's crying now, his face pressed into his desk. His back jumps with each wailing sob.

"But," I sigh, "you get to keep all your fingers today, Mr. Vaughn. I'm in a merciful mood. For your sake, I hope the FBI will feel the same."

Then I take the files, turn, and leave.

One former cop corrupted.

One more Trial completed.

Jasmine, the receptionist, is much less interested in me as I leave the office. Her eyes are locked instead on the FBI agent sitting in the chair in the waiting room.

The agent wears a killer skirt with a matching jacket and a tight-fitted white button-down underneath. Around her neck hangs a remarkably real-looking FBI badge.

Considering Gennady only had half a day to scrounge the outfit together, I'm impressed.

Arya meets my eyes for a moment as I pass. There's a twinkle in her eye. But she never breaks character.

36

ARYA
AN HOUR LATER

"I think we broke him." I drop my power suit jacket in a pile on Dima's bedroom floor. "He was pathetic and I'm not even a real FBI agent."

"Did he crack?" Dima is laying on his bed in a pair of gray sweatpants and a fitted black t-shirt. Somehow, he looks just as good in this as he did in the suit, which is saying something. He looked incredible in his suit.

"I thought he was going to pee on himself. He dripped sweat all over the desk and his hand was so damp when we shook. Pretty sure he cried when I left."

Dima throws his head back and laughs. "I had no idea you were so ruthless. I always imagined you as the good cop type."

I gasp in mock offense. "Excuse you! I may be small, but I can be scary."

Dima reaches a hand out towards me, curling his fingers. "Are you sure he wasn't just smitten? That pencil skirt does things to a man..."

I wrinkle my nose. "He'd better not be. I have a feeling that wouldn't sit well with you."

Dima's blue gray eyes flare. In one graceful move, he grabs me around the waist and yanks me onto his lap so I'm straddling him.

The skirt rides up my legs. Dima slips his fingers under the hem, drawing lines of fire up my skin. "Show me how you interrogated him."

My face flushes. "I just asked him a few questions. It was nothing."

"I said, show me."

I can feel his hard length against my inner thigh. I bite my lip. "I just want to ask you a few questions, Mr. Romanoff. Standard procedure."

"Procedure?" he growls. "Does that mean we're doing this the easy way… or the hard way?" There's a laugh dancing on the edge of his voice. But the fire in his eyes is deadly serious.

"Depends on whether or not you cooperate," I say in my most professional voice. It's getting harder and harder to do that with Dima's hard cock pressing against my inner thigh. "Will you cooperate, Mr. Romanoff?"

"That remains to be seen, Agent George." Dima slides his hands up my sides and around to the buttons on the front of my shirt. He undoes them slowly. Each one undoes me a little at the same time.

"Mr. Romanoff!" I yell, swatting at his hand. "I'll be the one stripping you down today."

"Is that so?"

I grab the hem of his shirt and tug it up. "Yes, that's so. I'll be stripping away the lies and revealing the truth," I say, dragging my fingernails across his chest. "No matter how long it takes."

Dima hisses and raises a dark brow when I dig my nails into his abs. "I thought you said this wouldn't be painful."

"It might be." I lean forward and swirl my tongue around his nipple before I nip the sensitive flesh with my teeth. He sucks in a breath.

When I sit back up, his eyes are darker than they were a moment ago. "But I don't believe pain and pleasure have to be mutually exclusive, do you?"

"I think you've convinced me otherwise."

"Good. Now, Mr. Romanoff, you stopped unbuttoning my shirt."

"Is there a question in there, Agent George?"

"Yes. The question is… Why?"

With a clench in his jaw, Dima seizes each side of my shirt in one hand and rips it wide open. Buttons go flying across the room.

Beneath the blouse, I'm wearing a white lacy bra that barely covers my nipples. Dima sits up and buries his face between my breasts.

"Mr. Romanoff," I sigh, "I'm worried you are losing focus. Are you still with me or are you lost in a fantasy?"

"I'm with you," he purrs. Goosebumps are spreading across my chest as he licks and sucks. "I'm right here with you."

"Good. Because the details of this case are still bound up tight, but I would like them to be released as soon as possible."

There's a moment's hesitation before Dima reaches around and unhooks my bra. He drags the straps down my arms painfully slowly. When the material is gone and my breasts are free, he drinks in the sight of me on top of him like I'm a work of fucking art.

Then he palms my breast, leans forward, and flicks his tongue over my pebbled nipple.

"I would love to handle the details for you," he whispers, his lips brushing against my sensitive skin. "I'll go over them as many times as necessary until you're fully satisfied."

I spread my knees further apart, bringing our bodies closer, and roll myself against him. Dima tips his head back and sighs.

"I am not easily satisfied, Mr. Romanoff. But I would love to watch you try."

He smirks. "As you wish."

He grabs me by the waist and rolls me over so I'm on my back and he is laying over me. Then he finds the zipper at the side of my skirt and slides it down before peeling the skirt down my legs.

My panties are the same delicate lace as the bra. Dima runs his fingers over the material. Shivers dance up my spine.

Then, in one swift tug, he tears them away.

The material rips and falls in tattered shreds to the floor. Before I can complain about the loss, Dima hooks my knees over his shoulders and lowers his face to my center.

He starts to devour me. All I can do is groan.

"Look at me," he orders. "Watch me lick you until you scream."

His head bobs between my legs, his lips sucking at my clit, wet with my juices. I curl my fingers in his hair and grind my body against his face.

I lift my hips as he starts to finger fuck me. That plus his tongue is short-circuiting my brain and my body at the same time. I feel like I'm melting and burning simultaneously.

I grab a fistful of his hair and lower his face back down. "Don't stop. Please."

Dima adds two more fingers and continues devastating me with his tongue.

"Oh my God, yes!" I cry out. "Please. Please."

He works faster and my body climaxes hard, clenching his finger, drenching him in a wave of pleasure.

When Dima pulls away from me and unhooks my knees from his shoulders, my body is too limp to react. I feel like an old rag doll, used and spent.

"I want to be inside of you." His voice is deep and velvety. "Now."

He presses a hand into my chest and lays me down on my back. Then, in one gentle slide, he's inside of me.

Like always, it's a stretch to accommodate him. But fuck, it feels so good. A moan escapes my lips once we're completely connected. I've never felt so full.

"Harder. Touch me," I beg. "Make me come."

At those magic words—the words that started all this shit in the first place—a low growl rumbles through Dima's chest.

He flips me on top of him, then lifts me effortlessly and spears me with one upward lunge of his hips. He sucks and kisses and bites my skin while he pounds into me.

It's so much. Too much.

And yet, I want more.

I slide my hand between my legs as Dima moans in my ear, "Get ready to come for me, *krasavitsa*."

I'm paralyzed with the next thrust—and then my legs start to shake. Dima doesn't stop. Neither do I. Even as my stomach clenches and my muscles start to contract, I climb higher and higher.

Then the dam breaks.

"I'm coming," I cry. I'm squeezing every ounce of me so tight that I'm worried I might snap his length off inside of me.

"I'm close," he pants. "So fucking close."

I stroke my fingers through the hair at the back of his neck and whisper, "Come with me. Fill me up."

Dima shakes to an orgasm, kissing my shoulder blades and my spine as he erupts again and again inside me.

When he finishes, he lifts me off of him and lays me down on the bed next to him. We curl against each other, sweaty and utterly wrecked.

So many times over the last few months, we've been on different pages. But today, we were a team. In and out of bed, we were in sync.

"You're my *krasavitsa*," Dima whispers in my ear like something out of a dream. "My queen. Never forget that, Arya."

37

ARYA

After we make love, Dima and I fall asleep. I wake up a few hours later and sneak over to check on Lukas. It's early in the morning, so he's sleeping soundly. I sit next to the crib to stare at my precious baby boy —and wonder what the hell I'm supposed to do.

I have our passports, so if we wanted to, we could leave. The only reason I stayed before was to get Lukas back. The only reason I helped Dima try to get his Bratva back from his brother was so I could find and save Lukas.

Well, he's found. He's saved. So what now? Why are we still here in Dima's mansion?

The obvious answer sits in my stomach like a rock.

Because I don't want to leave Dima.

Fuck. It feels like I've thought myself in circles so many times I can see the worn tracks in my mind.

I love Dima, but he's dangerous, so I have to leave him, but I can't leave him because I love him. And around and around it goes, irritating and endless. I'm getting pretty damn sick of it.

I feel a presence behind me and turn around to see Dima, huge and shirtless. I press my finger to my lips to signal we shouldn't talk too loud.

"Couldn't sleep?" he asks.

I shrug. "I slept some."

"I know. You drooled on me."

"I absolutely did not!"

Dima chuckles. I feel it as much as I hear it—a warm, pleasant rumble in my bones. Why do the simplest of his mannerisms make me feel like this? He winks and I melt. He smiles and I evaporate. He laughs and every cell in my body laughs along with him.

"So what's next?" I ask, eager to change the subject.

"I throw you over my shoulder, carry you back to bed, and fuck you until you can't walk right."

I smack him on the shoulder, although my cheeks are burning and my thighs are tingling at the thought. "I'm serious. What's the next trial? We should start preparing for it as soon as possible, right? Is it just whoever completes the trial first or what happens if—"

Dima presses a finger to my lips. "Later. Not now. I just want to be with you and not think about all of that shit for a second."

When I sigh and stay quiet, he nods, satisfied. Then he pads over to Lukas's crib. It amazes me how quiet he can move for such a massive human being.

"He looks like you when he sleeps," he whispers.

"Do I also have dried milk on my chin?"

Dima laughs. "It depends what your bedtime snack is."

"Again with the innuendo. You have the most one-track mind known to mankind."

He laughs quietly—then, quick as a flash, he whips me around so my back is pressed against his front. With one huge, strong hand, he palms my throat and forces my head back so he can claim me with an aggressive kiss.

Nothing has the ability to wipe my mind clear like the press of Dima's lips to mine.

The noise of my thoughts is still there, but I can't hear it. Can't care about it. For a little while, everything goes quiet and I feel perfectly at peace.

We waltz forward like that, back into the adjoining bedroom. He's pawing at my clothes. Everywhere his touch goes ends up burning like fire.

"I'm so fucking hungry for you," he growls into my open mouth.

"You've had your fair share," I retort with a grin.

He smirks. "It's not enough. It'll never be enough."

Grabbing my hand, he pirouettes me again like a dancer. Then he shoves me backwards. The bed hits me in the back of the knees and I collapse on it with a surprised, "Oof!"

Before I can even process what's happening, he's on me. He pulls aside my pajama shorts and licks me up and down.

I gasp and then bite my knuckle to stifle it. "Dima, if you get me worked up and then abandon me again like you did on the plane, we're going to have a serious problem."

"That doesn't sound like something I'd ever do," he murmurs. His voice is muffled between my legs as he laps me up.

"It—oh, fucking God—it absolutely does. You did. I'm still mad about it."

"How can you be mad at me when I can do something like this?" Just then, he adds his fingers to the mix. I can barely tell what's happening down there anymore.

All I know is that one second, I'm capable of functional speech and rational thought—and the next second, all those abilities are gone. I'm a humming blur of a crackling orgasm.

"That's what I thought, *krasavitsa*," he murmurs. His lips brush against mine as he sucks my clit in and releases it with a soft pop, over and over again.

I come hard once barely a minute after he starts and then a second time right on the heels of it.

Then, to my massive disappointment, he pulls away and stands up. His short beard glistens with my juices. I'm one thousand percent sure it's the sexiest sight that has ever existed.

"Come with me for a second," he rumbles.

"Uh, I just came twice, actually. So—"

He shakes his head. "I mean it. I want to show you something."

I feign frustration, but hold out my hand for him to take. He pulls me off the bed and I smooth my shorts back into place. My face is burning hot. I can still feel my slickness between my thighs and the throbbing need to be filled.

But it'll have to wait, apparently. Mr. Mystery himself has something else cooked up.

I'm wary. Last time he did this, I ended up locked in a storeroom while he went on a suicide mission.

I also don't want to leave Lukas unattended for long. That Mama Bear anxiety hasn't left me since he came home. Maybe it never will.

Dima catches me looking backwards over my shoulder and tugs on my arm. "He'll be fine, Arya. We aren't going far."

He's telling the truth. At the next door, he stops and pushes it open. I'm not sure what I expect, but it isn't what I find.

Dima stands aside as soon as he walks through the door. I walk ahead into a grand ballroom.

There's no other way to describe it. The floors are a deep, rich brown with a high polish on them, the ceilings are vaulted, and a massive crystal chandelier hangs from the center of the room. The walls are wood-paneled with every other panel being replaced with a thin floor to ceiling mirror.

It feels like stepping inside of a music box. It's magical.

"What is this place?" I breathe.

Dima shuts the door and hits a button. Soft string music emanates from who-knows-where. I can't see any speakers.

He extends a hand to me, bowing low. "May I have this dance?"

I laugh. "You don't usually ask questions like that. You just do what you want."

He nods. "True." Then he snatches up my hand and my waist in one motion, pulling me into a slow pirouette with him.

I laugh. "So it's a ballroom?" I ask as we revolve around the room to the pace of the music.

"It is," he says. He's shockingly good on his feet. I guess I should've expected that. He's full of surprises, Mr. Romanoff. "My mother loved to dance, so my father had this room built for her. She spent a lot of her time in here."

"Was she a professional dancer?"

Dima wrinkles his nose. "No, she just liked the music and having fun. And she liked my father best when he was dancing. That's how they met."

"Sounds romantic."

"According to her, it was," Dima says. "She claims the spotlights turned to my father when he walked through the doors of the party where they meet. He found her eyes instantly and they danced the night away. They were married three months later."

"Love at first sight."

"That's how my mother told it. But she could be a bit of a romantic."

"How did your father tell it?"

"He didn't."

"Ah. Not a romantic, then."

Dima's eyes are dark and cloudy under the amber light from the chandelier. "Love was weakness in my father's eyes. He wouldn't be caught dead waxing poetic about the night he first saw my mother beneath a disco ball."

I frown. "That's sad."

"That's why I think my mother had this room built. Because when she and my father were alone in here, he was different. He had to be. Otherwise, I don't think she would have spent so much time with him."

I want to know more, but I also want to be cautious. Dima never talks much about his parents, about his past. It's dangerous territory.

"Were your parents not happy?"

Dima tips his head to the side in thought. The motion is simple, innocent. For a brief moment, I can picture him young, living in this house.

"I don't think they knew the meaning of the word," he says sadly. "Happiness wasn't ever really their goal. They just settled on safety, I guess. Security."

I frown again. "That's also sad."

"Like I said, it just wasn't something they cared about." He looks around the room. "But this room is where they'd come to make up. When they had a power struggle, when my mother wanted more from my father than he could give, or when my father pushed my mother too far—my mother would lock herself in this room until my father broke down the door. And then when they came out, everything was okay again."

I'm not sure if the story is supposed to be sweet or not. To be honest, I don't know what good looks like anymore. What love should look like.

Dima saved me from Taras. Is that love?

Dima told me to run so he didn't have to kill me. Is *that* love?

I don't know. I really, really don't. But I'm glad he's sharing this glimpse into his past with me. It feels… important.

I lay my head on his chest and breathe in the musky scent of him. I wish I could bottle it up and spray it on myself like perfume.

We dance in silence for a while. Then Dima starts to talk while he continues to stare over my shoulder into the middle distance beyond.

"My brother and I used to play in here, too," he murmurs. "When it was empty and our parents were busy, Ilyasov and me, we'd come in here and played with cardboard swords and fake guns. We pretended we were dons fighting over territory or pirates stealing treasure. Kid stuff."

I love the image of Dima playing. Of him carefree and smiling.

But my heart tugs at the mention of his brother. It's hard to square the Ilyasov I've met with a young, reckless boy. All I can see is the tattooed monster trying to ruin his brother's life.

Dima has those memories in his head, though. The two versions of Ilyasov—the old and the new—are at war in his head. I can't help wondering which one is going to win.

38

ARYA

When the song ends, Dima takes me by the hand and leads me back to the bedroom. My mind is still racing with thoughts of what he was telling me. About his parents, his brother. Tiny glimpses into the life that molded the man he is today.

I want to know that man. I want to help that man transcend the shit he was born into.

Because he's done that for me.

But I don't think I've earned that right yet. He's so guarded about his past that I fear pushing him to reveal things before he's ready would only make him clam up that much tighter.

Maybe it's best to let some things lie in the past. That way, we can focus on the present.

God knows I have enough I want to forget.

Besides—right now, I just want to be with him.

"Is the little one still asleep?" I ask as we tiptoe back in.

Dima crosses his fingers and pulls back the blankets. "I hope so."

He's in a pair of gray cotton pajama pants with a white shirt and he is gorgeous. The most attractive man I've ever seen.

He leans over Lukas's crib to check on our son. As he does, I spy a dark stain on his shoulder. "Lukas left you a little present," I laugh.

"There's a lot more laundry with a baby than I imagined." Dima smiles and peels the shirt off in one pull, tossing it in the corner of the room.

He's not trying to seduce me, but he doesn't have to try. Just the act of breathing is enough for me to want him. The fact that he looks this good and exists is enough to make my knees weak.

But throw in him being a wonderful, caring father, and I'm done for. Doomed to a cursed existence of constant arousal.

I trace my hand over his muscled back. "Who needs pajamas, anyway?"

Dima looks over his shoulder, blue eyes sparkling as he takes in my satin shorts and matching button-down top. "I've been thinking the same thing. I'm not sure why I even bothered buying you these pajamas. I'm sure you'd be much more comfortable out of them."

I begin unbuttoning my shirt slowly. "You're right. I have blankets. What do I need clothes for?"

Dima grins. "A question as old as time."

I slide the shirt off my shoulders and bite back a smile when I hear Dima inhale sharply at the sight of my bare breasts.

I kick the blankets off and arch my hips high in the air as I hook my fingers into the waistband of my shorts and begin sliding them down.

Dima swallows a groan when he sees I don't have any underwear on, either.

When I throw my clothes in the pile with his, I turn to him. "Much better with no pajamas on, but now I think there might be better things to do in bed than sleep. What do you think?"

He nods. "I've got a few ideas…"

I roll over and crawl towards him. I throw one leg over his waist, then the other, until I'm straddling him with my heat lined up over his stiffening cock.

My nipple is already hard, but when he tweaks it between his fingers, it gets painfully sharp. I try to bite back a gasp and mostly fail.

His other hand slides between us and cups me. "Do you like being on top, Arya?" he asks. "You're already wet."

My legs are shaking from just the little bit of friction from his thumb, an orgasm anxious to burst out of me. But I'm not ready to be done yet.

I take slow, deep breaths as Dima slides his hand around to work a finger into me and then another.

I plant my hands on his chest and clench my entire body, trying to fight off what I know is coming. Trying to draw out the pleasure.

"I don't want your hand," I groan.

"What do you want?" Dima taunts. "Tell me what you want. Maybe I'll even give it to you."

I drag my thumb over his bottom lip and bite my own. "Your mouth."

Almost before I can speak the words, Dima has me on my back, my knees over his shoulders, and his face between my legs.

His beard tickles the insides of my thighs, but my giggles die in my throat when he presses the whole of his tongue against me in one long lick.

I slide my fingers into his black velvet curls and hold his head where I want it, thrusting against his sucking lips and the delicious flicks of his tongue.

Then he slides his fingers into me again, just like he did earlier before we danced.

And just like I did earlier, I cry out.

"Oh, fucking God, Dima, you're going to make me…"

I burst, slowly and silently in a series of mini-orgasms like a lightning storm. Dima pins me to the bed and licks me until each one blurs into the next and my throat gets raspy from stifling screams.

When he finally lifts his head, his lips are shiny with my juices and his hair is mussed from my hands.

I like knowing that I did that to him. Some primal part of me feels like I've marked my territory, and I'm anxious to mark it some more.

He crawls over me, but before he can pin me to the bed, I flip over onto my stomach and lift my hips.

"Yes, just like that," he sighs. "Put that pussy in the air for me."

His hands clamp down on my hips as he runs his hard length between my cheeks.

"Take me," I beg, face against the sheets. "Fuck me like I'm yours."

"You don't have to ask me twice."

My pussy is wet and desperate. He slides in like he was always meant to be there.

Dima slides his hands up the curve of my waist and cups my breasts in his hands, using them like handles to pull me onto him.

"Like that," I gasp. "Oh, fuck yes."

Dima circles his fingers over my nipples and pinches harder than I ever thought I'd like—but fuck, I like it so much I almost come again from that sensation alone.

My body is liquid heat. Every thrust feels like a wave moving through me. All I can do is cling to the mattress and wait for the next delicious onslaught.

"Fuck me as hard as you can, baby," I gasp. "Make me come again."

Dima curses under his breath and grabs my waist in a tight grip. He spears me onto him harder and faster than I've ever felt before. It takes every ounce of self-control in my body not to scream out in absolute ecstasy.

And then that self-control is gone. One thrust blends into the next. I'm practically weightless, levitating as he bends me how he wants and takes me how he wants.

And what he was is what I want. Every thrust feels like another orgasm. I lose count. I lose my voice. I forget to breathe.

Until, at some point, it all ends. We collapse onto the bed in a sweaty tangle of limbs, and suddenly Dima is kissing me everywhere, pressing his gentle lips all the way up and down me again and again. It's like being carried back down to earth in a cloud.

He's gentle. Tender. Delicate. Enough to rock me into the softest sleep of my life.

Then he whispers in my ear that he loves me.

And just like that, I'm ready to go all over again.

39

ARYA

When I wake up later in the morning, Dima isn't there. Instead, there's a note.

Back later. Business to handle.

Before I can even process his absence, there's a knock at my door. "Who is it?" I call.

No answer.

I throw on some clothes rapidly and then open it, wondering who's knocking on my door first thing in the morning. I wrench the door open to find…

"Ernestine! June!"

I sweep them both up in a crushing hug. It's so good to see their faces again. Dima has been keeping them protected away from the action. But God, I've missed my makeshift family.

"Wait a second. Why on earth are you here?"

"That's not nice!" June protests.

I laugh. "I'm sorry. I mean, of course I'm glad you're here. But…"

"Dima had a lot to do today," Ernestine explains, "so he mentioned you'd be free. We thought we'd come over and keep you… company. Brunch and makeovers for us ladies this morning."

Ernestine looks away. I notice June hiding a smile.

"What am I missing here?" I demand.

"If you don't hurry up, young lady, it'll be brunch that you're missing," Ernestine says with a mysterious twinkle in her eye and a laugh in her voice. "Now, let's go!"

On our way out, we run into Gennady in the hallway.

I start to say hi to him when I notice something in his hair. I pluck it out for him, thinking it's a piece of fuzz, but it's a piece of gold confetti. "What is this?"

Gennady rips it out of my hands. "I went to a, uh… strip club?"

"This morning?"

He nods slowly, though he doesn't look convinced of his answer, and backs towards the ballroom door.

I shake my head and grab his sleeve. "Okay, why is everyone being so weird today? Is there something in there?"

I try to move towards the door, but Gennady blocks my path. "The stripper. Is in there. Behind me. In the ballroom."

I roll my eyes. "You're the worst liar in existence. What is going on?"

Before I can press Gennady for answers—and I feel confident he would crack under my interrogation—Ernestine interrupts.

"Time to go!" she bleats. She hurries me to the foyer and out the door.

From there, the morning is a whirlwind of brunch and manicures and a much needed haircut. Taras Kreshnik may have been richer than sin, but he bought shit quality shampoo for his sex slaves and my split ends are crying for salvation.

When I leave the salon to head back home, I'm so pleased with my cut and blow out and my pale pink nails that I don't even notice Dima until I'm right in front of him.

Ernestine and June hang back, so I have a full, unobstructed view of him standing in the entryway with a large bouquet of flowers.

He looks unbelievable in a crisp white button-down rolled to his sleeves and fitted navy blue trousers that hug all the best parts of him in all the right ways. It looks like he has had a haircut, too. His beard is trimmed down to just a shadow of stubble.

I wolf-whistle. "What on Earth is going on?"

"I could say the same," he says, reaching out to take my hand and spin me around. "You look gorgeous."

"*Somebody* arranged for me to get my hair cut and my nails done." I narrow my eyes. "Any idea why that may be?"

He smirks, his full lips pulling into a pout. "I might have a few ideas. These are for you."

The bouquet is huge with blue carnations and chrysanthemums with pockets of babies' breath and yellow daisies. It's a bright, cheerful bouquet—but I have no idea why he's giving it to me.

"What are these for?"

Dima reaches around the bouquet and pulls a card from between the flowers. It has a cartoon picture of a stork carrying a baby with the words *"You had a baby!"* typed next to it in a word cloud.

"I had a baby over two months ago."

"And I never got you flowers," Dima says, wrapping an arm around me and leading me down the hall. "There's a lot you never got to do as a new mom, and a lot I wish I could have done for you. So…"

His voice drifts off. I'm still looking up at him, waiting for an explanation, when he grabs my shoulders and turns me towards the now open doors of the ballroom.

"Surprise!"

I almost scream in shock as a crowd of people shout at me. They're surrounded by blue and gold streamers and balloons dangling from the ceiling. Tables fill the room, each with a bouquet much like the one I'm holding in my hand, and covered in the same gold confetti I saw in Gennady's hair earlier this morning.

"It's a baby shower," Dima whispers in my ear, pushing me into the room.

Ernestine and June are at the front with Lukas in their arms, but next to them is Marsha from the vet clinic I used to work at, along with two of the other nurses. And next to them is Lauren Malone. As I go around the room embracing everyone, thanking them for coming, Lauren tells me Dima called her and flew her out.

"You came all this way for a baby shower?" I ask, shaking my head in disbelief.

"I wanted to meet the baby I helped save," she says with a casual shrug. "Plus, I needed a vacation, and your man flew me here for free."

My man.

Dima is standing with Gennady, sipping on pastel-colored punch and smiling at me whenever our eyes meet.

He is my man. My rock. My partner, with all the pros and cons that come along with that. I'd say today is a very serious pro.

~

I'm two cups of punch and a slice of cake into the party when Dima pulls me aside and asks me to come with him.

"You planned this party and you want me to leave already?" I tease.

He smiles and wraps my arm around his. "I have another surprise for you."

I'm not sure my heart can take another surprise, but today has been one magnificent reveal after another, so I trust him and let him lead me towards our room.

I think we are going into our room—which would be perfectly fine by me—but Dima keeps walking and goes one door over. He pauses for a second for dramatic effect, then pushes it open and stands back.

It's a nursery.

The dark walls have been repainted a pale yellow with white wainscoting on the bottom half of the wall. There is a long white dresser with a changing pad on top, a cushioned rocking chair with a cloud pillow, and a raincloud and rainbow mobile hanging over a white crib.

It's beautiful.

I press a hand to my mouth and blink back the tears trying to force their way out. I don't want anything to impede my view of this gorgeous room.

"I know you want Lukas close to us right now, and I do, too," Dima explains. "But when we're both ready, this could be his room."

"Right next door to ours."

Dima wraps a hand around my waist. "Yes. Right next door to ours."

"Dima, I don't even know what to say…"

"You are the best mom, Arya. You put Lukas's needs first, and you've fought hard to protect him and take care of him. Hearing you doubt yourself breaks my heart. So, I figured, maybe I can't convince you you're the best mom, but I can give you the best nursery. It's a step."

This is a whole other level. This isn't just taking care of me.

This is *loving* me.

I turn and bury my face in Dima's shirt. I'm probably smearing makeup on the white material, but I don't care. I wrap my arms around him and hold on tight.

"You like it?"

"I love it," I whisper. "I love you, too."

Dima grabs my chin between his thumb and forefinger so he can tilt my face up to his. The kiss he plants on my lips is sweet and lingering, and I don't want it to end.

On the other hand, if it doesn't, I'm afraid we will christen the nursery in a way that would be wholly inappropriate.

"We should get back to the guests, don't you think?" I whisper.

Dima shakes his head and kisses me for another minute before finally agreeing.

"I can't believe how many people you got here," I say as we walk back to the party hand-in-hand. "People from the vet clinic. Lauren. You invited people you'd never even met before."

"I wanted all of the important people in your life to be here. They were all more than happy to come."

Two faces appear in my mind unbidden, and suddenly, my perfect day has a big gray cloud.

Dima notices instantly. "What is it?" I try to brush it off, but he insists. "Tell me, Arya."

I sigh. "I thought of Rose. She'd be here if she could. She should be here."

"I'm sorry. I wish she could be."

"I also thought of Brigitte," I admit. "I know she did horrible things, but... she was my friend. Or, I thought she was my friend. I don't know. I'm just so mad that so much has happened. That there is so much bad in the world. Bad that killed Rose. Bad that took over Brigitte and turned her evil. I hate it so much and I also hate that I still miss them. Both of them."

Dima pulls me aside to face him. "There is bad in the world, Arya. You and I know it better than most people. I used to think the bad outweighed the good, but someone changed my mind about that."

"Who?"

He pulls away and looks down at me.

"Oh," I say, realizing what he meant. "Me."

"You have always been so good. You see the best in people. You're loyal. You're kind. You are the kind of person most people strive to be, Arya, and you give me hope that the world isn't lost. If people like you can exist, then there has to be a whole hell of a lot of good out there somewhere."

Once again, tears are prickling at the backs of my eyes, but I fight them back.

I don't want to cry. Especially right before we go back into the party.

Instead, I stretch onto my toes and kiss Dima. "Thank you."

He grins and tips his head towards the ballroom door where it sounds like Gennady is singing karaoke to a chorus of laughter. It's the Spice Girls, if I'm not mistaken.

"You ready?" he asks.

I grab his hand. "Absolutely."

40

ARYA

"This is a great party. And a beautiful house." Lauren takes a sip of punch and looks around. "I've never seen a house with a ballroom before."

"Me either," I admit, laughing. "Dima's life is… different from most other people's."

"Which means your life is different now, too, right?"

We've been so busy since I moved in to the mansion that I haven't really had time to consider that I live here. At first, it seemed like a temporary solution. Yet another place to crash on the long list of places I've crashed in the last few months. Granted, this was by far the most extravagant of the bunch.

But now that my stuff is unpacked in the closet and Lukas has a nursery, it feels like it could be… a home.

That's bizarre.

"I still can't believe you came all this way for a baby shower," I say again. "After everything you've done for me, I never would have asked you to come all this way."

Lauren waves my words away. "Please, this is great. Like I said, your boyfriend is very generous. He paid for my flight and booked my hotel. It has been way too long since I've taken a vacation anyway. It's hard to ask for time off when your dad is your boss. It's like being in school again and trying to convince them I'm too sick to go."

I laugh. "That can't be fun."

She nods. "No, but it's great, too. I love spending so much time with my family. It keeps us close."

"I bet that's nice," I say, even though I have no fucking idea if it's nice.

What do I know about family? My mom cared more about drugs than me, my fiancé turned out to be a drug dealing mass murderer, and the best friend I loved like a sister betrayed me and tried to kidnap my son.

They aren't exactly citing my life story in "How-to-be-a-parent" textbooks.

Lauren must be able to see the torment on my face because she reaches out and lays a hand over mine. "I know there's a lot about your life I don't know or understand, but you can talk to me if you need it."

Her kindness makes my throat constrict with unshed tears. "Thank you. That's… really nice."

"I like to think we are sort of friends now. I mean, I helped find your son, which I think makes me an honorary godmother or something, right?"

She laughs and assures me she's kidding, but it isn't a bad idea. I owe Lauren everything.

"We are totally friends. Absolutely," I tell her. "If you ever need anything, I'll be in Chicago in a flash. No questions asked."

Lauren looks around the room again. "I'm sure you will be. I try not to make assumptions, but you and Dima seem like you live a pretty comfortable life here. I bet you could both afford to go anywhere you wanted at the drop of a hat."

I'm not used to being wealthy or having people comment on it. My whole life, I scraped by. I made do. I worked my ass off and saved pennies. This will take some getting used to.

"We are definitely comfortable."

Lauren takes another sip of punch and then turns to me, eyes wary. "Is it rude if I ask you what he does for a living? I'm really not trying to be nosey, but I've grown up around doctors my whole life, and I've still never seen anything like this."

"You aren't being nosey," I assure her. "We invited you to the house and it's a normal question to ask. Unfortunately, it's not a question I can easily answer."

She sighs. "I thought you might say something like that."

"It's not that I don't trust you, but I mean, you know what happened with Lukas. There are risks with our lifestyle. I wouldn't want to… involve you anymore than you already are."

Lauren holds up her hands in surrender. "Enough said. I'm happy to live my life in ignorant bliss. As long as you are taken care of and Lukas is safe. And from everything I've seen here, he is more than taken care of."

"Really?"

Lauren looks at me, brows knit together, like I'm crazy. "Of course! It's obvious he is surrounded by people who love him, and that is all any kid could ever hope for. Believe me, I see all kinds of kids at my practice, and money doesn't mean anything. The happiest kids are the ones who have loving parents at home. You and Dima are certainly giving him that. You're doing great."

I squeeze her hand. "Thank you."

Lauren excuses herself to the bathroom and I sneak away to check on Dima. He hasn't been gone too long, but he has certainly been gone long enough for me to miss him.

I pad down the hallway and go into our room, but they aren't in there. Then I go next door.

My hand is on the doorknob when I realize there are voices coming from inside. Not just Dima's, but Gennady's, too.

I press my ear to the door, trying to hear what they are saying, but their voices are soft. I have to strain until I can make out some of the words.

"...There's no way to do this... covertly. You'll have to announce what you... did," Gennady says.

Being the klutz that I am, I promptly lean too hard into the door. It squeaks under my weight and I have no choice but to pretend like I meant to do it on purpose.

I walk in with a fake smile plastered on my face. "Playing hide and seek?" I ask innocently.

Gennady spins around and grabs a tall slender gift bag from the top of the dresser. "I, uh, got you this gift. I didn't want you to open it at the baby shower. It's a special gift. Just for the two of you."

I take it from him, feeling distinctly like I'm missing something. Dima seems hesitant to meet my eyes.

"Another gift? You already got Lukas the bouncer seat."

"Like I said, this is for you," he says.

I pull a ball of crumpled tissue paper out of the top of the bag to reveal a liquor bottle. I grab the bottle by the neck and pull it out of the bag.

The bottle itself is shaped like a skull with intricate detailing around the teeth and the nose. There are even manufactured chips in the bone around the eye sockets. The liquid inside is clear.

"It's vodka," Gennady explains. "*Good* vodka. Lukas will love it."

"Gennady!"

"Just kidding. It's for you, obviously. For when Dima really pisses you off."

I chuckle. "Thanks, Gen."

To my surprise, he then slaps a hand on his forehead at once, startling me. "Dammit!"

"What's wrong?" I ask in alarm.

"I should have gotten you gin from Gen. Damn it, damn it, damn it. Missed opportunity. Next time."

Dima and I both execute simultaneous eyerolls.

"Who doesn't love a good pun?" Gennady complains as we all start to head out back to the ballroom.

"Everyone," I say. At the same time, Dima says, "No one."

We laugh as we go back. I try to remind myself of what Lauren said. Lukas is surrounded by love. Me, Dima, Gennady, Ernestine, June, and many, many more. So many people love him.

That is enough.

At least, I hope it is.

41

DIMA

Lauren Malone is the last to leave the party. "Are you sure you all don't need any help cleaning up?" she asks.

"I have people for that," I assure her.

Arya nods. "Yeah. Please don't worry about it. You've done more than enough. You are free to go."

Lauren bites her lip. "Actually, I can't check into my hotel for another hour, so I don't really have anywhere to go until then."

"Oh," Arya says, turning to me and then back to Lauren. "Then stay! By all means. You can hang out here. We are happy to have you."

"I don't want to be in your hair. Maybe I could just take Lukas off your hands for a little bit." Lauren leans forward and wrinkles her nose playfully, making Lukas giggle. "He dozed in everyone else's arms most of the party, so I doubt he'll take a nap and I'm sure you could both use one."

Arya starts to argue, but then thinks better of it and relents. "Okay, point conceded. I am exhausted, but you don't have to do that. We can go to the kitchen and chat and—"

Lauren shakes her head and holds out her arms for Lukas. I hand him over. "I'm going to go an entire week without touching a single baby while on vacation, which I'm pretty sure is harmful to my DNA. I need my fix. You two go nap. We will be… in the living room? If I can find it." She turns to Dima. "Do you provide maps of the establishment for your guests? Or is it more of a 'second star to the right and straight on 'til morning' kind of deal?"

I chuckle as I point down the hallway and to the right. "That way."

She grins. "Easy enough."

"There's a diaper bag by the front door," Arya adds. "And his formula is in the kitchen if he gets hungry. If that happens, you can always yell for me, and—"

Lauren rests a hand on Arya's shoulder and smiles. "I've made plenty of bottles before. I actually do this for a living, if you recall. Anyway, after footing the bill for my flight and hotel, this is the least I can do. You two, go take a nap or… whatever."

When she's gone, Arya turns to me. "What did she mean by that? *Whatever?*"

"I don't think she meant anything."

"She said it weird. Really weird."

"Something like this, maybe…" I lean down and nip at her neck.

But she swats my hand away, still frowning. "That isn't what she meant."

"That's what I heard."

"You're projecting."

"No, I'm reading between the lines."

Arya's eyes go wide as she stares at the door Lauren and Lukas just walked through. I can tell she doesn't want to voice her thoughts, but she does anyway. "What if Lauren is secretly working with Ilyasov?"

I snort. "What makes you think that?"

"Nothing specific," she says. "But it's happened before. It could happen again."

I grab Arya's shoulders and turn her towards me, pulling her close. "Lukas is safe."

She takes a deep breath, shuddering on the exhale. "I don't know…"

"You brought Lauren into this situation by luck and random chance," I remind her. "You asked her for help and she helped. I invited her here and she came. Lauren hasn't tried to force herself into our lives or push us or anything. If she was working for Ilyasov, she'd be either the luckiest spy on the planet or the worst one."

She sighs bitterly. "I know you're right. I know it. But still, I can't help worrying."

I wrap an arm around her back and kiss the top of her head. "I'm sorry you have to worry. But Lauren helped us bring Lukas back. She is the reason we found him. She's on our side."

Finally, Arya nods. We walk hand-in-hand down the hallway towards our room.

I close the door. Arya slips out of her heels.

"Next move is up to you," I say.

She makes a big show of thinking about it. Then, with a mischievous twinkle in her eye, she says, "Oh, I dunno. *Whatever.*"

I laugh, but all it takes is the tiniest cock of her hips for that laugh to deepen into a feral growl.

I slide the lock on the door into place and cross the room to where she's standing in front of the closet. I press her shoulders back against the wall, my hands wrapped around her trim waist, and kiss her.

Arya wraps her arms around my neck and kisses me lazily, her soft lips driving me mad. Her tongue slides against my lower lip and then dips into my mouth.

I drag my hands down her waist and over the swell of her hips. Then lower.

She put on a dress for the occasion. A long, flowing floral dress with high slits up the sides. I slip my hand between one of the slits and push the material back, bringing my hand to the warmth between her thighs.

Arya gasps against my mouth, and I love the taste of punch on her tongue. The vanilla sweetness of frosting on her lips.

The material of her panties is thin and I can already feel that it's damp when I curl my finger up her center. Arya shivers, so I do it again. And again.

"Touch me," she begs.

Happy to oblige, I shove the material aside and touch her with nothing between us.

Arya tips her head back against the wall and opens her thighs a little wider, giving me better access. I press kisses to the pulse in her neck and the silky skin beneath her earlobe. I lick a line across her collarbone and lavish her skin in kisses while my fingers explore her folds.

When my fingertip brushes over her clit, she gasps and grabs my wrist, holding me there. *More*, her body says without saying a word.

I give it to her.

I want to give Arya everything she wants. Everything she needs.

If she needs a distraction, I'm happy to let my body be that for her. Nothing brings me more joy than to wipe her mind of worries and fill it with dirty thoughts of the two of us.

I want to give her even more, more than she knows to ask for.

She still has my hand in a vice grip, but I pull my hand free, lift up the skirt of her dress, and drop to my knees.

I kiss my way up her thighs, noticing the way they tremble and we've only just begun.

Slowly, I peel her panties down her legs. The way Arya steps out of them, the muscles in her calves flexing and the soft curve of her thighs on display, makes me hard. I want those thighs wrapped around me. I want those muscles flexing for me.

I push my need down and focus on Arya's, blowing a warm breath over her center.

She squirms and I smile. Enjoying the torture. The anticipation.

When I do lean forward, though, pressing my lips to her center, sucking her into my mouth, the moan that escapes her lips is even better than I hoped for.

"Fucking heaven," she breathes, curling her fingers in my hair.

There's no sense of urgency when I'm between Arya's legs. No desire to hurry or rush to the next thing.

I love the way her body rolls against my mouth, the way her hands tug on my hair or push down on my head, directing me where she wants me. I especially love the way her thighs tense before she releases, shaking to an orgasm as I lap up every bit of her.

When I come out from under her skirt, Arya is leaned back against the wall with her eyes closed. Her cheeks are flushed, and even though it's been a while since we kissed, her lips are pink and swollen.

"Are you relaxed now?" I ask.

She sighs. "Oh God, yes. I'm surprised I'm still standing."

I stand up and unzip her dress down the back, letting it slip down her shoulders and puddle on the floor around her feet. Her bra is purple lace. I push down the cups just enough that I can bend down and suck her perfect pink nipples into my mouth.

Arya claps a hand on the back of my head and sighs. "Please take me to the bed and fuck me. If you keep doing that, I'm going to collapse."

Quickly, I undo my own pants and push them off along with my boxers. Arya reaches down to stroke my length once and then helps me slide a condom on. She still has hold of me when I wrap my hands around her thighs and lift her up. Immediately, she hooks her legs around my waist.

But instead of carrying her to the bed, I press her back against the wall. Her eyes widen, but they drift closed when I press myself at her opening and begin sliding into her.

Inch by inch, she takes me, and it's maddening to watch myself disappear inside of her, to watch her stomach clench and feel her legs tighten around my waist as she takes me. It's a sight precious enough to threaten all of my self-control.

But I manage to hold on and then I'm buried inside of her, lost in her warmth and her tightness. I drop my head to her shoulder and breathe.

"You feel fucking incredible. I'll never get over it," I whisper, kissing her neck. "I want to be in you all the time."

"We only have forty more minutes," she teases. "Will that do?"

I pull back and give her a devilish look. "It will have to."

Then, I slide out of her and thrust back in. Hard.

Her body bangs back against the wall, and then she arches her back, rolling herself over me.

Flexing her thighs, Arya lifts herself up to my tip and then drops back down, our bodies slapping together. She tips her head back, and I lean forward to suck on her hardened nipple.

"You're so big," she gasps, taking all of me inside her once again. "I want more."

I growl and spin around, moving towards the bed. I lay Arya just on the edge, her lower half still in the air, and hook her knees over my shoulders.

It's the way I took her the night we met. She was on an exam table in the vet clinic, and I stood in front of her, having no idea the delicious, tight woman in front of me would become so much more. So much more than a tight pussy to lose myself in for a few minutes.

Now, Arya is everything to me.

She and Lukas are my world. I want to show her that.

I grip the soft flesh of her hips, my fingers digging into the skin, and slam into her with everything I have.

Arya cries out and then bites her lip, nodding for me to keep going.

I do it again. And again. Increasing speed until she's clinging to the footboard with one hand and the comforter with the other, trying to ground herself. I don't care. I'll fuck her off the bed and onto the floor. Down the hallway if I have to.

I'm mad with how much I want her. With how much I need to release the desire and want inside of my chest.

"You're mine," I grit out between clenched teeth.

Arya lets go of the comforter and drags her hand down my chest, her nails leaving light marks across my skin. "I'm yours, Dima. Fuck me like I'm yours."

I pull out of her and flip her over in one fluid movement. Arya bends over the bed and spreads her legs, unfazed. I push back inside of her and then she brings her legs together, making the hold even tighter.

"Fuck," I moan. I grab Arya's hands and fold them across her lower back, using them like a leash, like a grip to better direct my movement.

As I thrust, I pull her back, and it feels so good I see stars in my vision.

"Harder," Arya begs, her face buried in the mattress. "I'm close."

I'm close, too, and I'm ready to bring us both home. To set us both free.

Giving her everything I have, I thrust into her again and again, and just when I think I'm going to have to release without letting her finish, Arya's thighs turn to concrete against mine, and then her body goes fluid.

She's already squeezing me so tight, but as the orgasm moves through her, I feel the muscles inside of her clench and hold. It's the last straw.

I release into her, slowly thrusting my way through an orgasm that won't seem to end. When it does, I lean forward, resting my head on her back. Feeling the rise and fall of her ragged breathing.

I fucking love this woman.

I love the way I feel when I'm inside of her—but I love the way I feel with her, too. Now, in post-orgasmic bliss, but also first thing in the morning when I see her in the curtain-filtered dawn light. Or before bed, when she's bare-faced and sleepy.

I love her and there's no looking back. No denying it. No moving on.

It's Arya or nothing for me. Forever.

42

ARYA
A FEW DAYS LATER

The kitchen in Dima's house is incredible.

I haven't spent much time in here because he has a chef who delivers meals most days, and cooking has never exactly been one of my strengths. Still, I love the shiny granite counters and stainless-steel appliances. Even just making a sandwich, I feel more professional in this kitchen.

"One day I'll make you a sandwich, too," I say to Lukas, smiling at him. "Yes, I will. But right now, just milk. Do you like milk?"

He smiles and coos. It's the nicest thing anyone's ever said to me.

He looks more and more like Dima all the time, I think. Dima disagrees. He swear that Lukas looks just like me.

But I see Dima in his blue eyes and the curve of his upper lip. Occasionally, Lukas makes a frowny face that always makes me laugh because it looks just like Dima's annoyed smolder.

Dima is in a meeting downstairs with his inner circle. They've been cooped up all morning, so when I hear footsteps behind me, I assume it's him, finally finished with work.

"Hey there, you. I was just thinking about—"

But it's not Dima.

It's not Dima at all.

"Hi, Arya," Vera says.

I haven't seen Ilyasov's wife since Dima and I went to Chicago together to visit them. Just before Ilyasov kidnapped Lukas from me.

Immediately, I set down my sandwich and bend down to scoop Lukas out of his seat. I clutch him to my thundering chest, certain Vera is here to take him away again.

"What are you doing here?"

She holds up her hands innocently. "I'm not here to cause trouble."

Usually, I'd trust a heavily pregnant woman was not trying to harm my child. In this case, I don't trust her for a fucking second.

"What are you doing here?" I ask again.

"I was in the neighborhood, so I popped in to say hello," she says like it's the most natural thing in the world.

"I don't have the faintest fucking interest in saying anything to you, Vera."

Vera has the audacity to look hurt by my words. As if she's surprised I want nothing at all to do with a woman who was responsible for kidnapping my son.

"Truthfully, I'm only here because I'm due any day and Ilyasov wants me at his side in case I go into labor. Isn't that precious?"

I snarl at her, "Just darling. Now get the fuck out."

Lukas is starting to fuss in my arms. No doubt he's feeling the tension that is rolling off of me in waves. I begin to bounce him, humming a soothing song in his ear.

Vera smiles at us. "You're natural as a mom. It suits you."

"Is that why you decided to take my son away from me?"

Vera doesn't answer right away. She flips her long hair over her shoulder, checks her French tips, runs her hands over her belly. "Like I said, I don't get too involved in Ilyasov's work stuff. That is his business. He told me what he planned to do, and I told him what I thought about it, but—"

"But you did nothing." Long repressed anger is beginning to rise to the surface, making my hands shake with rage. "Instead of talking Ilyasov down or doing a damn thing to stop an infant being kidnapped from his parents, you sat at home and did nothing. You're a fucking bitch. No better than him."

"I'm sorry you feel that way." She presses her painted lips together. "I expected you of all people would understand it isn't always possible to control the man you love. Especially when that man is like the Romanoff boys."

"I don't *control* Dima. I work *with* him. He's my partner." I shake my head. "If your relationship is so fucked up that Ilyasov does whatever he wants without any thought for you, then I feel sorry for you. But not sorry enough to forgive you."

"I don't want your forgiveness." Vera's voice is cold, but her face is blank. "I'm not here to ask for it. Ilyasov did what he felt he had to do and I'm sorry if it hurt you, but I stand by him."

If the woman wasn't nine months pregnant, I'd punch her in the face.

How dare she.

"Get out, you two-faced bitch," I growl. "When we showed up at your house in Chicago, you knew what Ilyasov was planning. What he had already done. You knew that he would betray us, but you treated me like a friend. You welcomed us into your home and played along with your husband's games without a second thought."

"I like to be a good hostess," she says with an easy shrug.

I can't fucking believe what I'm hearing. "Good hostess? You're complicit! You're just as guilty as Ilyasov is in every way, no matter what you tell yourself. You stand by while your husband hurts people for his own personal gain. It's despicable. It's disgusting. You are a monster, and I want you out of my house. Now."

"*Your* house?" Vera looks around like she expects to see my name painted somewhere. "If that's the case, then you are just as guilty as I am, Arya."

Vera isn't worth the breath I waste talking to her, so I don't plan to ask her to explain herself. But she decides to continue unprompted.

"I know you've been helping Dima complete the Trials. You think your moral integrity is somehow escaping unscathed? Dima has killed people. And you've helped Dima. That makes you not so innocent, I think."

"He killed a white supremacist and blackmailed a corrupt cop," I bite back. "People who were hurting other people. And he only did it because your husband forced him into this in the first place."

She shakes her head. "Ilyasov didn't force anyone to do anything. Dima could have given up power. Isn't that what you wanted him to do when you two were in Chicago? You wanted him to leave this life behind and be with you and Lukas. You wanted to get your precious baby boy away from this life. Yet here you are. You're living in his mansion and calling it your own. You're a hypocrite."

Her words hit closer to home than I would like. My skin is bright with sweat and my heart pounds so hard it hurts.

"Everything I've done was out of necessity. I had to try and make the best of the mess you and your husband left behind. I'm not a hypocrite—I'm a survivor."

Vera throws back her head and laughs. "God, it's sad hearing you talk yourself into delusions. I'm dying to hear how you'll justify the third Trial to yourself. That one is a doozy."

I clench my jaw, trying not to show that I have no idea what she's talking about.

I assumed Dima would tell me what the third Romanoff Trial entailed when the time came, but he hasn't said anything yet.

Truthfully, I kind of forgot. With the baby shower and the new nursery and how close the two of us have been, the last few days have felt like a paradise. I didn't want to pop the perfect bubble by bringing up Ilyasov or the Trials.

"Wait." Vera tips her head to the side, her hair falling in a thin silky sheet over one of her eyes. "You do know what the next Trial is, right? After all, you and Dima work together. Isn't that what you said?"

I clench my hand into a fist, fighting the urge to slap her. "I trust Dima."

She smiles. "Of course. You'd have to trust him… if you plan to let him kidnap and sell an innocent woman."

Suddenly, it feels like I'm the one who has been slapped.

I actually stagger back, clutching onto Lukas to be sure I don't drop him.

Kidnap…

And sell…

An innocent woman.

Her expression turns soft and sympathetic, but her eyes are alight with amusement. No matter how much Vera plays the role of the innocent bystander, she enjoys the pain.

She's a wounded animal, deep in her soul. But she's the special kind of wounded I used to see in my clinic from time to time—the kind who hurts others to make her own pain feel better.

"You didn't know, did you?" She pouts out her lower lip. "Poor Arya. I guess Dima doesn't tell you everything after all."

The whispered conversation I overheard between Dima and Gennady the day of the baby shower comes back to me.

There's no way to do this covertly. You'll have to announce what you did.

Is this what Gennady meant? Have I let myself be blind to the truth?

I feel sick.

"And that begs the question," Vera continues, "what else has Dima lied to you about? If he didn't tell you something like this—seeing as how it's such a personal topic for you, given all you've been through—then what else has he kept from you?"

I want to scream at Vera, but I can't find the words or my voice.

I'm stunned.

But the worst part is… I shouldn't be. I know what Dima is. What he's done.

And I've accepted it all along.

Maybe I just thought I could change him. Isn't that every woman's dream? Change the bad boy with the heart of gold into someone worthwhile? Fix him?

I was wrong. Worse, I was stupid.

He knows what I went through at Taras Kreshnik's house. He knows what Rose went through. I've cried into Dima's shoulder night after night. Weeping over my lost friend. Over the horrors she endured.

And now this?

Suddenly, voices echo down the hallway. The meeting is over.

Vera looks towards the encroaching voices and smiles. Then she throws up a small wave. "Well, I have to run. As always, great to see you, Arya. We should do this again sometime."

Just as fast as she appeared, Vera is gone.

43

DIMA

After the meeting is over and the men clear out, I head straight back to my office to think.

There's a lot to think about. Ilyasov. Albanians. Arya and Lukas.

Before the final thought can fully form in my mind, my office door slams open and Arya is standing in the doorway, hands on her hips.

It takes me a moment to see the murder glowing in her eyes. "What is it?" I ask.

"I just spoke to Vera."

"You what?"

"Your brother's wife. Remember her?"

"Don't fuck with me, Arya."

"She waltzed right into my kitchen like there was nothing special about it."

"She fucking what—?"

"She told me about the third Trial, Dima," she interrupts. Arya crosses her arms over her chest. That's when I notice the puffiness under her eyes. The slight smudging of her mascara.

She's been crying.

Fuck me. This shit with the third Romanoff Trial has been keeping me up at night. There's no good way to handle it. At least, none that I can think of.

How would she ever understand? And could I really expect her to?

Now, I don't have a choice. I have to make her understand.

"What did Vera tell you?"

"The truth!" Arya yells. "Unlike you. What else are you lying about, Dima? I thought we were a team, huh? I thought I was your *queen*? What a fucking lie. You're a liar."

"Arya, you need to—"

"I bet you filled Gennady in, didn't you?"

I frown. "Of course. But Gennady isn't—"

"Isn't what?" she cuts in. "Gennady isn't a woman? Gennady isn't hysterical? Gennady isn't a victim like me?"

She's hysterical. I can't blame her.

But I also can't deal with this shit right now.

The headache that has been hiding behind my eyes all day comes out in full force. I need quiet and darkness. I need to think.

"We need to do this another time," I hiss.

Arya slams her hands on the desk. "We wouldn't be doing this at all if it were up to you, would we? You wanted to keep me in the dark until it's done. You wanted to lie to me and then act like everything was all rosy and perfect. What happened to your moral backbone? Remember when you told me you'd *never* sell someone? What happened to that?"

I stand up and crash my fist down on the desk. "This happened!" I bellow. "All of this shit happened. My Bratva was taken, my son was kidnapped, and my brother betrayed me. My world turned upside down, and suddenly, I became willing to make a few exceptions. I dare you to fucking blame me, Arya."

Her nostrils flare and her chest heaves as she stares at me. "Exceptions that don't hurt you. Exceptions that punish other innocent people. That's disgusting, Dima."

"Sit down." I point to the chair across from my desk. "Sit down and we'll talk."

Arya shakes her head. "I don't want to sit down. You Romanoffs are all the fucking same. You only care about yourselves and what's best for you. Fuck everyone else."

Finally, the thin hold I have on my self-control snaps. I jump to my feet again and this time, my chair clatters to the ground behind me. "Are you out of your fucking mind? How can you say that after everything I've done to help you? Do you think it was in my benefit to hunt you down at Taras Kreshnik's house and set you free? I saved your fucking life."

She gasps. "You blame me for having to look for Lukas? And here I thought you loved him."

"That isn't what I meant, goddammit!" My jaw is clenched so hard I feel like my teeth will crack. "Even when it's almost cost me everything, I chose to take care of you. To protect you. To protect our *son*. I'm not the same as my brother."

"Aren't you? I don't see a difference. You're willing to destroy anyone and anything in your effort to reclaim your Bratva. Sounds like Ilyasov to me."

"Ilyasov is willing to risk his own family. I'd never do that."

"How the fuck do I know that?!" Arya screams. "You know what I went through after Brigitte sold me like fucking cattle. And you know what Rose went through. You know how much that fucked me up, but you still agreed to these Trials knowing what you would have to do. Knowing you'd have to hurt people. It's… it's disgusting. *You* are disgusting."

"Thanks for telling me what you really think of me," I snarl. "If I ever get a comment box in my office, you'll be the first person I call to drop your thoughts."

Her eyes narrow to slits. "Don't make fun of me."

"Don't come into my office and call me disgusting. Don't stand in my house and insult me."

She leans away from me, eyebrow raised. "Your house, huh? I suppose it is *your house*, isn't it?"

"Last time I checked, yes."

"Maybe I'll just take Lukas and leave then. Find my own place. I never wanted him to grow up in this environment, anyway."

"Leave if you want." I wave a hand towards the door. "But if you think I'm going to let you take my son out of this house, you're wrong. If you kidnap him, I'll have the force of my Bratva on you in an instant. You won't even make it off the property."

Arya is looking at me like she doesn't know me. Like we've never met.

And I can't help but hear my father's voice over and over again in my head.

Love is a weapon.

Love is a weapon.

Love is a weapon.

He was dead fucking right. And right now, it's slicing me wide open.

Without another word, Arya storms out of my office, slamming the door behind her.

And I'm left here. The last of my world crumbling to pieces—just when I thought it was almost back together.

44

DIMA
A FEW HOURS LATER

When Arya leaves, I start to drink.

And drink.

And drink.

The room around me swirls in the sea of alcohol coursing through my veins. *How long has it been since I've drank?* I think, lifting the bottle back to my lips.

The vodka Gennady bought Arya for the baby shower is good shit. It goes down easily. Perhaps too easily.

My father was the drinker. Not me. He was the one who drowned his rage in vodka—only for it to rear its ugly head again as soon as he'd had enough. Ilyasov inherited that gene, too.

I've never needed anything to control my inner demons. I'm only just now starting to see that maybe it's because they've always controlled me.

I go to set the bottle back down on the desk. But everything is fuzzy and doubled. I miss and the bottle goes tumbling through the air.

It crashes against the ground. Expensive vodka glugs out onto the carpet. Shards of glass rain everywhere and, as I fall to my knees in a belated attempt to prevent the accident, they slice me open.

Blood leaks from the cuts in my hand. I fall on my ass and lean back against the desk with a grimace. One thought runs through my head again and again: *This is Arya's fault.*

I thought I loved her. I thought she needed my protection.

I was so fucking wrong about both of those things.

I don't love her and I don't need her. She sure as fuck doesn't need me. Maybe it's time to do what I should've done a long time ago. As far back as the day I turned down the wrong road and saw her giving birth in her car: gone my own way.

That's the final thought in my head before I succumb to the darkness intruding at the corner of my eyes.

In the morning, I'll say goodbye.

Forever.

~

In the morning, the headache is back—with a motherfucking vengeance.

Before I even open my eyes, I feel it pounding behind my lids, crashing through my temples, exploding through the top of my head.

There's also something jabbing into my hip bone. I start to lift myself up, but the movement makes my stomach jostle and my head swim. I slow down and grimace my way through the motion. At some point, I realize that I'm lying slumped across my desk.

"What the fuck?" My mouth feels like cotton and tastes like sour vomit.

I slide off my desk and lean back against the wall, a hand pressed to my forehead. As I do, the events of last night start to come back.

Drinking. Cursing Arya. More drinking. And apparently, smashing the vodka bottle to pieces and slicing my hands into ribbons.

I push myself upright with a pained groan. Arya didn't do this to me.

I did this to me.

My phone buzzes on my desk. I fumble for it up, squinting against the glare of the screen. It's a number I don't recognize, but the message is clear enough.

Trial #3.

That's all it says. But that's all it needs to say.

Ilyasov completed the trial. *Blyat.*

I have a choice to make now. The thought leaves a sick feeling in my stomach.

I'll do this for my Bratva. But it doesn't mean I have to like it. No matter what Arya may think of me, I don't enjoy causing pain. I'm not Ilyasov. I wouldn't throw my family into the fire just to gain power.

Suddenly, a thought occurs to me. If Ilyasov seems to be willing to sacrifice everything he loves to win…

Perhaps I should put that to the test.

I grab my keys and run for the car.

Arya is probably still in the house. Maybe she even heard me leave. But she didn't come out to ask where I was going and even if she did, I don't owe her any explanations. Not anymore.

It's clear everything in my life is in flux right now. The only thing I can control is whether I'm the don of the Romanoff Bratva or not. After today, I intend to be.

As I wait to see if the intel I'm using is accurate, I have time to wonder if I'm making the right move. She had to have known what her husband planned to do with Lukas. She isn't innocent. None of us are.

But the moment arrives before I can decide to abort the mission. The door to a boutique shop opens… and Vera steps out.

After she showed up in the kitchen and talked to Arya, I had one of my moles in the NYPD run a search on the plates of the car she arrived in. A little bit of recon later and my soldiers tracked the car here.

And then I followed.

Part of me wonders if this is all a mistake. It seems unlike Ilyasov to be so careless as to let his wife use the same car again and again. She ought to be changing cars, switching bodyguards, throwing any hunters off her scent.

But she didn't. And their mistake is my gain.

Her belly is huge, but she's still dressed in a sleek pair of black jeans with a long-sleeved maternity top and some knee-high boots. High heels.

She isn't paying attention. Her face is buried in her phone, and she's alone. No guards. No Ilyasov. Just Vera.

A sitting fucking duck.

"Need a ride?"

Vera's head snaps up. Her face is a surprised, friendly mask for a second before she realizes it's me.

Then I see her fear.

It's all in her eyes. A slight widening, a dilation of the pupils, a darting around to see which direction her help will come from.

Nowhere, I want to tell her. There will be no help.

I pull my gun from the holster on my hip and press it against her hip, keeping it hidden from onlookers' sight. "Come with me."

"You wouldn't shoot a pregnant woman, Dima. You're above that."

I shrug. "I thought you and my brother were above kidnapping an infant from his parents. We all make costly mistakes. Are you willing to lose your life for yours?"

Vera looks around again. "You..."

I prod the gun into her side again. "No one is going to help you. If you scream, I'll kill them."

She turns away from me, nose wrinkled. "Are you drunk?"

"Get in the car," I order, voice low. "Or I'll shoot you and anyone who gets in my way. *Now.*"

She must decide I'm deadly serious because she walks with me to the car. I help her into the passenger seat.

An older woman walking by comments on us to her husband. "Look at her. She's about to pop. How sweet."

If only they knew.

When I get in, my gun stays trained on Vera. "Move? I'll shoot. Talk? I'll shoot. Try anything and I shoot."

She stays quiet. I'm glad.

My head still fucking hurts.

45

ARYA

Dima must've passed out.

He stayed in his office all night. Even if he hadn't, he would have had to break the door down to get into our room. I locked it.

By the point in the night where he was shouting mumbled words at the ceiling and I could hear glass shattering, I thought he might be drunk enough to actually try to break the door down. But he didn't.

So when I woke up in the middle of the night, I tip-toed across the hall and checked on him. He was sprawled across his desk with a puddle of drool coming from his mouth and a bloody cut on his hand.

My first instinct was to take care of him. To rush forward and clean him up, get him to bed, give him some water.

That instinct needs to die.

Because I have to get out of here.

Dima told me he'd never let me leave with Lukas. I don't plan on asking his permission, though. I still have the passports Arnie Fleishman made for us and the last of my cash savings. It's not enough to get us overseas. But it's enough to get us away from here. Lukas and I could lay low while I work, save some money, and figure out a game plan.

Early in the morning, before Lukas is awake, I shove blankets under the crack in the bedroom door to keep my voice from carrying and call Arnie Fleishman.

"This is Arnie."

"Arnie, it's Arya."

There's a long pause. I know he's remembering the last time we met, when I held a knife to his throat. I crossed a line, but so did he. I was desperate and he pushed me. He shouldn't have done that.

"I know I shouldn't be calling you and I know you're probably pissed at me—"

"I'm not mad," he sighs. "I was backing out of a deal. I was a coward and I deserved your threats. I'm not happy about it, but I understand it."

Wow. That isn't at all what I expected him to say, but I'm grateful that's at least one less fire I need to put out.

"Great. I'm sorry, but you are the only person I could think to call. I just need you to do me a favor."

He sucks in a breath. "A favor? Arya…"

"I can pay you later, but I'm desperate, Arnie. I wouldn't call if I wasn't."

Another long pause. "Tell me what it is."

"I need you to book me a flight to Chicago. Under the names on the passports you made me. As soon as possible."

"You can't book your own flights?" he asks. "I'm a criminal, not a travel agency."

I've thought about this a thousand different ways, and I can't think of a single way to book myself a flight that doesn't end in Dima being able to track where I'm going. Gennady could probably get the information from my phone if I did it online, and I at least know Arnie's number is unlisted. Even if Gennady wanted to track it, he won't be able to. Arnie paid the best people in the business to make sure he was untraceable.

"I can't explain everything to you right now, but I'm not in a safe space and I can't book my own flight. I need you to do it for me. You call, book the flights, and I'll pay you back as soon as I can. I'm good for the money. You know I am."

"*Do* I know that?" He sounds dubious. "I like you, girl, but this is a lot."

"If you don't, I'm done." I don't like being helpless, but I level with him. "If you don't help me, I don't have anyone else to turn to."

Everyone in my life is too innocent to involve, too corrupted to trust, or dead. Arnie is the only one left.

Distantly, I hear him groaning, almost like he pulled the phone away from his ear to let out his frustration. Then he breathes into the receiver. "Fine. What time is good?"

"As soon as possible. I'm thirty minutes from the airport."

"I'll call you right back." He hangs up the phone. I sit on the floor next to the bed for a moment, trying to quell the shaking in my hands.

Then I get up and start to pack.

∼

Arnie calls me back and gives me the details for the flight. "It leaves in four hours. One-way trip."

I thank him for his help. He tells me not to mention it.

"Never mention it," he snaps. "And as far as favors go, you are fresh out, girl. I'm happy to take you on as a customer, but I'm not going to cross Dima Romanoff again."

"That makes two of us," I murmur.

We hang up. I pack a few outfits for Lukas and a few things of my own. And that's it.

I'm ready to go.

Most of my stuff is still hanging in the closet, but it won't take Dima long to realize we're gone. He is an observant man. As soon as he gets back to the house and comes in here to talk, he'll know what's going on and he'll come looking for us.

By the time that happens, I intend to disappear.

46

DIMA

I've been pacing in this godforsaken warehouse for what feels like miles. My thoughts are ping-ponging back and forth, back and forth.

This is wrong. This is necessary.

This is immoral. This is justice.

And the whole time, in the other room, I can hear Vera thrashing and wailing.

The question remains: What the hell am I going to do with her?

"I can't believe we're fucking doing this," Gennady mumbles for the tenth time since he arrived. "This is fucking crazy."

I whirl around and scowl at him. "I'm doing what's right for my Bratva. For my family."

"It's not you, Dima," he whispers in a hoarse rasp.

"I didn't ask for your fucking input, Gennady," I snarl.

He sighs and stands. "I'm going to go check on her," he says. He starts to stride away towards the door separating us from the cramped little room where Vera is chained and gagged while I decide who to sell her to.

But just before he opens the door, he pauses. He starts to speak, but he doesn't look back at me. "Dima, when we first met all those years ago, do you know why I followed you? Do you know why I was your friend before I was your ally?"

I don't answer. It's a trap question. He's playing fucking games with me, just like Arya does.

"Because you were a good man," he says, answering his own question. "A good man in a bad world. Now… well, I don't know what you are anymore. But worse than that, I don't think you know what you are. For your sake and for the sake of everyone around you, I hope you figure it out soon."

Then, before I can answer, he opens the door and slips inside. I hear chains clanking as he no doubt tries to make our prisoner comfortable.

I should tell him it's a waste of his fucking empathy. She's as bad as anyone in this whole goddamn underworld. She helped steal my son. She's bearing Ilyasov's spawn, helping him unleash more of himself on all of his enemies.

She deserves this.

But Gennady's words linger in the air. *I don't think you know what you are.*

What a ridiculous thing to say. Of course I know. I'm what I was always meant to be: don of the Romanoff Bratva. Unquestioned. Unchallenged. Untouchable.

Ilyasov tried to topple me, and look what happened? I have his wife in chains. The Albanians are dead or dying. The D'Onofrio clan has had its head chopped off.

And who's standing tall amidst all that bloodshed? Me. Dima Romanoff. The true heir to my father's legacy.

This is all I need. Not Arya, not Ilyasov—and if he's so uncertain about the path I'm taking, then I don't need Gennady, either. All I've ever asked for is undying loyalty. Anyone who doesn't give me that is extra baggage.

The door opens again. I expect Gennady to come out and guilt trip me again. *She's in distress* or *It's not good for her* or some other such bullshit.

But instead, he runs out into the space like he just saw a ghost. "Dima, come quick!" he yells.

"What is it?" I snap. "Does she want a fucking foot rub?"

"No," he says. "Her water broke."

My jaw drops. "You're fucking kidding."

Gennady shakes his head. "Her legs are wet and there's a puddle on the floor. She's been moaning for a while. I thought it was because she was tied up, but maybe she has been in pain. Like, in labor."

I race in the room. Vera's eyes are wide and terrified. True to Gennady's word, her black jeans are soaked.

"What are we going to do?" Gennady stands up and paces away from me and then back, nervous energy fizzling off of him like he's a live wire. "I don't know how to birth a baby."

"Shut up," I say again. "Let me think."

The hospital is out of the question. Too many loose ends there. Too many questions. Letting her give birth in an abandoned, dirty warehouse is an option, albeit not a great one. After all, Arya did it in the back of a car with only me to help her.

But Vera is pregnant with twins. Twice the risk. And even after coming this far… Even after everything she's done to me and Arya and Lukas… Even after everything Ilyasov has schemed…

I can't let this woman die.

Think, motherfucker! I roar at myself. *Come up with a plan.*

"Dima," Gennady warns, "she is not doing so well. What's the call?"

Vera is doubled over, her face red as she groans through what I now realize is a contraction. She's pulling taut against her chains.

I want to call Arya. She'd know how to make shit right.

But that ship has sailed. So I try a different route.

~

"Dima, hello!" Lauren says cheerfully when she answers the phone. "Are you calling to whisk me away on another vacation? This one isn't over yet, but I can call out of work again. I'm sure they can get on without me at the clinic."

"I need help."

"What is it? Where are you?" Lauren's voice shifts from casual to professional in an instant.

"I'll text you the address. Come now. Run, don't walk."

"Yes, of course. I'll be right there." She hangs up and I text her the address.

I call Sacha, too. He's the mafia doctor, mostly schooled in knife and gunshot wounds, but it's better than nothing.

"Should I untie her?" Gennady asks, hovering over Vera, who is writhing so hard the chair is starting to wobble around. If it tips over, she wouldn't be able to protect herself or her stomach.

I nod. "I don't think she's in any position to run away right now."

Even in the midst of her pain, Vera finds the energy to glare up at me. The second her hands are untied, she rips the gag out of her mouth.

"You son of a fucking bitch!" she screams, her anger transitioning into another contraction. "What did you expect to happen kidnapping a pregnant woman? Take me to a hospital!"

"No."

Her eyes widen in horror. "Are you serious? I'm giving birth *here*? Dima, are you out of your fucking mind?"

Gennady has gone white with the stress and from the force of Vera's grip on his hand. He's helping her to the floor, and she is squeezing his knuckles so tightly I'm sure she's going to break something.

"You can't do this to me," she cries. "And my babies. What about my babies?"

"What about my baby?" I snarl. "Where was your empathy then?"

Gennady pats her hand and looks up at me, clearly losing his shit. "When is the doctor getting here?"

"Soon," I mutter. "Hopefully, soon enough."

We suffer through ten more minutes of Vera's contractions and screams before the rusted out front door opens.

Lauren's voice echoes through the space. "Hello?" She steps into the warehouse timidly, looking around in confusion. When she spots me, she stops walking. "What's going on? Why are you here?"

"It's a long story, but—"

Before I can finish, Vera lets out a cry. Lauren sprints across the room and drops to her knees next to the prone woman. Then she looks back up at me, mouth hanging open. "What is happening?"

"She's having a baby. Two, actually."

She stutters over her next words. "Why—here?—she should… Fuck, she needs a doctor! A hospital!"

"You're a doctor," I remind her.

"A pediatrician!" she shouts. "I'm not an OB."

"I'm having twins," Vera says, grabbing Lauren's arm and pulling her close. "My water broke and I'm having twins. I can feel them coming."

"There's no time to get to the hospital. You need to help her."

Lauren growls in frustration, but I can tell she's scared, too. "You could have driven her in the time it took me to drive here. Or called an ambulance. What is really going on?"

Those questions will have to wait. Vera's cries are intensifying.

The rusted hinges on the front door squeal again and Sacha comes running in. When he sees the very pregnant woman on the floor, he stops short and then curses under his breath.

"Bloody hell, Dima. I've seen a lot of shit. But this is too much."

As if to punctuate the point, Vera throws her head back and lets out a loud scream that echoes off the cobweb-covered rafters.

"Start working," I order coldly. "You're running out of time."

47

DIMA

Somehow, it works.

Lauren and Sacha may not be OBs, but they know how to deliver babies. Gennady and I stand off to the side while they toil, comforting Vera while instructing her when to breathe and when to push.

"Holy hell," Gennady winces, holding up a hand to shield Vera's nether regions from view. "That's horrific. I'm scarred on female genitalia for life."

"I'm sure the world's women will rejoice."

He scowls. "Not funny."

"Trust me, you'll be fine. I—"

Vera's scream cuts me off. And a new scream: the scream of a newborn.

Lauren holds the baby up to the light. I can't help but be reminded of the first time I saw Lukas. And the way I saw Arya looking at him. Vera has the same look of wonder on her face.

That's when it hits me—a tidal wave of guilt like nothing I've ever experienced in my life.

Maybe it's because of how full circle this moment feels. I delivered my son from Arya with my own two hands and held him up to the light just like that. Did I look at him like Arya did? Like Vera is doing now?

What have I done? What am I doing? I've come so fucking far down the rabbit hole that I don't know if I'll ever make it back to the surface.

But if I don't, I'm going to burn in hell forever.

Because with all the things I've done, I'm no better than the people I did them to. Vera took my child—am I about to take hers?

Jorik Bogdanovich Jorik separated a mother from her newborn and sold Arya into slavery. Which, regardless of my reasons, is exactly what I'm planning to do with Vera. Am I like him?

I'm Ilyasov. I'm Jorik. I'm Giorgio.

Worst of all... I'm my father. I've become the one man I swore I'd never become.

Everything I ever wanted is right at my fingertips. But the price for having it is my soul.

A few minutes later, a second cry echoes through the warehouse. Both babies are both out.

Gennady sags with relief. "Thank God that's over."

Lauren and Sacha tend to Vera for a while, cleaning her up and checking her over, and then Lauren steps away, wipes a forearm across her sweaty forehead, and sits down on the concrete floor next to where I'm standing. Her arms drape across her knees as she watches the new mother nurse her babies.

"Now, is anyone going to tell me why in the hell I just delivered babies in an abandoned warehouse?"

I sit down next to her and shake my head. "It's better if I don't."

"Arya has said that about a lot of things. It makes me think you're not as nice of a guy as you seem, Dima Romanoff."

She's not wrong. But I don't say that. I don't say anything, actually.

Lauren groans and lays back, taking a deep breath. "You know, I originally wanted to be an OB. But it was too high stress. For all of the joy, there's a lot of heartache, too. I hated the idea of telling a woman they've lost the pregnancy or there's something wrong with their baby. That would be the worst. I love babies, but bringing them into the world is a big responsibility. So I switched to taking care of them once they're born. I am now confident I made the right choice."

"I'm glad you're here."

Lauren takes another deep breath. "Speaking of who's here, where is Arya right now? Does she know this is going on?"

"She's... not with me."

Lauren sits up and stares at me. "What does that mean?"

"We went our separate ways."

"Oh. Shit." Lauren frowns. "You two were so happy just a few days ago. What in the hell happened?"

"More than I could ever explain."

"More than your child being kidnapped and having to track him down yourself without the help of police?" she asks in disbelief. "Because after something like that, I would have guessed you two could get through anything."

"Apparently not."

I don't feel like talking about it. There are enough questions and doubts rolling through my own head without any external processing.

Lauren pats my arm. "I wouldn't write it off so fast. You two could find your way back to each other."

Without even thinking about it, I shake my head. "It's not worth it. Love is a weapon."

Hearing the words out loud, I realize how much I sound like my father. I hate it with a fucking passion.

Which is why I'm surprised by Lauren's immediate answer. "You're right."

My attention snaps to her. "What?"

"You're right," she says again. "Love is definitely a kind of weapon. It can hurt like a bitch. I see it all the time as a doctor. Pain in every size, shape, and color. Loved ones die. Pregnancies fail. Families splinter. In so many ways, love can hurt us worse than anything in the entire world."

I look at her, blinking, unsure how to respond.

"But then I also see the other side of it, too," she continues. "I see the couples who tried for years to get pregnant show up with a baby they love more than the entire world. I see sick people get better, families reunited. I see how much joy love can bring. So yes, it can hurt. But it's pain with a purpose."

"What purpose is that?" I scoff.

"Happiness," she says, smiling to herself. "Joy. The meaning of life."

Arya's face appears in my mind. No matter how hard I try to wipe her away, she stays put. One thing is undeniably true: whatever pain I'm feeling now is worth it when it comes to Arya. It's always been worth it.

I point at Vera. "Her husband is abusive," I tell Lauren. "I brought her here because he was searching for her and I didn't want him to hurt the babies."

It's a lie, mostly. But there's some truth in it. Enough for Lauren.

Lauren narrows her eyes, trying to see if she believes me or not. Eventually, she shrugs. "Okay. So can I take the babies to the hospital? They should still be seen by a doctor."

I nod. "Go." She and Sacha make quick work of getting the babies loaded up and to the hospital. Vera begs to go with them, but I refuse.

"What are you going to do with me, Dima?" she asks, her lower lip trembling. "If you're going to kill me, just do it."

"I'm not going to kill you."

Truthfully, I don't know what the fuck I'm going to do. Realizing I'm more like my enemies than I ever wanted to be is a wake-up call I wasn't ready for.

"Then what do you want?" she sobs. "This has been the worst day of my life. Is that what you wanted? If you wanted to punish me, you did it. Job well done. I'm miserable."

"I don't feel bad for you," I tell Vera. "The only reason I'm second-guessing my plan is because I don't want to live everyday knowing I'm as heartless and cruel as you and my brother. I don't want to be a monster."

Vera laughs. "Too late, Dima. It runs in your blood. You and your brother are both monsters."

"Not a very nice way to talk about your husband."

"Well, he's not very nice to me, either, sometimes."

"Then why stay with him? Why warm his bed and have his children?"

She bites her lip. "We have an… arrangement."

An arrangement. Like my mother and father. The love between them had died out long before, but they stayed together for the usual reasons. Power. Money. Control. They coexisted as best as they could until…they couldn't.

I never wanted what they had, but it doesn't surprise me that Ilyasov followed in our father's footsteps. Even after everything that happened between them, he always admired our father in ways I didn't.

Suddenly, the door bursts open. Gennady runs across the warehouse, his breathing heavy. He'd gone to deal with some Bratva business in the middle of the chaos.

"Do you have your phone? I've called you a million fucking times."

I pull my phone out of my pocket and realize it's dead. "Tell me now."

"I really didn't want to deliver this news in person."

My muscles clench. "What news?"

"Arya and Lukas are gone."

The jolt of fear that rockets through my chest is painful and sharp. It feels like my heart is being ripped out of my rib cage.

"Has Ilyasov called?" I demand. "If he couldn't get through on my phone, he would have tried to call someone else. Probably you."

Gennady shakes his head. "He hasn't called. But Dima… I don't think this was your brother."

I stop and stare at him, brows knit together. "What the hell are you talking about?"

"Clothes were missing from the closet, a suitcase is gone, and Lukas's diaper bag, too. It looked like someone packed them up. I doubt Ilyasov would have bothered. Plus, nothing was disturbed and no one saw anyone come or go on the security cameras… except Arya."

It takes a second for the meaning in his words to sink in. For me to fully understand what he's telling me.

"Arya left."

I don't know why I'm surprised. And I don't know why it hurts as bad as it does.

She's left before. More than once. But this one cuts deepest of all.

I spin around and reach out a hand to Vera, gesturing for her to stand up.

"I just gave birth," she snaps.

"Which is why I'm helping." I bend down and slowly pull her to her feet, wrapping her arm around mine. "We're leaving."

"Dima, come on," Gennady says, walking next to me as Vera and I slowly make our way across the warehouse. "You can't be thinking about going through with this Trial right now. You have to find Arya. Fuck Ilyasov and Vera. What about your family?"

"I'm not selling her. I'm ending this."

"What the hell are you saying?" Gennady demands.

I sigh. "I'm saying I quit. This isn't worth it anymore."

48

ARYA

I'm on my way to the airport when something grabs my attention out of the window: a familiar wrought iron gate set in the middle of a gray granite wall.

I pull to a slow stop in the middle of the road. Car horns scream as other drivers veer around me, giving me the finger and throwing curses in my direction.

But I don't care. I feel like I'm being summoned in this direction. I have to go in there, whether I like it or not.

So I turn into the graveyard.

It's like another world in here. The road is just beyond the borders of the low wall, but all the sound seems to stop at the perimeter. I park the car near a familiar patch of grass and get out.

Freeing Lukas from his car seat, I take him into my arms. He's been alternating between whimpers or wails since we left Dima's house. Even now that I'm holding him, he's still fussy. It's almost like he knows we're making a big decision and he's trying to let me know he isn't happy.

What little kid would be? I'm taking him away from his dad. I can look at Dima and his job and see the danger, but Lukas just sees his father. Even if he isn't old enough to know what that means yet.

Or maybe he does know, on some deep, cellular level. He always grins when Dima walks into the room. He settles for Dima easier than anyone else. When Dima talks, Lukas presses himself against his chest and falls asleep.

Now, he'll only have me. Forever.

I have to remind myself that I'm not alone. Not with Lukas. He and I will be our own family. We'll take care of each other.

That was my original plan, anyway. But no matter how hard and fast I've tried to run from my past, there's no escaping one truth: I also had a family *before* Lukas. Before Dima and before Jorik, too.

In the beginning, there was me…

…and there was Mom.

Still clutching Lukas like he might fly away if I let go, I walk down the path between the gravestones. It's a gray, windy day outside. My hair flaps across my face.

I pause at the headstone I came for. *Elira Georgeovich,* it reads. *Beloved Mother.*

I sink to my knees on the grass. "I always liked your name, Mom," I whisper—as if she can hear me.

"Elira" is Albanian for "the free one." Something about that always sounded so nice to me. Even back then, when I was too young to know better, there was an airy appeal to the idea of freedom. Of leaving all your shit behind and flying off into the blue sky.

And I liked yours, comes a voice in my head.

I shiver. She's been dead for almost twenty years and I can still imagine exactly what my mother sounds like. Maybe it's the stress or maybe I'm going crazy, but the wind in the trees overhead makes me think I'm hearing her right now.

Fuck it. The whole world is burning to ashes. Even if I sit here in an empty graveyard and have a conversation with my dead mother, I'm far from the craziest person I've met in the last few months.

Aryana means "the noble one," you know, Mom says.

"I know," I sigh, rolling my eyes. "You used to say that all the time when you were high."

It made me cringe back then. It still makes me cringe—but for different reasons.

When I was a little girl, Mom used to get high on her own supply. Those were the only times she told me she loved me. *You're my beautiful little princess,* she'd say. *That's why I named you that.*

Now, though, it makes me think of what Dima called me. *His queen.* Did Mom's princess turn into the don's queen?

"No," I say out loud. "Fuck that. I'm no one's queen. I'm not noble. I'm not special. I just want to be normal."

A single tear rolls down my cheek. It's all I've ever wanted—to be normal. To be the free one.

"But you're the only 'free one,' aren't you, Momma?" I snarl sarcastically. "You died and left me behind. Left me trapped. Left me to fend for myself."

I touch the scars on my jaw—the ones she gave me when she brought our house crumbling down on our heads. The salty tear mingles with my fingertips. God, the memories of my world crashing on top of me are so fresh that it's like they happened yesterday. What a sick and twisted metaphor for my whole fucking life.

Lukas is playing in the grass at my feet. He's weirdly quiet now, almost as if he recognizes that his mother is on the verge of losing her mind.

"What am I supposed to do, Mom?" I say as I stroke Lukas's velvety cheek with the pad of my thumb. "You left me and it broke my heart. Is taking Lukas away from Dima the same thing? Is it wrong to separate a child from their parent? Am I cursing him or am I saving him? I don't know what's right. And I'm so, so tired of trying to do the right thing all the time. It hasn't gotten me anywhere good. So please, just tell me what to do."

The wind swishes through the trees again. But this time, I don't hear a voice in it. No Mom. No nothing.

"Come on, Mom," I beg. "Please just give me some stupid sign. Tell me to run. Tell me to stay. Tell me *something*."

More silence. A lone raindrop hits the ground next to me. I close my eyes and let my chin fall against my chest.

Then: "Arya?"

I look up in alarm. That wasn't breeze in the leaves or my own fevered imagination. That was a real person. "Mom?" I say hopefully. "Mom, is that—"

"Not quite," Gennady says grimly.

I turn to see him standing next to my mother's gravestone. I freeze for only a fraction of a second before leaping into action. I snatch up Lukas and scurry away towards the parked car a few dozen yards away.

"Easy there," Gennady says, trying to calm me down.

"No!" I cry out. "No, you're not taking me back to him! No! Gennady, I—"

"Arya, relax. I'm not taking you back to him."

I'm almost to the car now. Lukas is crying again, no doubt because he senses me freaking out. But the calm in Gennady's voice slows me down.

"How did you even find me?" I gasp.

He holds up his cell phone. "A good spy always keeps his friends as close as his enemies."

"You tracked me?"

"Guilty."

I shake my head. "I'm not your friend, Gennady."

He nods sadly like he understands and expected that answer. "Maybe not, but I'm trying to be yours, Arya."

"What does that mean?"

"Honestly, I'm not even sure. Just thought it sounded kinda deep and cryptic. We're in a graveyard, after all."

I snort through my tears. "How can you be funny when the world is falling to pieces?"

Gennady tilts his head to the side. "Because it's the only way I know how to be. You'd know something about that, wouldn't you?"

"What does *that* mean?"

"Look at you," he says, gesturing to the car and the bags visible in the trunk. "You're running away. This isn't the first time you've tried that, is it?"

"Stop asking me these goddamn leading questions, Gen."

He chuckles bitterly. "Am I wrong?"

Lukas has quieted down and is looking back and forth between Gennady and me. My back is up against the cold metal surface of the car, but the frantic sense of fight-or-flight has receded somewhat since Gennady surprised me.

"No," I admit softly. "You're not wrong."

"We do what we've always done. I laugh because I don't know what else to do. You run because you don't know what else to do. And Dima—"

"Don't talk about him," I snap. "Don't even say his name."

He nods again, so empathetic that I want to slap him across the face and tell him to stop pitying me. "I understand why you'd say that."

I bark out another laugh. "No, you definitely do not. You don't even know the half of it."

"I know that he's suffering without you," he offers.

"Bullshit."

"He is," Gennady insists. "That's why I'm here."

"Oh, yeah?" I throw out sarcastically. "Is he expecting me to volunteer as a sacrifice for the third Trial?"

He winces. "Of course not, Arya. He would never."

"But you know what it is, don't you?"

"Yes," Gennady says. "I know what the third Trial is."

"He told me when we met that he'd never sell a woman. And look at what he's trying to do now. So don't say 'he would never,' Gennady. You can't promise me that. He's trampling all over the line he swore he'd never cross."

"For you! And for Lukas!" Gennady lets out a long breath. "Our life isn't always pretty, Arya. Dima has to make tough decisions. So many people rely on him. Ilyasov's leadership would destroy the city."

I roll my eyes. "Noble fucking Dima. A regular knight in shining armor."

"He saved you, didn't he?"

Gennady's words stun me. They're so simple and yet so accurate.

Dima *did* save me. Time and time again, he risked himself to do what was best for me and for Lukas.

"Maybe," I admit. "But that's in the past. He went too far this time, Gennady. There's no coming back from some things."

"In this case, I might be inclined to agree with you. What he did today is… not good."

I frown. "What did he do?"

"He kidnapped Vera."

My heart plummets. "He *what?*"

"He's desperate, Arya. I couldn't calm him down or anything. He just called me and told me that he'd tracked her after she left the house from talking to you, he picked her up, and he had her in a Bratva warehouse in the meatpacking district."

I can feel the blood rushing in my ears. My fingertips are trembling. Lukas is squirming again, too.

"She's… she's pregnant," I stammer. "He wouldn't actually…"

"She's not pregnant anymore," Gennady sighs.

"Oh my fucking God. She lost the babies?"

"No, no, no," he says hurriedly. "Nothing that morbid. She just… had them."

"So she's in a hospital?"

He winces again. "Well… not quite."

"Explain, Gennady," I snap.

He quickly tells me the rest of the story. How Lauren and the Bratva doctor came and delivered Vera's babies. How they took them to the hospital, while Dima and Vera split off and went somewhere else.

"Is he going to kill her?" I ask quietly.

Gennady shakes his head. "I don't think so."

"Is he going to kill Ilyasov?"

"I don't know."

"What *do* you know?"

"I know that if you don't come back and help me bring him back to his right mind, then lots of people are going to die, Arya."

"No," I say flatly. "No, I refuse. Fuck that."

Gennady stands silently in place and watches me melt down.

"I can't go back, Gennady. Not after what he's done. Not after what he's shown he's willing to do."

"He's trying to make things right, Arya."

"How is he going to do that?"

He takes a big breath and then finally delivers the line he's clearly been waiting to say since he first appeared here. "He's going to give it all up."

I freeze. I can't possibly have heard him right. "What?"

"Everything," Gennady explains. "The Bratva, the city, his legacy. His life, if necessary. He's going to give it all up, rather than cross the line in the sand he swore to you—and to me—that he'd never cross."

"You're lying," I accuse.

But one look in his eye says he's telling the whole-hearted truth.

"Ilyasov will kill him."

Gennady nods. "Probably. That's usually how these kinds of things work."

I look down at Lukas in my arms. My son looks back up at me with his father's fire in his eyes. That smolder that's so uniquely Dima is right there. We made him. We made this little slice of perfect. It was an accident and maybe it was a mistake, but Lukas is perfect and I will never, ever regret the things that delivered him to me.

I've said it since the beginning: I'm all he has now.

But I'm wrong about that. He still has Dima—for the time being, at least. And I owe it to my son to keep Dima in his life for as long as possible.

I glance over Gennady's shoulder to my mother's gravestone. I didn't have her. Even before she died, the drugs took her away from me in all the ways that mattered. I never had a chance at a happy ending.

But Lukas did. Lukas does.

So for his sake—for my son's sake—I'll go stop his father from walking into a suicide trap.

"We have to go stop him, Gennady," I whisper.

He nods. "Glad you agree. I'll drive."

49

DIMA

I drive back to the mansion. Vera is in the backseat, still bound at the wrists and too weak to fight, so I'm not worried about her attacking me and running us off the road.

I'm distracted enough that I might do that even without her help. My mind is fucking racing. With guilt. With memory. With anger. With the acceptance that the decision I've made might mean the end of my life.

I quit. I roll the words around in my head again and again.

I never thought I'd say them. Especially not to my brother, and especially not at a time like this.

But it's the only option left. The only honorable way forward. I've made so many fucking mistakes in the last days and weeks and months. If quitting can erase even one percent of them, I owe it to everyone in my life to do that.

As soon as we get back to the mansion, I'm going to call Ilyasov. I'll hand Vera back over to him and I'll concede. If he kills me, so be it. It just means my time has come.

A few minutes later, we pull up in the courtyard. "We're here," I say quietly.

Vera seethes and says nothing as I let her out of the car. She walks behind me, proud and haughty, as I go up the stairs and reach out to grab the handle.

It's unlocked, I notice. And actually, partially ajar as well.

I frown. Tentatively, I push it inwards. The house is spookily silent. I take one cautious step inside.

Where are the guards? Where are the maids? The Romanoff Mansion is never truly empty.

Except for now, it seems.

A strange kind of adrenaline starts to surge through my veins. I grab Vera's upper arm and pull her along with me.

"Don't touch me," she snaps, but I ignore her. We slink inside along the walls of the hallway. Not a single thing moves or makes a noise.

We round a corner... and that's when I see that the door to the ballroom is open. A triangle of light spills out into the corridor.

Somewhere deep in my bones, I know what's waiting for us in there. But I go forwards anyway. It's fate or stupidity or maybe a little of both—I don't know for certain. All I know is that I'm being called there. Like my whole life has been building to this moment. I don't have a choice, not really.

I press a single finger to the ballroom door and push it. It swings inward on silent hinges. I suppose I shouldn't be surprised when I take one step into the only place my parents ever loved each other...

And find myself staring right down the barrel of a gun.

"Hello, Dima," Ilyasov growls. "Thought I might find you here."

I tilt my head in greeting. "I had the same thought," I say. "Brotherly intuition, I guess."

Vera rushes over to her husband's side. "Oh my God, Ilya!" She throws her arms around her husband and he pats her back, his eyes still on me. "I had the babies," she sobs. "The twins. But he took them. I don't know where they went."

Ilyasov's expression sharpens. "Where are they, Dima?"

"At the hospital being seen by a doctor. They'll be fine."

Vera is full-on sobbing now, clinging to Ilyasov like he's the only thing keeping her upright. I can't help noticing that Ilyasov doesn't seem nearly as emotional.

"I didn't think you had it in you, brother," he rumbles.

"I don't," I say bluntly. "I was coming here to call you and tell you where to find her. You just happened to beat me here."

"Couldn't stomach it? Did your conscience get in the way again?"

I nod. "Something like that."

Vera's legs are sagging underneath her. She's losing strength—not such a huge surprise after everything she's been through. But Ilyasov doesn't seem to care.

"I hope you don't think this satisfies the demands of the third Trial," he scoffs. "You didn't even get close to completing it."

"I couldn't agree more," I say. "I failed."

Ilyasov laughs cruelly. "Then what are you going to do now, oh brother of mine?"

I shrug. "The only thing I can do: quit."

Finally, it seems I've shocked Ilyasov. His eyes go wide and he stares at me as though trying to read my thoughts. He thinks there is a trick hidden in my words, but there isn't. Not this time.

I'm done.

Arya was right.

This fight for power and control has corrupted me. It's turned me into a man like Jorik, like my brother, like my father. I'd rather die a failure and also a good man than to live with the power of the Bratva and yet not be able to look myself in the mirror.

I'd rather be a man Arya can be proud of in death than a monster she won't have in her life.

"You forfeit?" he asks slowly. "After everything you've gone through?"

"I'm done with this fight. I'd rather lose my Bratva than my soul."

Ilyasov hesitates for a moment and then laughs, throwing his head back. "Good God, the dramatics! Since the moment you stepped into my office, you've been insufferably philosophical. You've done worse things than this, brother. We both have. Let's not pretend otherwise."

He isn't wrong. But it doesn't matter. I don't want to be that person anymore. I haven't been for a long time. Not since I met Arya.

"People change, brother."

"So what now?" Ilyasov asks. "You forfeit and I trust that you mean it? I let you walk away and expect that you will hand over the Bratva to me?"

"You don't need to trust me. I won't be around to trust."

He raises a brow. "You're planning to give this all up for Arya, then?"

Vera shakes her head. "They broke up. She left him. I heard him admit it."

Ilyasov's mouth opens, and he looks truly amused now. "Oh my God. This is all over a broken heart? This is what a sad Dima is capable of—throwing away his Bratva and running off because his poor little whore won't suck his cock anymore. Holy shit. This is good. Well, you've made my job easy."

"It's all yours, Ilyasov," I say. "Everything you've ever wanted."

"You're more right than you know, Dima," he croons. He glances down at Vera, who's gone quiet with her face buried in his shirt. "I have my sons. I have my birthright. I have my arrogant brother groveling at my feet. I just have to tie up a few loose ends and then a decade of planning will finally be at its end."

I stand proud. "Pull the trigger then, Ilyasov," I sigh. "You win."

He nods slowly, sagely. Like he understands something I don't.

Everything that happens next happens so goddamn fast.

Ilyasov rips Vera's hands off his shoulders and gives her a hard shove. She cries out in shock and stumbles backwards. Whirling, he takes the gun away from my face, points it at her head, and pulls the trigger.

There's a bang.

And I swear that for a single moment, she's still looking at me. Eyes hazy and confused.

Then she drops.

"Fuck!" I jump back, back pressed against the door. "What the hell, Ilyasov?"

My brother just smiles at me, no sign of the atrocity he just committed on his face. "Like I said, just a few loose ends to handle."

"She was your wife, for fuck's sake!" I roar.

"She was a means to an end," he snaps in the coldest tone I've ever heard from another human being in my whole goddamn life. "She served her purpose. And now her purpose is complete. It's a nice thing I just gave her. Closure, you know? A neat ending."

"What the hell is wrong with you?" I say. I'm flaming with anger and shock and a million other emotions I can't name.

Mostly, though, I'm staring into my brother's eyes and wondering when he became this monster—or if he's been this way all along, and I'm only just now noticing.

Ilyasov stalks closer. The gun is loose in his fingers, casual and nonchalant. "Ten years ago, we committed a horrible crime, *sobrat*. We both did it. We both have the blood on our hands. But we took different lessons from that night. It weakened you, yet it strengthened me. I saw what had to be done to take the throne. To run an empire. I've never forgotten that lesson. You, on the other hand, have forgotten everything our father taught us. You don't deserve what you have. So now I'm here to take it all from you. Your empire is mine now. Your home is mine now. And who knows? Maybe, when my men find your backstabbing little whore, I'll make her mine, too." He grins, and it's the most sickening shit I've ever seen.

One thing is clear now: the boy I knew is gone.

The brother I loved is dead.

There's just a walking nightmare in his place.

When I stepped into this room, I did it knowing full well that I'd probably never step out. But the math has changed on that now. Vera was far from innocent, but she deserved a better ending than what she got.

Arya deserves better than whatever Ilyasov has planned for her, too. So does my son. And Gennady. And the million and one other people in this city who rely on me to rule with a conscience, with morals, with fairness and justice.

Ilyasov wants bloody, burning chaos.

But it's a thin line that separates us from the beasts.

So I'm going to wrap that line around his throat and choke the life from him.

Ilyasov starts to raise the gun. To point it at my face and deliver the final injustice. But as his hand arcs through the air, I move.

I've always been faster than him. When we were training as boys, I'd beat him again and again. And each time he lost, he'd demand that we fight again. "I won't lose to my little brother!" he would cry out.

He said I didn't learn the lessons of our childhood. But he's wrong. I learned them well. And I'm about to show him just what that entails.

My own hand lashes out through the space between us. His eyes widen, but it's too late to stop me. My fist collides with the butt of the gun and knocks it out of his grip. It hits the floor and goes skittering away across the ballroom.

We both freeze, eyes locked on the other for what feels like an eternity.

Ilyasov makes the first move. He lunges for the weapon. His fingertips stretch through the air.

But before he can reach it, I find his ankle and yank him backwards. The motion throws me off balance and sends me tumbling on top of him.

It becomes a blur of limbs. He punches me in the side of the head and stars explode in my vision. I elbow him in the gut and he gasps as the air is driven from his lungs.

I manage to roll on top. I deliver one, two, three quick punches to his face. His nose breaks under my knuckle. I feel the hot, wet spurt of blood.

Then, as I cock back to swing again, he lashes out. This one manages to clip me in the jaw. My head snaps to the side and I fall in that direction. It gives him the window he needs to shove me aside, straddle me, and start raining his own punches down.

My cheekbone cracks. I feel it give way in one nauseating CRUNCH that sends agony searing through the side of my face. The punch I was in the middle of throwing falls limply to the side.

Ilyasov has the opportunity he needs now. He turns his back on me and dives for the gun. I try to go after him. Try to stop him.

But this time, I'm not fast enough.

I hurl myself from my knees just as he grabs the weapon and rolls over to direct it at me. I can barely see, barely think. All I know is that only one of us can walk out of this room alive.

It doesn't look like it's going to be me.

The gun goes off for the second time in as many minutes. One deafening bang that echoes endlessly in this mirrored room.

This place is drenched in horrible memories. In pain. In bloodshed.

I'm about to add my story to that collection.

The bullet from Ilyasov's gun enters me just beneath my chest. It's like a hot poker being driven into me. I have just enough presence of mind to feel it rip all the way through, exiting out to the left of my spine and leaving agonizing fire in its wake.

I fall to the ground. My life's blood begins to pour out of me.

Ilyasov rises slowly to his full height. Just like me, he's always been huge. And right now, he seems taller than ever. Like a mountain standing over me. The blood from his broken nose drips all the way down to land on my face. His eyes are two black and burning coals set deep in their sockets.

"Until I see you again, brother," he says.

Then he turns away and leaves me to die.

50

DIMA

As I lay there dying, I dream.

No, it's not a dream—it's a memory. *The* memory. The fork in time where all this shit began.

∼

Ten Years Ago—The Romanoff Mansion

I'm standing over my sleeping brother with a knife in my grasp. Five minutes ago, Father pressed the blade into my hands and told me what I had to do.

But I can't fucking do it.

My whole life, I've been training for this moment. I've learned how to kill. How to lie. How to rule. And now, the Romanoff Bratva empire is right there for the taking.

All I have to do is plunge this knife into my brother's chest, and it will all be mine. I'll be the don I've always longed to be.

But I can't. Fucking. Do it.

"Faltering at the final moment, brother?" comes a voice from the darkness.

I blink in confusion. "You're awake?"

"I've been awake since the moment you came in here," Ilyasov says. He sits up in bed and pushes the covers off. His eyes are wide awake, but they're as dark as they've always been. Like a shark's eyes, cunning and alert.

"Then why didn't you do anything?" I ask. "Why didn't you try to stop me?"

He shrugs. "I didn't think you could go through with it. Looks like I was right, doesn't it?"

I let the hand holding the gleaming knife fall by my side. "Fuck."

Ilyasov clasps my shoulder. "It's okay, Dima," he croons. "I have something to show you, too."

He pulls the blankets off of his lap and shows me what he's holding: a sharpened knife of his own.

"Father gave me the same task," he explains. "'*Kill your brother and the Bratva is yours. Kill the thing you love most in this world and you can have it all.*' Does that sound familiar?"

My blood feels like ice in my veins. Word for word, Father told me the same thing in his office just moments ago before dispatching me to end Ilyasov's life.

Turns out it was a test. A lie. A scheme.

"Don't fret, brother," Ilyasov says. "I have a better plan, anyway."

He tells it to me.

I can't believe what I'm hearing. But when he's done, the only sound in the room is our mingled breathing. And I realize: there's no other way forward.

I can't kill my brother. He can't kill me. So this is what must be done.

Without saying a word, Ilyasov and I slide out of his bedroom. We go down the stairs and find the ballroom. This is where Father told us each to come meet him once our task was done. Some sort of twisted fucking symbolism in it that I don't bother to decipher.

In unison, we pause outside the door.

Ilyasov looks at me.

I look at Ilyasov.

Then he pushes it open.

Father is standing with his back to us, hands clasped behind him. At the sound of our approach, he doesn't turn. He just snarls in that savage, raspy voice of his, "Which one of you has come back to me alive?"

Ilyasov speaks first. "Both of us."

Father freezes. Then, slowly, he turns in place. His eyes go from me to Ilyasov, from Ilyasov to me, again and again. Like he can't decide which one of us is disappointing him more.

Even as an old man, he's huge and intimidating. We both got our size from him. Those massive shoulders. Those smoldering eyes. The hands that can break a man's spine in a single snap.

But he's no match for what's coming next.

"I cannot tell you how much it hurts my heart to see you both here," he intones. "You let your love for one another blind you from what matters most."

"Love is a weapon," I repeat softly. It's what he's told us again and again. The one lesson that he's drilled into our heads above all.

He nods. "Love is a weapon, indeed. But you've both chosen to let it use you instead of the other way around."

"We chose not to let a deluded old man move us around like chess pieces," Ilyasov snaps.

The anger in his voice surprises me. Back in his bedroom, he seemed so calm and cool. Now, in the presence of our father, he's barely managing to restrain himself. The whites of his eyes are gleaming, his knuckles are tight, and he's fidgeting in place as if he can't keep himself still.

"It's all part of the game," Father whispers.

"You're right," Ilyasov snaps. "And down goes the king."

He rips the knife from my hand, takes one strong lunge towards Father, and plunges the blade right into his chest.

I stand frozen in place and watch as he withdraws the bloody knife and brings it down again and again. Five, ten, twenty times, he stabs our father in the heart. Until his hand and face are both drenched with the blood of the former Romanoff don.

Only when Father isn't moving anymore does Ilyasov turn to me. He looks like something from a nightmare. Glistening crimson head to toe. A fire in his eyes that I don't understand.

And then he grins. Slow and savage and cruel.

As if this was part of his plan all along.

Present Day—The Romanoff Mansion

I open my eyes. I'm still in the ballroom, and part of me wonders if I'm still in fact dead or dreaming. But when I try to move and the greatest pain I've ever felt rips through me like a lightning bolt, I know that I'm still alive.

Only life can hurt this much.

There's a smell in the air. Smoke, I think, although my senses are fucked up so I can't be sure. The heat radiating through the room makes the images in the mirrored walls waver like a mirage. I struggle up to my elbows, gasping with the effort.

"Ilya…" I groan. Speaking hurts. Breathing hurts. Moving hurts.

But I have to move. I somehow manage to flip onto my hands and knees and start crawling. Every inch feels like a mile. Every breath feels like being shot all over again.

The closer I get to the door, the stronger the heat gets. And when I reach it and nudge it open, I understand why.

Flames are running up and down the length of the hallway. Through the open door to the living room a few dozen yards away, I can see more fire engulfing the furniture and climbing up the curtains.

I use the doorframe to pull myself upright. Smoke fills my lungs on the first breath at this height. I hack hard. The motion makes fresh blood ooze from the bullet wound in my chest.

It's a miracle I'm alive. But the window for survival won't last long. Each cough costs me more seconds of my life. I have to get out.

I start to walk towards the front door, using the wall for support. One foot in front of the other. This hurts even worse than crawling did.

Somehow, I make it to the corner. I round it. And as I do, I see that the hardwood in the middle of the foyer has given way. There's a huge, ragged circle in the middle where the planks have burned up to a crisp. It's like a burning, open mouth, ready to swallow me whole.

I grit my teeth and start to edge around it. The front doors are in sight now on the other side of the gaping crater, though they're still impossibly far away for how fast I'm moving. The flames keep getting hotter, too. I'm running out of time.

"You can make it," I wheeze to myself. "Do it for your son. Do it for Arya."

I'm almost there—and then my older brother rises up like a ghoul in front of me.

His hands are wet with the gasoline he must've used to set the fires and he has a scrap of fabric tied like a bandana around his face. All I can see are his eyes. They still have that shark's violence in them. That inhuman cunning.

"You should have stayed dead," he growls.

"You should have killed me ten years ago."

He nods. "You're right about that, Dima. You're very fucking right about that."

With a fierce lurch forward, he steps forward and seizes my shirt in both hands. Then he starts to drag me towards the pit.

I can see his plan unfolding: throw me in. Let the fires rage.

And I'm fucking helpless to resist.

We're a yard or two away from the lip of the burning crater. Ilyasov's hands are clenching my shirt.

And then I trip.

It's a pure accident. Nothing but dumb luck. My foot catches a jagged hardwood plank and it pitches all my dead weight forwards. With my shirt being as soaked in my blood as it is, Ilyasov can't maintain his grip.

So I fall from his grasp. And as my weight descends towards the floor, I reach out for something. Anything.

My fingers close on the gold chain around Ilyasov's throat.

If it were cheaper, it would've just broken. But my brother has never settled for less than the best. So the strength of the chain is enough to act as a yoke.

Enough that I drag him down with me.

We both land right on the edge of the crater, him collapsing hard on top of me. My head is dangling over empty space. The acrid smell of burning hair and skin makes me want to vomit.

Ilyasov rears back. The collar of his shirt is on fire, but he barely seems to notice. He raises his hand above his head and I see that at some point in the scrabble, he managed to grab a burning spar of hardwood. It's as good as a knife at this close range.

He cocks it back. And as he does, past and future melt together.

I didn't think you could go through with it.

He starts to bring it down towards me.

You let your love for one another blind you from what matters most.

In the last moment before he pierces me through the face, I shift my weight to the side and buck my hips upward.

It's all part of the game.

It's just enough force to send Ilyasov somersaulting over my head—and into the depths of the raging fires below.

I turn in time to watch. The motion of falling is slow. Ilyasov seems to pause in mid-air for a second, burnt arms flailing, eyes wide and panicked.

Then, almost in slow motion, he descends down into the flames and smoke coming from the floor below.

He disappears, but I think I hear him scream for a second. Just a moment of wailing. Then the rest of the sound is lost in the crackling of the fire.

It's all part of the game, brother. All a part of the game.

51

ARYA

The house is burning.

As Gennady and I park out front, the smell of smoke hits my nostrils. I can see the flames licking at the front windows, too.

My heart throbs painfully in my chest. "Is Dima in there?" I cry out to Gennady.

"I don't know!" he roars back.

I'm torn. Do I run in? I can't leave Lukas alone out here, but I can't let Dima die in there. The flames are growing hotter and hotter with every passing second. Time's wasting. I have to decide.

Before I can make up my mind, I see motion out of the corner of my eye. Turning, I notice a pair of feet sticking out from beneath a massive hedge bordering one side of the property.

I race over and kneel down next to the body. It's Eduard, one of Dima's lieutenants. He's badly wounded and slicked all over with drying blood. But at the sound of my approach, he coughs and shoves himself upright with a pained grimace.

He's alive.

"What happened?" I beg.

"Ilya... Ilyasov came," he murmurs. He coughs again and spits up blood. "He got the jump on us. Took out me and a few of the... the others. They're... dead, I think."

"You need to rest," I say, putting a hand on his shoulder. "You're hurt."

He knocks my hand off. "I can't. Dima is in there."

He struggles to his knees, then presses a fist into the dirt and wobbles up until he's standing. He's wincing and scowling in pain the whole time, but he manages to right himself—barely.

"You can't go anywhere," I order. I hand him Lukas. "Stay here. Watch my son. I'm going in."

I don't wait for his protests. I just turn and run into the fire.

The smoke inside is even worse than I thought. The world has gone red and gray and black. I can't see a thing.

I bend into a crouch and try not to take deep breaths, but adrenaline is pounding through my veins and my heart is racing. I've only been inside for a few seconds and already my body feels starved for oxygen.

Dima needs me.

It's that thought that propels me forward.

Flames are tearing through the doors in the hallway now, filling the area with smoke, and the floor feels unstable beneath my feet. The fire is eating away at the foundation. One wrong step could send me plummeting through.

The smoke clears enough for me to get a glimpse of the foyer. In the center of it is a burning pit from hell. The hardwood is getting chewed up by flame and giving way to this yawning chasm, rimmed with licking fire and emanating thousands of degrees of heat.

I ease myself around the hole, sticking as close to the wall as I can. Everything is brutally hot. Sweat is pouring off my face and my arms are coated in so much ash I can't even see my skin.

When I'm almost all of the way around the circle, I trip over a dark mass on the floor. I think it's debris—until it moves.

"Dima!" I know I spoke, but I can't hear the sound of my own voice over the roar of the flames.

I drop down next to him, fear shooting through me as the timbers beneath us crack slightly. I lay a hand on his back and pull it away to see that he's covered in blood and ash. "Dima?"

I'm worried I'm too late. That he's already dead. But then he lifts his head and looks around.

He has soot smeared on his cheeks and burns on his arms, but Dima is alive. He's still breathing. There's still a chance.

"Dima, you have to get up. We can still get out of here, but we have to go."

His lips move, but I can't hear him. There's no time for talk, anyway.

I wrap an arm through his and do my best to help lift his large frame to his feet. Dima stumbles sideways into me. It's only when he pulls away do I realize that all the blood on him is pouring from a horrific-looking wound in his chest.

"Can you walk?" I'm not sure how he hears me, but he does.

Dima nods. Together, we make slow progress towards the front doors. It's a long walk and Dima is far heavier than I am. Dima groans with every step, but I keep moving.

His breathing is ragged, his eyes are bloodshot and rolling around without any clear direction. Dima looks more unlike himself than I've ever seen before, and I hate every second of it.

My whole world has narrowed down to this. Left foot in front of right. Right foot in front of left. Repeat. My muscles are screaming, my throat is raw from breathing smoke, my skin is baking and threatening to split from the heat.

But I can't stop. I won't stop.

We reach the doors. I touch the handle and hiss when it sears my fingertips. Rearing back, I kick it as hard as I can.

Nothing.

The floor behind us is beginning to crumble. Plank by plank, the hardwood is giving way and going tumbling down into the pit below. The space of floor we're standing on won't last much longer.

I rear back and kick the door one more time.

Still nothing.

"Fuck!" I scream, though there's no point since I can't even hear myself think amidst the roar of the fire.

I close my eyes and steel myself for one final attempt. This is my last shot. If this doesn't work, the fires win. Ilyasov wins. Fate wins.

My mind flashes back almost three decades. I'm a little girl again, lying trapped beneath the roof of a destroyed house. I didn't know it then, but my mother was dead just a few yards away from me. I found the strength back then to wriggle my way out of the wreckage. To build a new life.

I can do that again.

Opening my eyes, I let out a war cry. I load up my kick and drive into the door with my heel as hard as I can.

This time, the door bursts open. The motion carries me forward, off-balance. Dima and I tumble down into the outdoors. We collapse together on the ground, a tangle of ash and blood and sweat. I'm taking huge lungfuls of fresh air and crying, the tears scything down the ash still clinging to my face.

But we're alive. *We're alive.*

My head is swimming as hands start to lift me up, to pull Dima off of me. I want to scream, "No! Don't take him from me!" But my throat hurts to much to speak and I've breathed so much smoke that I can't distinguish reality from hallucination anymore.

All I know is this: my whole world changed when Dima kicked in the door of my clinic, almost a year ago.

It was my turn to return the favor.

EPILOGUE: DIMA

Before I open my eyes, my throat burns.

It's like someone slid a hot knife down my esophagus. Each swallow is like being sliced by the blade again and again.

"Dima?"

The voice is distant, watery. But I recognize it.

There's no other person whose voice is as close to honey as hers. No one else could say nothing more than my name and still spark excitement in my chest.

Even unconscious, I recognize Arya.

And I want to see her.

My eyelids are heavy, practically fused shut, but I force them open after a few tries. My vision solidifies, the fuzzy outline of her coming into sharper and sharper focus. Until she's undeniably in front of me. Solid and alive and radiant.

"Arya." My voice sounds like I've smoked two packs a day for the last thirty years.

She sighs. "Thank God. You're awake. I mean, I knew you'd wake up. The doctors told me you'd wake up, but still, it's good to see you."

Doctors? Then I notice the beeping. The distant sounds of metal carts rattling and voices.

I'm in a hospital.

I look down and groan. Arya laughs. "I knew you'd hate the gown. I told them you'd rather be naked."

"That would be more dignified."

"Your clothes were trashed," she says. "They had to cut you out of them to tend to the gunshot wound and the burns."

I move my arms and legs just to prove to myself that I can. Then her words register.

"Burns. There was a fire."

"Yes," she says softly.

"Did anything…?"

She shakes her head. "It's all gone."

I lay my head back on the pillow and try to process that. *It's all gone.* The Romanoff Mansion, burned to a crisp. The site of the worst crime of my life—standing by as Ilyasov murdered our father in cold blood.

Ilyasov's body is there now, too. It's fitting, in a macabre way. He died in the same place our father did.

I shudder.

There was something else lost to the flames, too. I search her face for any sign that she already knows, but I get distracted. She's beautiful. Perfect.

Her lips are pink and full, her green eyes are emeralds in sunshine, and her hair falls in loose curls down her shoulders and over the soft curves of her breasts. She looks incredible.

And I'm in a fucking hospital gown.

Something else occurs to me. "Did they get rid of my clothes?"

"No," she says with a strange frown. "Why?"

"Bring me my pants."

"Why?"

"Please, Arya." It hurts to speak. But this is important. It needs to happen now.

Arya walks over to a drawer. She opens it and pulls a large plastic bag out of it. Reaching inside, she retrieves my charred pants.

"The back pocket," I tell her.

"There *is* no back pocket anymore," she says with a frustrated laugh. "It's basically an ashtray."

"Just look," I insist. "It's in there."

She frowns more as she fishes around in the mess—until her hand closes around something.

She keeps her fist closed as she walks back over. Only when she's back at my bedside does she turn her hand palm facing upwards and open her fingers.

In the middle of her palm is a ring.

It's simple. Just an engagement band with two stones, one aquamarine, the other sapphire.

"Our birthstones," Arya says softly, her voice thick with tears. "Mine and Lukas's. You had this made, didn't you?"

I nod. "I wanted something special for you."

"As a gift?"

I look over and I see the uncertainty on her face. She's happy—thrilled with the ring—but she isn't confident it is what she thinks she is.

After everything we've been through, I wonder how she could have any doubt. Being with Arya has changed me, body and soul. I'm lost without her. I need her.

"More like a promise," I say. "And a question."

She lets out a tiny, breathy laugh, and smiles. It's breathtaking.

Then she frowns and slaps my arm.

"Hey," I say. "What the hell?"

"Don't *'what the hell?'* me. What the hell, you?! No more secrets! We talked about this!"

I can't help laughing. "It's a good secret," I say.

She sighs and relaxes. "Yes," she says. "It is." Something occurs to her and she glances up at me, brows furrowed. "When did you have it made?"

"As soon as you moved in."

She looks at me, eyebrows wide. "We weren't on the best terms when I first moved in."

"No, but that's the nature of our relationship, I think. I do something stupid, you get mad at me, we make up. I figured we'd sort it out."

"And when we did, you wanted to give me this?"

I reach out and wrap my hands around both of hers. "I never planned to get married. Not seriously. I knew it was a possibility, but I assumed it would be more of a duty I fulfilled to the Bratva than anything else. Then you came along, and everything changed. I changed."

Tears are rolling fat down her cheeks now. I reach out and brush one away before I continue.

"You took me in stride. You weren't scared or timid around me, and you didn't care who I was or what kind of power I had. You are a force, Arya. An unstoppable force. And I knew I wanted to marry you the second you walked away from me in Chicago."

She gasps. "We'd only known each other a few days."

"I would have denied it until I was blue in the face, but I knew it even then. Down deep. I knew I'd marry you one day. So I bought the ring to have for whenever I thought you'd have me. Which brings me to the question: will you have me?"

She opens her mouth to answer. But before she can, the door opens. Gennady waltzes in with his ever-present smile on his face.

"Santa's here!" he announces.

I turn to Arya. "Quick, unplug the life support," I drawl.

Arya giggles as Gennady sighs and puts a hand on his chest like he's been mortally wounded. "Don't be a sourpuss," he scolds. "You're lucky I didn't put on the nurse costume I bought for the joke. I figured that would be a bridge too far."

"So you *do* know when to stop?" I joke.

He raises an eyebrow. "You're one to talk. You've been shot, burned, strangled, and punched in the face."

"All in a day's work."

He turns to Arya. "What do you think about that, Madam President?"

I frown. "What does that mean?"

Gennady faces me again. "You've been out for almost a week and there were a lot of decisions to be made. Arya here has been helping me sort through some of the leadership stuff. Eduard and the others, too, of course." He jerks a thumb over his shoulder. I follow the motion to see Eduard and the other lieutenants clustered outside the doorway, looking in at me. "But Arya has a knack for this stuff, believe it or not."

I gaze at her. She meets me with her green eyes, cool and intelligent and feisty as hell. The same eyes that drank me in the night we met. The same eyes that have loved me again and again.

"I believe it," I say softly. "I really fucking believe it."

∼

Eduard and the rest of the inner circle join us, and we talk for a while about all the shit that's happened while I was out.

The Albanians are a mess without Ilyasov's backing and leadership, so Gennady's taken the opportunity to rout them out of several key territories.

The Chicago Romanoff Bratva contingent have pledged their loyalty to me, meaning my empire has practically doubled overnight.

The remnants of the D'Onofrio clan are pissed, but that's fine—they're small potatoes and wouldn't dare threaten me. Especially not now.

Things are good and it's good to hear everything. But I'm grateful the nurse shows up when she does to kick all of the guests out of the room.

When the room is quiet again, Arya nestles into the bed next to me and lays her head on my chest. "Lukas is with Ernestine and June. They're watching him for the night."

"So you can tend to my wounds?"

She winks and then smooths a hand down my chest. "And I asked around and found out Ilyasov's twins are here, actually. In this hospital."

"Are they?"

She hums a yes. "I went and saw them. They're perfectly healthy, Dima. Beautiful babies."

"They're Romanoffs. Of course they're beautiful."

She laughs and then grow serious. "What's going to happen to them now that their parents are both dead?"

I know where she is headed with this. It doesn't take me more than a second to make my decision.

"Their parents aren't dead. They're right here."

She stiffens against me and then sits up. Her green eyes are glassy with unshed tears. "Are you sure?"

"They're my family," I say firmly. "If anyone should take care of them, it should be me. I'd understand if you don't want to. After everything Ilyasov did, I'd understand if—"

"Ilyasov," she says softly. "Everything *Ilyasov* did. Those babies are innocent and precious. They did nothing wrong and they deserve a good life. We can give them one."

I wrap an arm around her and hold her close. "Then that's what we'll do."

Arya starts excitedly talking about baby names and nursery designs and how close in age our three kids will be. When she gets to the topic of finding a new house, I wave her away.

"It's too early to talk about that. I just came out of a near-coma."

"You weren't in a coma," she scoffs. "And you just agreed to adopt two babies! How could buying a house feel more momentous than that?"

"Because I hate moving. It's too much work."

She laughs and shakes her head. "You're ridiculous. You run an entire Bratva, but you can't handle furnishing?"

"A real man knows the limitations of his talents, Arya," I intone. "Which reminds me… you're hired."

She wrinkles her nose. "I'm hired?"

"Yes. Queen Empress of the Bratva. The title is a work in progress, but the duties are simple: you're in charge of everything."

Her jaw drops. "Dima, I'm not… I can't…"

"You can and you will," I say. "I meant what I told you before: you're my queen, Arya. Let's make the world in our image."

She doesn't answer. Just snuggles up against my shoulder.

It's good enough for me. More than good enough. More than real enough. More than pure enough.

It's immaculate.

EXTENDED EPILOGUE

Thanks for reading IMMACULATE CORRUPTION—but don't stop now! Click the link below to get your hands on the exclusive Extended Epilogue to see Dima and Arya's family a year into the future!

DOWNLOAD THE EXTENDED EPILOGUE TO IMMACULATE CORRUPTION

MAILING LIST

Sign up to my mailing list!
New subscribers receive a FREE steamy bad boy romance novel.

Click the link below to join.
https://sendfox.com/nicolefox

ALSO BY NICOLE FOX

Romanoff Bratva
Immaculate Deception
Immaculate Corruption

Kovalyov Bratva
Gilded Cage
Gilded Tears
Jaded Soul
Jaded Devil

Mazzeo Mafia Duet
Liar's Lullaby (Book 1)
Sinner's Lullaby (Book 2)

Bratva Crime Syndicate
Can be read in any order!
Lies He Told Me
Scars He Gave Me
Sins He Taught Me

Belluci Mafia Trilogy
Corrupted Angel (Book 1)
Corrupted Queen (Book 2)
Corrupted Empire (Book 3)

De Maggio Mafia Duet
Devil in a Suit (Book 1)

Devil at the Altar (Book 2)

Kornilov Bratva Duet

Married to the Don (Book 1)

Til Death Do Us Part (Book 2)

Heirs to the Bratva Empire

Can be read in any order!

Kostya

Maksim

Andrei

Princes of Ravenlake Academy (Bully Romance)

Can be read as standalones!

Cruel Prep

Cruel Academy

Cruel Elite

Tsezar Bratva

Nightfall (Book 1)

Daybreak (Book 2)

Russian Crime Brotherhood

Can be read in any order!

Owned by the Mob Boss

Unprotected with the Mob Boss

Knocked Up by the Mob Boss

Sold to the Mob Boss

Stolen by the Mob Boss

Trapped with the Mob Boss

Volkov Bratva

Broken Vows (Book 1)
Broken Hope (Book 2)
Broken Sins *(standalone)*

Other Standalones
Vin: A Mafia Romance

Box Sets
Bratva Mob Bosses (Russian Crime Brotherhood Books 1-6)
Tsezar Bratva (Tsezar Bratva Duet Books 1-2)
Heirs to the Bratva Empire
The Mafia Dons Collection
The Don's Corruption

Printed in Great Britain
by Amazon